Open Your Eyes

A Novel By
Schelle Holloway

Open Your Eyes © 2011 by Schelle Holloway

This book is a work of fiction. Names, characters, places, and incident are the product of the author's imagination or are used fictitiously. So if by chance you see yourself in any of the aspects of this novel...good for you.

Printed in the United States of America

First Edition

ISBN-13: 978-0-6154471-0-0

Cover Design: immaculatedesignstudios@gmail.com
Photography: Jackie Smith, owner of Photograph by Jackie
Editing & Typesetting: Carla Dean of U Can Mark My Word

For information regarding special ordering for bulk purchases, contact Schelle Holloway at info@openyoureyesbook.com.

Website: www.openyoureyesbook.com

ACKNOWLEDGEMENTS

Let's just get it over with. You have thirty seconds to say whatever you want to say about Schelle Holloway writing an erotica novel and being so dedicated to her Christian background. Go! Twenty seconds … fifteen seconds … only ten seconds left… 5…4…3…2…1. Boom! Do you feel better now? I hope so. Because say what you want about me, but yes, I can write a faith-based stage play AND write something so hot and steamy that your panties will be soaking wet with desire or have the men's penises rock hard looking for a target. Just that talented, I am! Don't be mad at me. HE blessed me with all this, so take your drama to Him!

It started one Friday after I purchased my home and figured out how to work my fireplace. I really wasn't in the mood for sex; I just felt like writing. So, I poured myself a glass of wine, got a blanket, fixed my ottoman and chair right in front of the fireplace, and started writing. The people came to mind, and the words hit the screen almost as if the keys were pulling my fingers down without my help. I didn't want to be disturbed as I moved the words along. So, I paused, got the whole bottle of wine, and placed it next to me as I continued writing.

Shortly after I had about fifteen pages, I called a dear friend of mine and asked him to listen. I read what I had written as if it came out of a book that had already been published. His reaction was, "What the f*ck is that? Who wrote that?" I responded, "Me." He came back instantly, "Stop lying." He told me to hold on, and when he came back to the phone, he said, "Read it again." I wanted to know why, and he said, "I had to close my door." I asked, "Why?" He said, "Just read it again." I knew he wanted to take advantage of my words and masturbate, friend-to-friend, and when I asked him, he laughed devilishly because he knew I had found him out. I told him I would not help him get his rocks off and that he'd better pull out a DVD or call his honey. Still, just the thought that I intrigued him enough to get out of bed and want me to do it again let me know I was well on my way to something big.

Same story as above, but I called one of my best girlfriends. When I said I wanted to read something to her, she gave her undivided attention. I read in the same sultry voice, with the same passion and commitment, and after I finished, she said, "Sh*t! Who is that?" I laughed and said, "Me." She blasted right back, "Shut the f*ck up! Oh my goodness, Holloway, you did not write that sh*t!" I admitted shyly that I did. She demanded that I keep reading, but there was no more. I had given all I had, and as I was about to speak, she said, "Read it again." I laughed because I thought about my homeboy who wanted the same pleasure. "I have to write some more," I told her, to which she responded, "Damn. Okay. Call me back." As if she were telling me, "No time for talking; get back to writing." I was warm on the inside. Nervous or scared even. I just didn't know where I was going with this. But, I do now!

The story is an erotica fiction novel that just came…and you will too once you get in it. Orgasms are good. Trust me, I know. Just when you think you know the story, you don't. Just when

4

you think it's all good, it's not. And just when you think you are about to explode in your body, you will! Thank me by telling a friend about the book and demanding them to purchase their OWN copy. Don't let them get off on your dime! Tell them to invest in their own night of pleasure! Be selfish!

This book was *written* by the fire, only to send that burning flame through your body. It was *edited* with care by Editor Carla M. Dean. How many "cool off" breaks did you have to take, girlfriend? And it was *published* because He gave me talent without limitations. Thank you!

Thank You Connie For your support!

Happy Reading

Your Author,

Schelle Halloway

3/19/11

DEDICATION

This book is dedicated to my family and friends, who encouraged me, loved me in spite of what others thought, and helped dust me off after people tried to beat me down. To my daughters, who stepped out on faith with me in our move, I love you! My parents who supported EVERY decision I made (good/bad), I love you! My brother who gave me the funniest look when I told him what I was writing, it's too late now. My sister who was dying for a copy early on, the finished product is so much better, right? I love you both! To my keep-on-writing, don't-get-discouraged, forget-what-they-will-have-to-say, pray-about-it family and friends (you know who you are), thank you for the late nights, early mornings, midday chats, and emails. I love you!

God forced me to tap into something HE gave me that I didn't even know existed. HE gets my praise daily, and HE sent me an angel. I love you, honey! I love our family. Here's to you ALL!

Schelle Holloway

Chapter One
Sunday After Service

"Thank you, Deacon Fredricks. I don't know where Rashad is with my car. He said he was going to take his break and come pick me up from church. Then I was going to take him back to finish his shift."

"No problem, Wendy, and call me Mark, please. That's why we have a transportation ministry."

"Well, you tell Mrs. Pam that I really appreciate her letting you bring me home."

"Sweetie, this is God's work. This has nothing to do with Mrs. Pam. She understands my position at the church. Now, do you need anything else? What you gonna eat for dinner today?"

"I put something on before I left this morning so Rashad would have something to eat when he got home from work."

"Signs of a good woman."

"Thank you. I just know how he is if there's nothing ready for him to eat when he gets home. Well, at least I've learned to have something ready for him."

"I don't want to pry…"

"Then don't, Deacon Fredricks. New member or not, I don't tell my personal business to anybody but the Lord."

"I understand, but if you ever need someone to pray with you, I'm your deacon."

"Thank you."

As we turn the corner, not to my surprise, my nosey neighbor Chrissy was cleaning out her car.

"Hi, Chrissy."

"Hey, girl!"

"Thanks again, Deacon Fredricks," I said, using great emphasis on the word *Deacon* while getting out and trying to rush inside so I wouldn't have to hold a conversation with her.

"Do you mind if I use your restroom, Wendy?"

"No, not at all. Come on in. See you later, Chrissy."

As usual, making it her business to be in my business, she came across the yard as I let Deacon Fredricks in and give him directions to the restroom.

"Girl, you know if Rashad finds out you let another man in that house he's going to have a fit."

"Mind your business. He's a deacon at my church."

"It will be my business later on tonight if Rashad finds out. But, I guess you will take that to the Lord in prayer like you do everything else."

"I sure will."

While walking in the door and trying to ignore the fact that she was trying to make sure the deacon was really a deacon, I thought about how right Chrissy was. So, I planned to Febreze the living room and Pine-Sol the bathroom down as soon as he left.

"Thank you, Wendy. There was no way I could have made it all the way back to the church."

"No worries, and thank you again."

"You know, we're so glad you decided to join the church, and the singles ministry is one you may want to look into joining."

"Well, I'm not really single, but I will think about it."

"I know you don't think just because Rashad may be paying the bills here that makes you exempt from shacking in God's eyes?"

"I don't think what I do with Rashad is any of your business, and as a man of God, you shouldn't be judging me anyway."

"Oh, I'm not judging you, but I do care about where your soul spends eternity."

"Thank you for your concern, but I think me and the Lord are working out this whole Rashad thing. So, you better get back to the church before Mrs. Pam begins to worry."

"Just think about what I've said, and be sure to invite Rashad to church again next Sunday. We're looking forward to meeting him one day. A man and a woman should be evenly yoked in order to maintain a healthy, stable, loving, unconditional relationship."

Now mind you, all the while he was standing there preaching his trial sermon, I couldn't help but notice he forgot to zip his pants, and the good Deacon Fredricks wasn't wearing any underwear. So, do I (a): Say "Amen" and push him out the door in hopes that the summer breeze will let him know his penis is penetrating through his unzipped pants? (b): Let my sexual emotions take over by reaching down and helping him put it back in his pants. Then send him out the door embarrassed at the fact that now not only Mrs. Pam knows he's abundantly blessed, but so do I? Or perhaps (c): Make Chrissy's potential lie a reality by "doing" him and giving her something else to talk about when her little stank friends come over and sit on the back of their cars like the hood rats they are? No, how about (d):

"Deacon Fredricks, you forgot to zip your pants and your partner is peeking at me." I laughed and then headed into the kitchen to check on my dinner.

"Oh my God, I'm so sorry and embarrassed. Lord, please forgive me."

"I know you didn't do it on purpose," I yelled to him from the kitchen. "So, there's no need to apologize. See you next Sunday, and I promise to have a ride."

In the back of my mind, my body was stuck on the word *ride* because Deacon Fredricks is not your ordinary deacon. This man is fine as hell, clean shaven, and built like a professional athlete training for a marathon. I'd do him in a minute, hands down or up, with them tied behind my back or to the bedpost, closet door, wherever. He could get it.

"Be blessed, Wendy," he said, then slammed the door.

With intent, I said to myself, "You, too, Deacon Fredricks."

I looked at the time and saw I had exactly two hours before it was time for Rashad to be off work. After going upstairs, I turned the shower on as hot as I could stand it because that's how I was feeling at the time. I stripped my clothes off and looked at myself in the mirror. I am 5'10", with mocha brown skin, full lips, shapely hips, and my own silky jet-black hair. I'm carrying a set of D-cups that won't smother you, but just enough for you to nurse on if you even get a little hungry late at night.

My picture-perfect smile is a result of the three thousand dollars my mother paid for my braces while I was in high school. I won't even mention this ass. I'm so blessed. To some women, I'm a threat, but to a man, I'm a secret weapon. *So why am I with this fool?* I wanted to be free so bad; to explore, to live. Damn.

I jumped in the shower and let the water run down my face. Closing my eyes, I turned around to let it hit my back. That's when I thought I heard Rashad calling my name. So, in frustration, I tried to hurry and get the orgasm that I really wanted, while thoughts of Deacon Fredricks' dick ran through my head.

However, the voice calling for me was not Rashad's voice at all. It got closer and closer, and I rubbed myself faster and faster. I knew I could get it before being interrupted if I just concentrated on what I wanted to feel from Deacon Fredricks. The faster I moved my finger over my throbbing clit, the louder the voice got. Feeling myself about to erupt, I turned the calling of my name into something nasty and lustful. I began to say, "What's my name?" And the voice coming up my stairs answered on key. I said it again. "What's my name?" And I heard the voice say, "Wendy," just the way I wanted to hear it, as if I were demanding the deacon to call it before he came.

I rubbed faster on my clit, and as I began to cum, I moaned, "Yes," to what I was releasing. The voice and a knock on the door clearly let me know my release was not in vain, as it was Deacon Fredricks calling out to let me know the car he used to bring me home would not start. In my embarrassment and pleasure, I licked my lips, smiled from behind the door, and told him I would be right out. I had to wash away my lustful thoughts and the guilt of mentally cheating on Rashad before I could look Deacon Fredricks in the face. I just hoped Rashad didn't bring his ass home early to ask why I had to take a shower right after church. Of course, I would have to lie, because saying I fucked one of the deacons in the shower, mentally, just wouldn't sit well with him.

Chapter Two
Monday, That Bitch

It's Monday morning, and I had to put my white face on to deal with the people I worked with, but not before cursing Rashad out for almost tripping over his work boots on my way into the bathroom.

"Rashad, this is why we have closets in this house. Damn. Last week, I was your momma when you were sick. I refuse to be your maid this week."

"Good morning to you, too. I was just so tired last night when I came home. Plus, you cooked that good food that put a brother down."

"Whatever. Move. I don't have time to play house this morning. You gonna make me late."

"Well, in order to play house, we need some kids 'round here. Come on. We can practice right now."

"Rashad, move. I have to pick up Jessica this morning."

"Why you picking her up?"

"Because when you took my car for a week and I had to find a ride to work, she picked me up every day. Now the stupid bug that lived in you during that week has jumped into her man, so she needs a ride this week."

"That's cute, but don't get knocked out for breakfast."

"Won't be the first time, will it?"

"Come on, baby. I'm just playing. I meant it when I said I wasn't going to ever hit you again. You're my baby, and I want you to have my baby."

"You think just because you promised *again* not to hit me that automatically qualifies you to impregnate me to bear little physically, mentally, and verbally abusive offspring. I don't think so. Plus, I'll get pregnant when *I'm* ready, just like you'll come to church with me when *you're* ready."

"That mouth. That's always been your problem."

"No, my mouth has always been your problem when I disagree or tell you when you ain't right. That's the problem. Rashad, you do understand I'm going to leave you one day, right? I just don't know what day."

"I tell you what. The day you do you'll know about it."

Then he tried to kiss me after the sly threat. *Negro, please!*

"I'm gone, Rashad." *Please don't let him say I love you.*

"I love you, baby."

Damnit! If I don't say it back, he'll call me all day wanting to know why I didn't say it back. Why not keep the lie alive?

"I love you, too." Well, I would pretend to love him until he made my last car payment the next month.

When I got in my car, I was shocked to find it had a full tank of gas. Sure, it would be those thoughtful things that I would miss when I leave him, but I would take the rising gas prices over the aches and pains any day.

I had just left home and my phone started ringing already. *Why is he calling me?* Since my display screen on my phone was not working, I couldn't see who it was calling, but I was pretty sure it was Rashad.

"What, Rashad?" I answered with irritation.

"Good morning, Sister Wendy."

"Deacon Fredricks?"

"Did I catch you at a bad time?"

"Uh, no, but how did you get my phone number?"

"The paper you filled out yesterday when I gave you the ride home asked for it. I was responsible for you yesterday, and I'm just following up today to make sure you didn't need a ride to work."

"Thank you, Deacon Fredricks, but no, Rashad came home late last night. Actually, I'm on my way to be as nice to my co-worker as you were to me yesterday."

"Well, bless the name of Jesus, and I said for you to please call me Mark."

"It's a respect thing, that's all. I know all the other deacons by their first names, too, but I still call them Deacon."

"Well, I guess I understand that. I'm glad you were able to get to work and you are ministering to someone else."

"I guess you can call it that, but she just needed a ride to work."

"Does she know Jesus?"

"I don't know, Deacon Fredricks. We don't talk about that much."

"Well, never miss an opportunity to bring somebody to Jesus."

"Ain't this 'bout a bitch?"

"Excuse me?"

"I'm sorry, Deacon Fredricks. I just pulled back up to my house because I forgot my work badge, and my neighbor just went into my house with what looks like her bathrobe on. I have to go."

"Wendy, wait. Don't go in the house. Just calm down. Is Rashad still at home? Well, I guess so if you say she just went into the house. Do you need me to come over there?"

"No. I just needed one last reason to get him out of my life. I finally prayed the right prayer yesterday, and the Lord has delivered this morning. I knew she was dirty, but I just didn't know how dirty she was."

"Well, it takes two to tango, and who knows? She just may need to borrow some sugar or use the phone."

"She has two cell phones, Deacon Fredricks, and I watched her unpack a car full of groceries on Saturday. So, if she didn't get sugar, that's not my problem. I'm just trying to give them time to really get into whatever they may be doing in my bed before I go in."

"Wendy, listen to me. Just go on to work."

"Not gonna be able to do that, Deacon Fredricks. Have a good day."

"Wendy?"

After ending the call, I took off my shoes right there in my car. I had to call Jessica and tell her I wasn't going to work so she could find another ride. Next, I called work and told my supervisor, Mr. Wallace, I had been sick all weekend and still wasn't feeling my best. He said no problem, but little did he know, the problems were about to start.

I opened the door so quietly that I felt as if I were breaking into a house like a professional thief who was careful not to set the alarm off or alert the family dog.

As I took one step at a time, while trying not to bump the wall or rattle my keys, I could hear the moans of pleasure from Chrissy. When I got closer to the top of the stairs, I heard Rashad beg her to turn over so he could fuck her from behind. In that instant, I paused because that's how I liked it...from the back. Hard and fast, then slow, then harder. *How could he be doing this in my house, in my bed, in my favorite position?*

On the verge of going into a rage, I leaned up against the wall. My knees got weak, and I slid down the wall while my ears burned when her moans turned into desperate cries of the pain and pleasure I knew so well from Rashad. I found myself taking advantage of the disgusting betrayal of my man and the begging for more from Chrissy. Running my hands in my panties, I found myself wet from the sounds of Rashad and Chrissy fucking in my bed. I positioned myself on the top step, opened my legs the width of the staircase, and leaned my head back to form a heavy arch in my back. While he banged her harder and harder, I rubbed faster and faster against my clit as juices ran down the crack of my ass on to my dress.

As she called out his name and begged him not to stop, my fingers went in and out of my throbbing pussy deeper and deeper. With each finger thrust inside myself, I envisioned Rashad giving it to Chrissy like he had done to me in the past. I didn't want him to stop either. I wanted him to fuck her harder and faster because I wanted to cum at the same time they did. Once I climaxed, I let out a heavy sigh of pleasure that immediately caused Rashad to pause.

"Did you hear that?"

"Hear what? Boy, that was me."

That's when I pulled my dress down, got up, went into my bedroom, and told her, "No, bitch, it was me. Now get the fuck out of my house."

Chapter Three
It's Friday. What Now?

"I guess I'll go, Jessica, but I'm not the type of females who has to go out to the club and look for an immediate replacement after they break up with a man."

"I know that, girl, but you can't pretend sitting in the house is helping you get over him any faster either. You even said you haven't talked to him in six days. Hell, that calls for a drink all by itself. In the past, the three days it took Jesus to raise from the grave was the same amount of time before you let that thang back in the house. So, yes, let's celebrate."

"Fine, Jessica. I'll be over there in one hour, and no, I'm not coming in so your nosey momma and sister can be in my business, because I know you told them Rashad and I broke up again."

"For your information, I only told Momma. I don't know how Casey found out."

"Bye, Jessi."

I hadn't been out to a club in so long. Rashad said the only reason people went to a club was to find who they wanted to sleep with that night, and since he and I were together, there was no need for me to go. Funny thing is he went out all the time and managed to come home before the sun came up. So, did he spend the night with someone all those nights?

Hell yeah. Who am I kidding?

He'd probably been sleeping around the entire time we were together. Well, two broken ribs, a couple of black eyes, a busted lip, broken finger, few patches of missing hair, a pregnancy termination, and five STDs later, I finally walked away.

I think I will have a drink tonight. Maybe two, and hell, if this bra works like I plan to make it work, I'll get three or four drinks on somebody else's tab.

"Damn, Jessi, did you have to spray the whole bottle? What is that?"

"Girl, something called His Last Words that I found in Casey's room."

"You damn right it's called His Last Words, because he gonna pass the hell out after inhaling that mess."

"Don't hate that you have to wear knock off Gucci to even come close to smelling like what I'm wearing tonight."

"Please! I'd wear Crisco as opposed to what you smell like right now. Let that damn window down."

When we pulled up to this new club, the line was around the building. Of course, they wanted you to pay seventy-five dollars for VIP to get free watered down drinks, but as cute as my shoes were, they only had a three-minute wait limit before my feet would start crying out for freedom.

"I hope you cashed your check yesterday, Jessica, because I am not standing in line."

"I took fifty dollars from Travis' pants tonight. He ripped up a shirt of mine and knew he would have to pay for it eventually."

"Ma'am, step to the side, please."

"Oh no, we're paying for VIP. There's no way I'm standing in that line."

"Mr. Hamilton saw you coming across the street and is on his way down to escort you in."

"Mr. Hamilton? I'm sorry. I don't know a Mr. Hamilton, and I don't need an escort. I just want to pay so my friend and I can go in."

"I'm sorry, but I have instructions not to let you in until he comes out."

"Look, there must be a mistake. Mr. Hamilton doesn't know me, and I don't want to wait on him. So, call him, text him, or whatever and let him know I don't need his assistance."

Just then, a voice behind me said, "I know you don't need me, but I would love to make sure you have the best seat in the house tonight."

I turned around to find this 6'5", clean-shaven, yellow-ass man with a tight haircut and wearing a tailored made suit with nice shoes. *You just couldn't give it to me all the way 'round Lord, could you?* I thought. I don't like yellow men. Plus, their penises are two-toned, which causes me to be distracted when giving them head. I like mine the same color all the way around. *Damn.*

"Mr. Hamilton is it?"

"I am."

"Thank you for your kind attempts to make my evening run as smoothly as possible, but I'd like to pay for my entrance into the club. So, tell your boss that I decline whatever pimp game he may be trying to run this evening."

"My boss? I'll make a note that the next time you come to this club you would like to pay, but tonight, your money is no good. Now, if you and your friend will follow me, I have a table already waiting for you."

"Did you hear me? I said no thank you."

"Bring yo' ass on here, Wendy. We're right behind you, Mr. Hamilton. And please tell your boss that I apologize for my friend's rude behavior. She doesn't get out much."

"Well, I hope she enjoys herself enough tonight to come back again."

I couldn't believe it. We were escorted to the middle of the club, up a flight of stairs, and to the center of the dance floor. The gentleman even had the nerve to have food and drinks already in place.

"Jessica, I'm ready to go. I don't know what the hell is going, but I'm not eating or drinking anything that has been set up from a complete stranger. So, come on. Let's go."

"Look security said he saw you walking from across the street. He knows you or wants to know you. Either way, you need to sit your ungrateful ass on this leather sofa and relax."

"Ma'am, can I get you something different to eat or drink? I see you haven't touched anything on the table nor drank any of your drink."

I pulled the little waitress down on the couch beside me. "What's going on with this whole set-up? You can tell me. I won't tell on you. I mean, does the owner always randomly pick his booty for the night from the parking lot and put them up here on display?"

"No, ma'am, he normally sits up here alone. This is the food he normally eats, and he doesn't drink. So, the bartender made you the special for tonight."

"You mean to tell me this is not his way of saying I'm going to bang who's in the VIP circle?"

"No, ma'am, and actually, you're not even in VIP. This is the owner's box. VIP is the section on the bottom behind the glass. I heard him radio down that he was coming to greet you, and that's when he put in the food and drink order."

"Damn, Wendy, you a bad bitch!"

"Shut up, Jessi."

"So, Mr. Hamilton is the tall, light-skinned man that brought us up here?"

"Yes, ma'am."

"And this is his club?"

"Yes, ma'am, and he has five other clubs in five other states. Mr. Hamilton is a very nice man and very particular. So, whatever you did to catch his eye, congratulations."

"But I didn't do anything except put on a new bra."

"Trust me, ma'am, if Mr. Hamilton saw something in you, it wasn't your bra. Now, can I get you something else to drink or do you want to try the special?"

"No special. Just bring me four shots of Patrón, because either he pays you a hell of a salary or Mr. Hamilton is crazy."

The waitress laughed before replying, "He's not crazy. I'll be right back. Anything else for you, Ms. Jessi?"

"Hell, bring me four, too. We came together, so we might as well get tore up together." Right after the waitress walked away, Jessica turned to me and said, "Wendy, what in the hell?"

"I don't know, and I haven't seen him since he pushed us off to the waitress. I bet he's sitting somewhere watching my every move right now."

"Probably so. Hell, get up and drop it like it's hot or something. Didn't you hear her say he has five other clubs in five other states? He has a $75 VIP section here that is packed, and regular admission is $25 that people are still wrapped around the building waiting to pay. Everybody in here drinking and having a good time. Add all that up times five, and bitch, I said drop it like it's hot!"

"Shut up! And stop trying to pimp me out."

An hour later, clearly Jessica had too many drinks because she was sitting on the floor. When the waitress came to check on us again, I told her that we were headed out.

As I tried to leave her a nice tip, she said, "Oh no, ma'am, my tip has been taken care of. Thank you, though. And if you'll give me your keys, someone will bring your car to the front for you."

"What? Look, I don't know what... No, I can get my own car. I just need help with my friend."

"Please, Ms. Wendy, let us get your car and someone will be up to help with Ms. Jessi."

"Stop being so nice and stop calling me Ms. Wendy! What is wrong with you?"

"I'm just doing my job, ma'am. So, may I please have your keys?"

"I apologize for yelling at you. Here are the keys, but you tell Mr. Hamilton to bring his ass here right now."

"Yes, ma'am."

At the same time I demanded to see him, Mr. Hamilton was coming up the stairs with another gentleman.

"Walter, please take Ms. Jessica to the lounge and get her some coffee. Then let her lay down until Ms. Wendy is ready to go."

"Yes, sir."

"Now, you needed to see me?"

"Who do you think you are? You don't know me. You come out and make this scene about how you want to make sure I had a good night, and then you disappear. You have a woman wait on me and my friend hand and foot, and then you show up for what? To tell me what I really owe you for this night?"

"You requested to see me. So, I guess the real question is what can I do for you, Ms. Wendy?"

"Brooks. Wendy Brooks is my name. And you can excuse me so I can go home. Thank you for a very surprising evening."

"You haven't seen anything yet, Ms. Wendy Brooks."

"I'm telling you now not to waste your time. I just ended a relationship, and I'm not looking for a Mr. Hamilton at this time."

"But what if a Mr. Hamilton is looking for you? Okay, I won't push it. I'll let Walter know you're ready to go, and he'll get Ms. Jessica to the car."

"Bye, Mr. Hamilton."

I walked down the stairs and didn't look back until I got across the room. When I did finally look back, he was still standing at the top looking down at me as if he were a king overseeing his kingdom. By the time I got to the car, Jessica was laying back in her seat.

"Girl, how did I get in the car? Did I walk?"

"Hell no, you didn't walk, you drunk heffa. You left me to look at the light-skinned Denzel Washington all by myself."

"Stop pretending you weren't impressed with that man. He has it going on, Wendy. Don't let your broken heart keep you from something that may be good for you."

"My heart is fine, but your damn breath is killing me."

"Did you at least get his phone number?"

"No. For what? I told you that I was only coming out because you made me feel like I was trapped in my own home."

"You so selfish."

"How am I selfish?"

"Do you know we were the envy of that entire club tonight? When I went to the restroom, do you know there was a security guard at the bottom of the steps?"

"Stop lying."

"I wish I were."

"Whatever his deal, he need not think he can buy me."

"Hell, he can buy me. I'll sell myself half price if he wants it."

"You are sick! Get out of my car. And thank you for getting me out of the house."

Jessica is a mess, I thought after I had been driving for a while. *Why is my only true friend a white girl with whore tendencies? And where is my phone? I know Rashad's begging-ass has called a hundred times. I'ma kill Jessica. Who feels like driving back to her house, then back to mine? Damnit. Now I have to knock on the door and pray her momma don't answer it. No such luck.*

"Hey, Momma Reins. Can you ask Jessica for my phone, please?"

"Sure. You want to come in?"

"No, ma'am, I'm going to stay out here. You know I'm afraid of your dog."

"Okay."

A couple minutes later, Jessica appeared. "Girl, I thought you got it off the seat at the club."

"You left it at the club?"

"I thought I told you to put it up after I called Momma to see if Travis was sleep."

"Damn, Jessi. Now I got to… Ugh! Goodnight."

I can't believe it's still a line of people trying to get in here, I thought while pulling up. *It's one o'clock in the morning.*

"Excuse me."

"Yes, Ms. Wendy."

How is it that all of a sudden everyone knows my damn name?

"Mr. Hamilton said you would be back. If you get out, I'll park your car and escort you to his office."

"Unbelievable," is all I could say.

Once inside the club, we traveled down a long hallway to an elevator, and then down another long hallway. Too much for one man.

"Mr. Hamilton, Ms. Wendy made it back."

"Thank you, Walter."

"I think Jessica left my phone in your booty bowl upstairs."

"What an inappropriate name you've given it, but if that's how you feel?"

"Look, I know you have my phone. I just want it so I can go home."

"Do you really want it?"

"My phone, yes."

"I want to give it to you."

"Then give it to me."

All the while I'm making my plea for my phone, he is walking closer to me and looking me dead in the eyes. My heart began to race. I don't know if I was afraid of what he would do to me in his office or if it was racing because he wanted to, "give it to me". I began to back up until I was against the wall. He came so close to me that I could feel him breathing on my face, and as he reached in his pocket and pulled out my phone, I closed my eyes only to capture a thought of him lifting my leg around his waist and pressing his warm dick inside of me. I never desired a light-skinned man until that very moment.

He called my name and I answered yes in a deep breath, but I couldn't open my eyes because he was still pushing inside of

29

me. He was so close to my lips that when he called my name again, I took his breath in my mouth and exhaled as I mentally felt his dick going deeper. I felt his hand move my hair from my eyes, and that moment, his touch caused me to cum so hard that the juices began running down my leg. I felt like a child who had a terrible accident while trying to wait patiently on her mother as she shopped the clearance table in a department store.

When I opened my eyes, he said, "Rashad called you six times."

I grabbed my phone and tried to walk away, but he grabbed my arm.

"Are you okay, Wendy?"

"Yes. Please, I have to go."

"But I want to see you again."

"Maybe."

As I pushed through the crowd to find my way to the restroom, I could still feel him breathing on me. I finally got into a stall and wiped the lust from body, which had run down into my shoe. While washing my hands, a girl stared at me in the mirror.

"You're the woman that was in Mr. Hamilton's owner box, right?" she asked.

"Yes, I was there tonight."

"Are you a celebrity or something?"

"No, I work for a bank. Why?"

"Women would die to be where you were tonight. No one gets up there. So, we figured you were an up and coming star or something."

"No, I'm no star."

"There must be something about you that caused him to put you up there. Well, congratulations."

I looked at her as if she were as crazy, just like everyone else I had come in contact with that night. For some reason, I wasn't surprised to find my car waiting at the door when I came out of the club.

"Goodnight again, Ms. Wendy."

I turned, and it was Walter standing there with a smile.

"Goodnight, Mr. Walter," I replied, returning the smile.

I drove off and turned the corner only to find a business card from Mr. Hamilton on the front seat. His personal information was on the front, and on the back, it read: *Now that you know where my office is, feel free to cum anytime.*

Chapter Four
Church

"Where do I sign up to join the singles ministry?"

"Good morning, Sister Wendy."

"Oh, hi, Ms. Gibson. I didn't know that was you. Wearing a new hat?"

"Yes, ma'am. Got it on sale, too. You know we're so glad to have you here at the church. Pastor said he can't wait until you find the perfect ministry to work in, and the singles ministry is a great start."

"I heard."

"Well, Deacon Fredricks is in charge of the singles ministry."

"But he's not single."

"He was at one time. And hopefully you won't be long after you join either."

She laughed, but there was no way I could sit and listen to him minister to me after mentally fucking him in my shower. *How uncomfortable is that? I mean, I've seen the man's dick for crying out loud. How do I get out of this now?*

"Deacon Fredricks, Sister Wendy is joining the singles ministry."

"Well, praise the Lord. I see you took my advice."

"Uh…yes, sir. I guess I did."

"We have to have a one-on-one like I do with all the new members. Then I'll let you know when the next group meeting is. Seeing how you are joining, you must be single now?"

"If you're asking about Rashad, Deacon Fredricks, I am okay, and yes, Rashad and I are over."

"I guess I prayed the right prayer, too, and I know you are going to be just fine. Pam and I are having dinner at Henry Shoemaker's Country Kitchen. Would you like to join us?"

"Oh no, I can't do that."

Ms. Gibson interjected with her loud ass. "Girl, you don't know what you're missing. Old Shoemaker been cooking since he was fifteen years old. Ain't nothing like it."

"Come on, Wendy. Pam and I insist."

"Okay, you twisted my arm."

"Good deal. I'll go and get Pam so we can get there before the crowd picks up."

"Thanks, Ms. Gibson."

"No problem. By the way, Pastor wants to know if you would be willing to teach a Sunday school class next Sunday."

"I don't know about that, Ms. Gibson."

"He thinks the teen girls could use a change from Elizabeth Dunlap, who's sixty-seven."

Giving in, I replied, "I guess I can do it."

"Stop guessing and claim yes you can to things. Say a prayer and just do it. Now, I'll put you down for next Sunday, and we'll see how it goes. A pretty girl like you should be more confident about the things she can do."

"Yes, ma'am."

"Ready to go, Wendy?"

"Yes, I sure am."

"Go 'head, girl," Ms. Gibson shouted out like she had just

validated me.

She is a trip, I thought while walking with Deacon Fredricks.

"Oh, Pam has to take Sister Wilson home, and then she's going to the mall to take back a suit she bought that's too big. She said enjoy dinner, and she promises to catch us next time."

"So it's just you and me?"

"Yep. We can talk about the singles ministry and kill two birds with one stone. Is that okay?"

"Sounds good to me. I'll follow you because I have no idea where the place is located."

There were so many people at the soul food place. Men were dressed in suits and ties, and women were wearing their Sunday's best skirt suits and dresses. Kids played and enjoyed the restaurant's feeling of being at grandmother's house. I immediately embraced it all. A tall, skinny man came to the counter as we walked up.

"Who do you have here, Deacon Fredricks?"

"Henry, my main man, this is Ms. Wendy Brooks. She's new to the area. She is also the newest member of the church and singles ministry."

"Singles ministry? That won't last long. Pleased to meet you, Ms. Wendy."

"You too, Mr. Henry. You always have this kind of crowd?"

"Tuesday through Sunday, yes, ma'am. Now that you know, we expect to see you more often."

"Yes, sir."

"Where's Pam at today, Mark?"

"Running errands, and she said she's going to the mall."

"Spend his money, Pam!"

"Trust me, she is."

"Well, enjoy your dinner. Tabitha, take Deacon Fredricks and Ms. Wendy here to his table."

"You have your own table, Deacon Fredricks? That's a shame."

"No, that's a good thing. Did you see that line?"

We laughed and followed the young lady through the stuffed restaurant. As we sat at the table looking like the perfect couple, I couldn't help but to notice the men looking at me and then at him as if they were silently questioning our relationship. I crossed my legs in discomfort, because even in watching the men watch me, I couldn't help but notice how smooth Deacon Fredricks' lips ran off his fork with every bite of food he took. I tried not to give him too much eye contact, but he just kept on talking. When we laughed, he flashed the prettiest smile and the most beautiful teeth. *Oh my God, this man.*

I tried not to close my eyes for too long because my pounding heart was turning into something sinful right there at the table. Earlier that day, I prayed I would not encounter him in any way other than passing by him during church service, but I see God was away from His desk when I sent up that request.

And if this man to the left of us eats another piece of that potato pie and licks his lips while looking at me, I'm going to explode.

"Wendy?"

Open your eyes and answer him, fool.

"Wendy?"

"Yes?"

"Are you okay?"

"Yes."

"Why are you smiling?"

Damnit. Open your eyes, please.

"You want to talk about you and Rashad?"

"No."

"You want to talk about the singles ministry?"

"No."

"Are you done eating?"

"Yes."

"You gonna be okay to drive?"

"Yes."

"Do you take medication?"

"No."

"Well, what's wrong?"

"I want to fuck you."

His tone changed immediately. "Excuse me?" I opened my eyes in shock. "Oh my God. I'm so sorry. I didn't mean to say that. Please forgive me. I have to go. Thank you for dinner. I'm sorry."

Quickly, I grabbed my purse and took off running to my car, only to realize I left my damn keys on the table. *How in the hell am I going to go back in there and get them? Shit. I'm just going to walk home. I can't. I just can't.*

Then I looked up and walking towards me with a grin similar to the Grinch who stole Christmas was Deacon Fredricks, rattling my keys.

"You won't get far without these."

I dropped my head; he lifted it up.

"It's okay."

"No, it's not. I'm so, so sorry."

"You thinking it is one thing, but us acting on it is something else. You're human. Not that I'm all that or worthy enough to deserve the compliment you just gave me at the table, but thank you."

37

"I have to go. I don't want to talk about this ever again."

"We don't have to. And if it makes you uncomfortable to be in the singles ministry, I understand. Just know that we all have thoughts, but it's the acting on them that gets us in trouble. Some people believe if you thought it, you might as well have done it. Not me. You don't think I fantasize about things? Shoot, Halle Berry is my biggest setback. I have to ask the Lord to forgive me when it comes to her. So, get over it."

"Thank you for trying to make it okay, but I openly said the words of the thoughts in my head. How about that for a setback? So, have a good evening."

"Drive safely, and I'll check on you tomorrow."

"That won't be necessary, Deacon Fredricks."

"Yes, it will be. Now, goodnight."

All the while I was driving home, I kept thinking about what if his wife would have been at the table. All kinds of hell would have broken loose. *How could I be so stupid?* My phone rang, interrupting my thoughts. *Not now, Rashad. Does the ignore button not mean anything to you? Ugh!*

"Hello?"

"Baby, I want to see you."

"No, thank you."

"But why, Wendy? I miss you, and I know you miss me, too."

"Were you missing me about six days ago when you were knee deep in Chrissy's pussy in my bed?"

"Baby, that was a mistake."

"And me taking you back again will be another mistake. A mistake I refuse to make. Don't call me anymore, Rashad. It's over."

"Don't say that. Plus, I need to get the rest of my clothes in the other bedroom."

"Don't worry. I took them over to Chrissy's house, too."

"Wendy?"

"Bye."

Deciding to rent *What's Love Got to Do with It* and call it a night, I pulled up at my favorite video rental spot.

"Hey, Mr. Phillip."

"Ms. Wendy, you must be taking it in early this Sunday evening?"

"Yes."

"Rashad got you picking up a good movie to cuddle with tonight?"

"Not at all. Rashad and I are done, Mr. Phillip. So, I need a male bashing movie."

"Well, you know we have plenty. Enjoy your search."

"He must be crazy," a voice says from behind me.

I turn around to find a very well-dressed Mr. Hamilton. "If memory serves me right, you have a debt to pay, Ms. Lady."

"I don't owe you shit." I turned back around to Mr. Phillip. "Excuse me, Mr. Phillip." I then pull Mr. Hamilton towards the back of the store. "What, you stalking me now? You don't control enough stuff at night you have to follow me around and try to control my day, as well. Wow. Talk about power tripping."

"Why pick up a movie and go home when I can take you to a movie and dinner?"

"I've had dinner already, thank you. I'm not in the mood to be around a lot of people, so no thank you. I'm going home."

"Let me buy you a drink then. Pick your movie, and let me take you around the corner to Michael's and buy you a drink."

"Michael's? What does your high-profile behind know

about Michael's?"

"I own Michael's. That's what I know."

"So you're the club Robin Hood? Got them for the rich and for the poor?"

"No. I just know sometimes people don't like to be around a whole lot of people as you just so sassily put it. They want to just sit back, listen to something peaceful and smooth, and just chill out. Now, can I buy you a drink or not?"

I looked over to see Mr. Phillip giving me the head nod of his approval. See, Mr. Phillip has been around for a long time, so if he says okay, then it must be all good.

"Fine, Mr. Hamilton, one drink. Mr. Phillip, I'll be back to get my movie."

"Take your time. You know where I am."

"Have a good evening, Mr. Phillip."

"You, too, Little G."

"Let me guess. You own Mr. Phillip, too?"

"Funny. Mr. Phillip and my father were good friends before we moved away."

"How convenient."

"Why are you so mean, Wendy Brooks?"

"You think I'm mean?"

"It's only a sign of hurt that you shouldn't wear on your shoulders. It takes away from your outfit."

I shook my head and smiled. "Mr. Hamilton, what do you want from me?"

"I just want to buy you a drink."

"If memory serves me right, you bought my entire evening yesterday. So, let's cut to the chase. Tell me what it is that you really want."

"To see you smile daily."

"Oh really, and what else?"

"That's it. Now go on and tell me where you're going to be tomorrow so I can be there, too?"

"And who says I'll be smiling tomorrow if you're around?"

"Trust me, if I'm there, you'll smile."

"Cocky does not look good on you."

"Does confident?"

"Damn. Do you have an answer for everything?"

"No, but maybe you have an answer to why you would stand in my office and take advantage of the fact that I'm a gentleman?"

"What do you mean?"

"What happened last night? When you were up against my wall with your eyes closed, you weren't there. I mean, you were there, but you weren't there. And at my touch, something happened that caused you to run out like a child that was caught stealing from a store. Tell me about that."

"I have to go."

"You said that, too."

I felt myself getting antsy in my seat, and a throbbing sensation began to muster inside of me. I needed to leave or it was going to be the second time I put my foot in my mouth that day.

"Wendy? Talk to me."

"I'm going home. I'll just call you later."

"Let me take you home."

"Okay. Wait! I mean, no." I said that shit so fast that I scared myself and then tried to take it back. "I meant to say no thank you that won't be necessary."

"Too late. I just want to make sure you get home okay."

"I'm fine."

Ignoring my reply, he proceeded to call Walter and give him instruction. "Hey, Walter, can you get Louis to bring you over to Michael's so you can take Ms. Wendy's car to her house? I'll leave the keys and her address here for you. She'll be riding with me."

Damnit. He said riding, derived from the word ride. I can do this. It's all about self-control.

"Come on." He extended his hand as if he were saying, "Just trust me."

On the ride home, I let my seat back to enjoy the view of the sky due to the fact that Mr. Hamilton was driving a convertible Mercedes. He had some nice Jazz music playing, and the breeze was just right. It calmed me down enough for me to close my eyes and envision I was running through a field of flowers in the springtime. I finally opened my eyes after the car completely stopped. We were in the yard of one of the most beautiful houses I had ever seen in my life.

"Mr. Hamilton, is this your house?" I asked.

"Yes. Would you like to come in?"

"I think so."

We walked into his house that was fit for a royal family. I wanted to ask him what else he did on the side, and pray he didn't admit to selling drugs.

"Mr. Hamilton, now do you want to tell me what you want from me? I mean, we are in the privacy of your home."

"Are you smiling?"

I shyly smiled. "No."

He looked at me and said, "Come to bed with me."

"Excuse me?"

"Just come and lay down with me. I'm not going to touch you, I promise."

I took his hand and followed him upstairs as if I were a girl about to have sex for the very first time. However, I became so confident by the time we reached the top of the stairs that I went ahead of him to the double doors in front of us.

When I opened the doors, nothing could have prepared me for what I saw. It was a bed big enough for two bears. You had to walk up five steps to reach it. Walk-in closets, a bathroom straight out of a five-star hotel. The man even had a waterfall in the corner that displayed crystal rocks at the bottom.

He led me up the steps to the bed and said, "Lie down and get some rest. I'll be back in a few hours."

"No. You can't just leave me here."

"Dawn is here if you need anything. You haven't slept well in about five days, if you let me tell it. Get some rest. I'll be back."

Okay, now I'm really scared, because how in the hell does he know I haven't slept since Rashad has been gone? I watched him walk away as if he were a genie that had granted my last wish. Before exiting the room, he turned, looked at me, and winked his eye.

Dawn (I assume that's who she was) knocked, stuck her head in the door, and said, "If you need anything, just pick up the phone and speak. I can hear you from any room in the house."

"Thank you."

"My pleasure, Ms. Wendy."

What the hell? She knows my name, too? This is some freaky shit, but who can argue? I crawled to the middle of the bed, took off my dress and shoes, and before I knew it, I was stretched out listening to the water run over the rocks. I felt a light kiss on my head, but when I turned, no one was there.

When I turned back over and closed my eyes, I was kissed again, only this time on my lips. Once again, I opened my eyes. Still, no one was there, but I wasn't afraid. The next time I closed my eyes, the lips kissed my neck so gently that I exhaled in delight. They didn't stop there, though. Down the middle of my chest was the path those lips traveled. Then they went to my left breast and a tongue teased my nipple enough to get my right nipple hard. Next, the lips went across to my right breast, teasing it enough for me to take my panties down for more lip service. I never opened my eyes. I just enjoyed the lips all over me. I didn't know who they belonged to, and I didn't care.

As they began to go down the center of my body to my navel, I bent my legs at the knees to make a suitable path for the lips to continue their journey. They released the tongue that stroked over my pussy with such ease that it sent a chill down my spine, causing me to arch my back enough to receive more. The entire mouth then took my swollen clit in, while my hips begin to wind slowly. Then, it happened. The mouth overpowered my clit, pressing it hard between my pussy lips and the tongue. My moans insisted it was good and I wanted more.

The tongue that had been giving so much pleasure to my clit began going in and out of my pussy without hesitation. I couldn't help but to wonder what human being possessed a mouthpiece that could go in and out of a pussy deep like a regular dick on a good day?

My legs were then slowly pushed towards my head to the point where my body was openly exposed. The lips took my clit again, sucking and pulling. Then the tongue went in and out of my pussy again. Before I could beg for more, the warmth of a hard dick was pressing its way inside my body. My pussy was so tight at first that I began to scoot back to ease the pressure, but the dick only came after me with a stronger determination for me to feel it completely inside of me.

I laid there with cries of pain and pleasure coming from my mouth as the lips silenced me with kisses. Hands caressed my breasts, and the dick that powered its way into my pussy made music with my hips. The music I heard in my head from the pleasure my body was receiving only grew louder as the dick became harder while pushing deeper inside my pussy. I could feel a body close to mine, grinding and pushing, going deeper as I put another arch into my back. I couldn't catch my breath because the lips were all over my face and breasts. Soon, they were on my pussy, but I could still feel the hard dick plunging inside me.

What in the fuck is happening? Why do I feel so many things at the same time? I can't breathe. Oh my God, I'm about to cum, but I can't breathe. I'm gonna cum. I can't bre...shit, I'm cumming.

I took three short breaths and opened my eyes to Mr. Hamilton sitting at the foot of the bed completely dressed. Dawn stood nearby holding a glass of ice water.

Smiling, he asked, "Are you okay?"

Chapter Five
A New Week

"Momma, I'm fine. This is not the first time I've broken up with a man."

"Yeah, but this is the first time you've broken up with Rashad and meant it. What are you doing to occupy your time?"

"Reading."

"Reading what?"

"The Bible."

"Stop lying. You pick up the Bible on Sunday during service, if that. Who do you think you're fooling?"

"Momma, I'll have you know I joined a church downtown, and I'm part of the singles ministry there, too."

"Sharon told me she thought you joined a church on 18th Street, but I told her not my daughter."

"You got people spying on me, Momma?"

"No, but Sharon has a friend who has a cousin named Linelle that dates a girl named Kelly that goes to the church on 19th Street, and she said she saw Rashad dropping you off a few Sundays ago."

"Dang, Momma."

"Whatever, little girl. I'm just glad you're going. I'm glad you didn't let Rashad keep you from going like you did when you first moved over there."

"A lot of things have changed since I moved over here away from you, Momma."

"What are you trying to say, Wendy?"

"I'm just saying, Momma, since I moved out, I have a new independence. You've always told me that I had to find Jesus for myself. So, joining this church was my first step."

"Well, I'm proud of you, baby."

"Honestly, Momma, I didn't do it for your approval. I just knew I needed to make some changes in my life, and I knew God needed to be top priority. Then I figured He would give me the strength to leave Rashad if I had to and mean it."

"How have you been since the breakup?"

"Getting better every day. He calls. Sometimes I answer and sometimes I don't. Just depends on how I'm feeling that day. It's over, Momma, and whether he understands that or not, I'm moving on."

"Well, baby, what happened?"

"That's not important, Momma. Just know that I am fine. I'm in my right state of mind, and like I said, getting better and better every day."

"Then I'll leave it alone."

"Good, and if I stay on the phone with you for one more minute, I'm going to be late for work. So, I love you, but I have to go."

"I love you, too, baby. Call me later."

"I will."

*****

What a great way to start my week. Number one in recalls in our division. Wendy Brooks, you are a bad bitch! What will I do to treat myself? I could take this bonus check and take the rest of the week off if I wanted to. You know what; I think I will make an appointment to have a massage at Pandora's Box this evening. Hell, I deserve it.

Why are they sitting outside? Damn. I'm just going to walk in my house and act like I don't see them.

"Oh, what? You ain't speaking these days, Wendy?"

"Angela, don't pretend you give a damn if I speak to you or not. You sitting over there with Chrissy, and I'm sure you know she's been fucking Rashad in my house. So, no, I'm not speaking. Now what?"

"I ain't got nothing to do with who Chrissy is sleeping with. She's grown."

"Then her grown ass ought to know that sleeping with someone else's man makes her a whore."

"Why you talking like I ain't even sitting here?"

"Because you don't matter, and Angela started talking to me. So, I addressed her."

"But you're talking about me."

"Girl, please, everybody is talking about you."

As I turned to walk in my house, she had the nerve to say, "Rashad came to get his stuff you put in my yard."

"He should have, because I told him his shit was with his bitch. I see he had no problem determining who that was."

I turned the key in my door, shook my head, and closed the door behind me after entering my house. I knew she wasn't going to come off that car because she still didn't know what state of mind I was in from catching her ass in my bed. She's too nervous to run up in my face. So, I proceeded to take my shower, shave, and head out to Pandora's Box.

*****

Now this is nice.

"Ms. Brooks?"

"Yes, and call me Wendy, please."

"Right this way, Wendy. Titan will be doing your massage today. He is very experienced, and when I told him that you were celebrating a bonus at work, he said you deserved the best."

"And he's one of the best?"

"Well, at least that's what we've heard."

"Then, thank you."

"It's our pleasure." She escorted me down the hall that was filled with the aroma of pure essence. "If you just undress to your comfort level and hang this red knocker on the outside of your door when you're ready, Titan will be right in."

"Thank you."

Okay, she said undress to my comfort level. Hell, if I get butt naked, he'll think I'm a whore. If I undress halfway, he'll think I'm nervous and uncomfortable. To hell with it, you smell good and you look good. You're single and carrying around a bonus check that can buy Titan's time for two weeks. Naked it is. Hang the knocker and now under the sheet. But why is my heart beating so fast?

The door opened, and it was the young lady from the front counter.

"Ms. Wendy, Titan had to leave for an emergency, but Panther is here now. He's just as good as Titan."

"Why do all of your men have exotic dancer names?"

"Truthfully, it's an exotic experience that's provided here at Pandora's Box. So, if you will have Panther, we will only charge you half price because of the delay and since the person we assigned to your massage had to leave."

"Then, Panther it is. Thank you."

Before she could even close the door good, I closed my eyes

and began envisioning what a panther looks like. Sleek, powerful, black, fast...damn, what a beautiful creature. When I opened my eyes, he was standing there...sleek, black, hot, and fine as hell.

Then he did it. He opened his mouth to speak, and the most beautiful set of teeth money could buy were displayed.

"Hello, Ms. Brooks. I'm Panther, and I'll be taking care of you this evening."

Say something fool before he thinks you're retarded. Hello. Speak.

"You have the most beautiful smile I've ever seen."

"Thank you. And thank you for letting me take care of you in Titan's absence."

"If you're what I get when Titan is not available, I hate to see what they offer if you're not available. How can someone enjoy a massage from a man as fine as you without having some of the most impure thoughts known to man?"

"Your time here is supposed to be pleasurable. That's one thing we believe in here at Pandora's Box, making the guest feel good. And if you're ready, I want to make you feel good."

I took a deep breath, looked him in his eyes, and said, "Please do."

Then, I closed my eyes. Just smelling his cologne made me relax as if I'd been there with him on numerous occasions. When he began explaining what he would be doing to me, I immediately stopped him.

"Shhh. Just do it, please."

"Yes, ma'am."

I felt the softest touch to my right leg as he reached under the sheet to pull my leg out. He started at the very top of my thigh, far enough up to determine if I were wearing panties or

51

not. It was so pleasant, and it didn't make me jump in discomfort at all. In fact, I wanted to scoot down so his fingers were close enough to accidently glide inside of me. He caressed my leg like you would caress a newborn baby.

He took my other leg out with the same care. Again, he was so close to my pussy that it had already began to juice up. I exhaled at his touch. He then positioned himself at the side of my arm and placed my hand on his belt buckle. I grabbed hold and didn't let go until he took my hand and glided it down the front of his pants to an erect penis. I licked my lips in excitement. My pussy tightened, squeezing like I was already on his dick. This time, my exhaling turned into a slight moan.

"I'm going to hold the sheet opposite of my body, and I need you to turn over on your stomach," he whispered.

I guess I did, because I felt him straddle me right below my ass. I didn't even care what massage technique this was, because my pussy was so wet that he could have put his big toe inside me and I would've cum instantly. I felt his warm body through the sheet. He started at the back of my neck, and I could have sworn those were his lips so warm on me. Still, I didn't budge.

He went down the center of my back, pushing with both hands. I wanted him to keep pushing since I could feel his hard dick up against me with his every motion. As his hands made it to the top of my ass, I thought he was going to skip over it and go straight to the back of my legs, but not this Negro. Arching his back, his dick fell perfectly between my legs as he began to rub my legs backwards with both hands. I could feel his hard dick pressing up against my wet, jumping pussy. I moaned so loud that it must have turned him on, because he leaned back even further to reach my ankles, which gave him a more direct aim at my pussy. When I felt his dick pushing against my clit, that was it for me.

"Please, don't stop," I told him.

"Are you okay, Ms. Wendy?"

Ignoring his question, I repeated, "Please, don't stop."

The sheets were so thin by design, I'm sure. Still, I could feel him, hot and hard, and I knew I was going to cum if he kept leaning back rubbing my legs with his dick piercing through the sheet.

"Please, don't stop."

His rubbing got faster, and I could feel myself about to explode because of the friction in between the sheet and his dick. Why did it feel like his dick was out of his pants and right there for me to take? I wanted to reach down and see for myself. It was so hard I wanted it inside of me. *If I could just turn over, I'd grab his waist and pull him inside this pussy that is so ready to receive him.*

I could feel his hands on my legs, but as they got closer to my thighs, I could feel him coming down to reposition himself. That's when something eased inside of me. *What is that? Shit. I don't know, but don't take it out.*

"Ahhh," I moaned louder as it went in again. "Yes."

That has to be his dick. Fuck, I'm about to cum.

"Don't stop. You're going to make me cum, Panther. Oh my God. Shit. Shit, I'm cumming. Yes, I'm cumming now."

I shook in sheer pleasure and forced my eyes open to find Panther standing over my head, watching as I plunged the lotion bottle I had taken from him into my pussy, giving myself pleasure like I had never before. He kissed me on my forehead as I lay there in embarrassment.

"Welcome to Pandora's Box," he said with a little smirk,

then left the room so I could get dressed.

I took the lotion bottle and put it in my purse. *Ain't no way in hell he's gonna use it again.* Then I headed to the counter to pay.

"How was it, Ms. Wendy?" the receptionist asked.

Before I knew it, I blurted out, "I want him next Monday at the same time."

"I'll schedule it right now," she said while taking the money from my hand. "Oh no, you only owe half. So that's $150.00."

"Can you give the rest to him, please?"

"You want to leave him a $150.00 tip?"

"That doesn't even come close to covering what that man's hands can do."

"Thank you for coming today, Ms. Wendy."

"No, thank you for allowing me to."

During my drive home, I began to think how I must have embarrassed myself or made Panther uncomfortable with my actions. However, he kissed my forehead. So, either it happened all the time or he got off, too. *I can just imagine the number of women who go in that building and come out feeling as good as I feel. I can finish my workweek with no problem now.*

My attention was drawn to my ringing cell phone. *Didn't I tell Rashad not to call me? Why? Why, Lord? Do I need to speak it in Spanish?*

"Hello!"

"Hey."

"Hey what, Rashad?"

"Don't be mean, Wendy. I want to come over to see you."

"For what? We don't have anything else to say to each other. Why is that so hard for you to understand?"

"I just need to see you. I won't even stay that long. I just need to say what I have to say to you in person. Please?"

"Fine, I'll be home in fifteen minutes, and you only have five minutes upon arrival to get out all that you have to say."

"Thank you."

I don't know why I want to fuck up my night with this mess, but fine. And it just couldn't get better for one second, because his trick is now outside. I wish she was standing in the street; I'd accidentally not see her. Wonder if my insurance covers that?

"Hey, Wendy."

"Why, Chrissy? Why do you pretend like you didn't sleep with Rashad and that we're supposed to just be cool after that? Make me understand it."

"I'm sorry!"

"You got that right, and stop speaking to me. Get this for the last time. You can have him. What the two of you did was foul, and I don't appreciate it. You couldn't be satisfied with the five other men I knew you were sleeping with. You just had to have mine, too. You're pitiful."

"But, Wendy…"

"Fuck you."

I slammed my door as hard as I could. Moments later, my doorbell rang. *This better not be her.*

"What?" I yelled while swinging the door open.

"You told me I could come over." Rashad said, standing there.

"Oh, I thought you were Chrissy."

"Y'all had words?"

"Why?"

"She just sped off in her car."

"She probably sped off because she saw you pull up, so don't even go there. Now, what's so important that you had to see me to tell me?"

"You know I love you, right?"

"What now, Rashad? Who's pregnant? You might as well tell me. If not Chrissy, who? The girl who use to do my hair? The lady at the cleaners where you pick up our dry cleaning? Or no, wait. The lady who use to work the service desk at the mall? Who?"

"Nobody is pregnant."

"Then what is it?"

"I think Chrissy burnt me. I went to the clinic on Friday and got treated. I wanted you to know so you can go and get checked."

Smack!

"What the fuck you slap me for?"

"Get out!"

"What? I didn't have to tell you."

"You nasty and you dirty. And you gonna learn the hard way about not wrapping your dick up. HIV is real, asshole! I'm glad we're done. Now you can just gamble with *your* life. In all these years, all your cheating, I'm glad you only brought me something home that I could get some pills or a shot for. You don't give a fuck about yourself, so what in the hell would make me think you would give a fuck about me? You're weak. Get the fuck out of my face!"

"Baby, I'm sorry. I just wanted you to be okay."

"You wanted me to be okay? You're a joke. Where you staying at, Rashad? You ain't got shit. You move in with every woman you date. Get your own shit. That way, when a woman puts you out, you'll have somewhere to go. Grow the hell up. It trips me out that you'll go and spend a hundred dollars on some shoes, but won't spend ten dollars on a box of condoms to cover your dick. You know why I hadn't slept with you in over three months right before we broke up? I had to get treated for another STD from your stupid ass. What you think, I want to die fucking around with you?"

"So you weren't gonna tell me?"

"Hell, you didn't think enough of me to tell me. That's how I knew you didn't love me. You said you did, but you didn't. I'm glad it was something I could get cured, yet again. I'm working on getting over you, so I suggest you do whatever you need to do to get over me, as well. Maybe you need to go over there and tell Chrissy about your little problem, but you're done here."

"Man, fuck that girl."

"Man, you already did. That's why you over here now. Get out!"

"Wendy..."

"Bye, Rashad!"

"But..."

Slamming my door twice in one day felt so good, especially slamming it in his face. *Sure, it's been three long months, but I'm gonna save this good stuff for someone who deserves it. From this day forward, I vow to give only to the needy, not the greedy!*

I laughed as I walked upstairs, only to look out my window to see Rashad and Chrissy outside arguing. *Guess she didn't go far after speeding off. Hell, ain't no telling. He might have given something to her as opposed to her giving something to him. Let them deal with it. It's not my problem anymore. I'm going to bed. Goodnight, Panther.*

Chapter Six
Another Saturday Night Out

"No, Jessica. The last time I went out with you, I ended up being macked from the parking lot."

"Don't pretend like you didn't like Mr. Hamilton's VIP treatment. Hell, I know I did."

"I just want to chill tonight. I thought maybe you would come over so we could watch a movie or something. Then I could tell you about my trip to Pandora's Box on Monday."

"You went to Pandora's Box? I can't believe you kept that from me all week. You ain't right."

"Well, we needed something to talk about this weekend, so I saved it. Plus, if I had told you about my experience, you would have been trying to get some money to run up in there."

"I ain't going in there. People say that place is forbidden."

"The massage parlor? Girl, please!"

"No, women who go in there don't come out the same."

"Well, I went in, and I'm fine."

"Says who?"

"Go to hell, Jessica. I'm fine."

"I bet he was, too."

"Who?"

"The man who massaged you. I bet he was the shit."

"Girl, he was. I dreamed about him until like Wednesday."

"See what I'm talking about."

"Hey, Wes from work asked me to an all-black party tonight. If I go anywhere, I think I want to check his party out."

"Hell no. That's a big step down from Hamilton's club. I want to go back there."

"No, Jessi, because then he'll think I want him or something."

"You can't be serious, Wendy. His professional behavior didn't turn you on one bit?"

"No."

"You a damn lie. I know you, Wendy. You were hot and bothered by it. You're probably getting excited right now."

"I've seen him since then, thank you."

"Bitch, and you weren't gonna tell me that either?"

"There was nothing to tell."

"Please! You already told me that you hadn't slept with Rashad in almost what, three months? Then here comes Mr. Fine-Ass Hamilton with all these perks, and you didn't fuck him? Don't try to play me."

"Jessica, you're the only one who gets turned on with 'perks', not me. I've always been simple to please."

"Whatever. And calling me easy doesn't take away from the fact that if you didn't sleep with Mr. Hamilton, you will."

"Are we going to Wes' party or not? I have tons of sexy black stuff that I've been buying and hiding since Rashad and I started dating, but now I can bring it all out."

"I'm not going over there, Wendy. You know how lame Wes' ass is at work. Please!"

"I have something you can wear that will make those D's stand up and dance."

She paused before replying, "I'll be over there in fifteen

minutes."

"And don't go in Travis' wallet. I'll take care of drinks tonight if we need them."

"Hell, it's the Waffle House that I want after we leave."

"See you in a few, crazy."

"Bye."

*****

"This can't be the right address, Wendy. Hell, Wes works on the 2nd floor. Ain't no way in hell he lives in this neighborhood."

"Well, this is the address on the invite he gave me. Jessi, look."

"Bitch, he got valet parking. I'm gonna fuck his lame ass tonight."

"Shut up, stupid." As we approached the person checking names off on a guest list, I provided our names. "Wendy Brooks and Jessica Reins, thank you."

"Girl, Wes is showing out!" Jessica said as we entered the party.

Now mind you, Wes is the lamest Negro at our job. He's a cross between Steve Urkel and Mr. Rogers with muscles, but his party seemed to be slamming. *And what'da you know, here's Wes coming towards me with two fine-ass women. He is either fronting tonight or he has a damn alter ego.*

"Wendy, glad you made it. Jessica, damn, you looking good tonight." He turned to his arm candy. "Ladies, if you will excuse me, I need to speak with Wendy alone, please?" Once the women dismissed themselves, Wes looked me up and down. "I told myself if you showed up tonight, I wasn't going to hold anything back. Jessica, can you excuse us, please?"

I looked at him kind of confused and grabbed Jessica's arm.

"Hold anything back? Wait. Anything you want to say to me you can say in front of Jessica. I will more than likely tell her what you've said anyway." I smiled and then paid close attention to what he was about to say because I had a feeling it was going to be good. *Hell, he cleared the area for this speech, so it has to be something good that he wants to share.*

"Fine, then! I want to fuck you. I want to fuck you so bad that it kills me to clock in every day, because when I see you at work, I immediately get a hard dick and want to put it inside of you. I want your pussy on my face when I see you walk past my door. I gave you the invitation with the intent to have you tonight. I...want...you."

I swallowed hard before walking right up to him and kissing the side of his face. "Have a good night, Wes," I said. Thank you for the invite, and your honesty is greatly appreciated."

"Wait. Please don't leave. I just had to tell you. I couldn't help myself. I have a party like this every three months, and I just got the nerve to invite you after a year and a half. So, I know you can just imagine how long it has taken me to muster up the nerve to say what I just told you."

Before I could say anything, Jessi said, "Well, if you ask me, I think it was rude and downright disgusting for you to think for one minute that you can say how you want to take someone to bed after you just shook two women off your arm. What kind of woman do you think my girl is? The party was not whack until you came over here and opened your mouth with that nasty-ass proposal. Let's go, Wendy. And when you see her at work, think what you want to think, but keep your damn mouth closed."

I looked back at him, feeling like a twelve-year-old that just got caught kissing outside the mall or something by her parents.

Even with Wes being lame as hell, it was a hot-ass party, and I can't pretend I wasn't turned on by his interest in me. Take off his work attire and his glasses, and maybe...just maybe!

During the entire ride home, I didn't hear one thing Jessica said. I had blocked her out so hard that I thought she had gone to sleep. When I pulled up to my house, she got out and slammed my door.

"What the hell is your problem?"

"You tell me, Wendy. I've been talking to you for twenty minutes, and you ignored me the entire time. If you call yourself upset about what I said to Wes, I'm sorry. There's no way he should have been able to say all that to you. He ain't even that cute either. I mean, yeah, he had valet parking at his lil' party, but who cares?"

"Jessica, this is the same man that you declared you were going to sleep with when we pulled up. And now that you find out his attraction is not to you, but me, it's a problem?"

"He's disrespectful."

"No, you're jealous. I can't believe you. But, sweetie, you can have Wes. I don't want him."

"Say whatever you want to say, Wendy. I'm gone. I'll bring your dress to work."

"Jessi, are you serious?"

She walked off, leaving me standing by my car in awe.

No she is not pulling off. Well, this is one mess that I will not let bother me. I reached in the car to retrieve my purse and phone. *I'm going in this house and have myself a drink since "Mother-May-I" dragged me out of the party before I could have one there. Then I'm going to bed. This is ridiculous. Now here this bitch comes.*

"Hey, Wendy, can I talk to you?"

"Nope!" I said, slamming the door behind me.

No she didn't request permission to speak to me again. Why is this so hard for her? Lord knows I have to go to church tomorrow. My mouth is bad; my attitude is bad; and my mind is bad as hell. Yeah, I'm going to church...early.

Chapter Seven
Sunday Morning

Who could be ringing my doorbell at this time of morning?
The Witnesses are at church already.

"Rashad? Why are you dressed like that?"

"I want to go to church with you. Is that okay?"

"I'll never deny anyone Christ; that's not me. But why didn't you just go to the church?"

"I wanted to go with you."

"You never wanted to go with me before, so why now? Are you sick?"

"Sick of being alone."

"Rashad, please. We've only been apart for two weeks? And if there is one thing I know, it's that you have NOT been alone."

"Well, I'm not with who I want to be with, so I might as well be alone."

"Hey, Chrissy!" I called out as she was exiting her house. "You look nice this morning, girl. I was just about to send him over to go to church with you, because obviously he's at the wrong door. Bye, Rashad."

I didn't even slam the door this time. *You better not cry. Man your ass up, girl. You're over him. Take a deep breath, get your purse, and go on to church. Lord, please don't let*

Rashad still be standing outside my door or I won't make it to church. He had on square-toed shoes, Lord, with a tie. Please don't let him still be at this door. Damnit.

*****

"Whose dick is this?"

"It's yours, Wendy! I'm sorry for giving your dick away, baby. Tell me you forgive me."

"I forgive you, Shad!"

"Say it again."

"I forgive you, daddy."

"How you want this dick?"

"Harder."

"Yeah?"

"Yeah, fuck me hard, Shad, please!"

"Let me taste that pussy!" He picked me up off his dick and sat me on his face.

"Oh shit!"

"Uh huh!"

"Yeah, baby, don't stop! Yeah, yeah, eat that pussy, baby."

He turned me over on my back and shoved his dick inside me again.

"Uh-uh, bring that pussy back here. Stop running!"

"Wait."

"Shut up. I missed this pussy. You should've never opened the door."

He knew he was turning me on even more by being so damn rough with the pussy.

"Uh, yeah, Shad! Yeah!"

"Is that dick deep enough for you, baby?"

"Yeah! Harder, baby!"

"If I hit it harder, you gonna be mad!"

"Shut up and fuck me harder. That's what you came over here for, all dressed up and shit. Come on! Fuck me then! Cum for me if you missed me."

"Shit, girl, stop squeezing my dick. You know I can't take that shit."

"Whose dick is this, nigga?"

"Shit, Wendy, you know it's yours! Don't do that...shit! Fuck. Baby, I'm about to...ugh. You gonna make me bust! I'm cumming! Fuck! Damn, girl, I'm cumming. I missed this pussy so much! Please let me come back home."

I sat up on the side of the bed and smiled at him. "You've been a bad boy, Rashad."

"Don't play with me, Wendy. I fucked up, and I know that. But, I'm sorry. I should have never crossed that line with Chrissy."

"It's okay, but listen, get your condom wrapper off my floor, go in the guest bathroom, and wash up. When I get out the shower, you need to be gone. I have to go to church, pay my tithes, and pray for your ass."

"What the hell is your problem?"

"You are! I've fucked better men in my dreams. I did you today because whatever pleasure you got from fucking Chrissy in my bed can't beat my cumming in your mouth and making your dick cum in two minutes simply because I can. You slapped me around a few times because you are a weak-ass man that won't hit a real man. I let you treat me like shit, but for what? Negro, you ain't shit. Even dressed up in a shirt and tie, you're still weak and your dick is still easy."

"So you think you can just talk to me any kind of way?"

"What you gonna do to me that you haven't done already, Rashad? I'm not afraid of you anymore. That shit is played out, and so are you. So, if you want to fight, we can, or you can just leave with your well-fucked dick. I know pretending to be grown can be difficult for you, but if you try really hard, you can do it. Who knows? I might call you later if I feel like it."

"Fuck you, Wendy."

"You did, and baby, it was better today than you have ever done in the past. You must have known this would be your last time in this pussy. Good job! Now, bye."

I got up, jumped in the shower, and listened for him to slam the door while leaving. *I told you! Stupid! Lord, forgive me for I have sinned! He got me all late now. Damnit. I hope I didn't miss offering.*

*****

"Hey, Sister Brooks!"

"Mrs. Pam, good morning!"

"We missed you in Sunday school this morning. The girls' class really enjoyed whatever you shared with them last Sunday."

"I enjoyed them, as well. I may be able to teach that class more often now that I have my car back in my full possession."

"Praise the Lord, and forgive me for not having dinner with you and Mark the other Sunday. He said he took you to Henry's place?"

"Yes, ma'am, and we had an enjoyable time. The food was great."

"Well, he loves that place, and the eye candy in there ain't that bad on Sundays either."

No, she did not! Now that is funny.

"Well, I'm going to run on in so I won't miss offering."

"Speaking of, they need an extra person to help count offering today with another trustee. Mark told me to find someone to help, and who else other than the person running in to pay hers?"

"Oh, Mrs. Pam, I can't do that. I'm not a trustee or anything like that."

"No, they need one other person in there with the trustees because they can't be trusted all the time."

Why is she laughing like that is something to brag about? This lady is crazy as hell.

"Okay, then. I guess I can do it."

"Good. I'll let Mark know."

I hope I don't have to be in that little bitty-ass room I saw them in last Sunday.

*****

I'll be damned.

"Hey, Deacon Fredricks, looks like we're counting money today."

"Yeah, Pam just told me, but it's going to have to wait a few minutes. I have to get the buses ready for the choir and Pastor to go to another service. People are clearing out pretty fast today so they can go eat and get on over to the other church. So, just hold tight."

No, I'm not hungry as hell, and no, I don't want to be held hostage after church counting money.

"Bye, Sister Wendy."

"Bye, Ms. Gibson."

Please let her keep walking, Lord, before she signs me up for something else. Okay, wait a minute now. The church is pretty much completely empty. Where in the hell is Deacon Fredricks?

"Hey, Sister Brooks."

"Hey, Pastor, how are you?"

69

"I'm good. Thank you, and thanks for staying around to help count the offerings for today."

"Oh, it's my pleasure, Pastor."

"I have to take Trustee Berry with me, so it'll have to be you and Deacon Fredricks. But, you count behind him. His math gets bad after two o'clock."

"Yes, sir. Enjoy the other service."

"Oh, you're not coming with Deacon Fredricks?"

"I hadn't planned on it."

"Nooo, you don't want to miss it."

"Um, okay. I might be able to stop by for a minute."

"Well, I hope to see you there, and if not, I'll see you next Sunday at Sunday school again, right?"

"Yes, sir."

"Good girl," he said, while walking away.

Why did I almost tell the pastor I'm damn near twenty-five? My daddy use to say good girl when I put my plate away as a child.

"Okay, I just double checked the church, and everyone is cleared out. We can begin the count and get this done so I can make it to the next service."

"Then let's do it. I mean, let's count the money."

"I knew what you meant. I hope you're not uncomfortable about being alone with me after what happened at the restaurant. All of that is behind us. We both agreed that we are human."

"I'm fine. I don't know why I was so fast in correcting what I said. So where do we do it? I mean, count the money."

"Come on. It's back here. The space is very limited in here. I hate counting with Deacon Mosley. He seems to let his breakfast get the best of him and passes gas the entire time we're back here."

"That can't be good."

Now mind you, we were in the very same room I didn't want to be in with him. My ass is so big that no matter which way I turned it would either rub against him or the damn table. Both are hard as hell, so I can easily get off. That's why I didn't want to be in there.

Breathe deep and calm down. Shit, he took off his damn jacket. White shirt and tie only. Don't look down to see if his dick is pressing up against his dress slacks. Don't, stupid! I'll be damned.

"You okay, Wendy?"

"Yes, I'm fine. How do you like it done? I mean, I'm just going to stand here and be quiet and wait on direction."

"Wendy, I'm a married man, and I love my wife. As beautiful as you are, I will never take advantage of the fact that my wife trusts me. So, no matter what you say, I'll always respect the both of you. Therefore, don't feel like you have to walk around on eggshells when you're with me."

"Thank you, Deacon Fredricks. Then let's get it on."

I smiled and put my purse down. When I turned back to get started, he was so close to me that I could smell the mints manufactured in the gum he was chewing. I wanted to put my tongue so far down his damn throat it was ridiculous. My heart started beating uncontrollably, and my pussy began to jump with every word I tried to say at that moment. He probably thought I was having a damn seizure or something. *Get your shit together, Wendy.*

"Okay, Deacon Fredricks, stacks of ones, fives, tens, and twenties, right? And checks over here, correct?"

"Yep, and I'll sort all this change that our little tithers put in.

Pass me the coin sorter on the other side of the table on the floor, please, ma'am."

I bent over, not thinking I didn't have on any panties. And no, I didn't squat down to get the sorter. I bent my stupid ass over. When I turned around, he was gone. *Do I go and see where he went or do I just sort the damn coins myself? Maybe I'll just call his name.*

"Deacon Fredericks?"

He can't hear that damn whisper shit.

"Deacon Fredericks?" I said a little louder.

Since he didn't answer, I started walking down the hall in search of him. That's when I heard a bump in the hospitality room. I slowly opened the door to find him leaning against the wall with his dick in his hand, masturbating with his eyes closed. He had his bottom lip in his mouth, and his dick was just like I remembered it that day at my house, but it was erect. *My goodness, this man is so blessed. How old is he again?*

So, do I (a): Gently close the door back and let him enjoy the view he got from me bending over? Or (b): Walk in bold as hell, take his dick from him, and show him my hospitality by putting it in my mouth and then my pussy that's already wet from watching him beat his long, hard dick? Or (c): Just get in my car and leave, never to return to this church again?

But, I love the pastor, the people are so nice, and the Sunday school needs me.

"Deacon Fredricks?"

"Oh my God, Wendy!" He tried to put his dick away, but I walked up to him and took it in my hand.

"Let me help you with this."

"Wendy, no."

"Shhh."

I let it glide inside my dripping wet mouth so slow, keeping my lips tight on it so no air could get in. I wanted it to stay warm as I pulled it back and forth.

"Wendy, I'm sorry."

"Shhh."

I took his dick to the back of my throat, and he let out the very first sign that he was ready to do me.

"Fuck."

I turned around, bent over the lounge chair, and pulled him close to me. "Now do it. Fuck me."

His dick went in my pussy with a little hesitation. Then he began to enjoy the wet, hot walls of my insides. He went deeper with his next stroke before reaching around to pull my breasts out of my dress.

I thought he would squeeze them hard, but he just held them in his large, masculine hands. He leaned in closer to my body for me to feel he had come out of his shirt, his hot body pressing against mine. He pushed all the way inside my pussy and did a slow grind that made me explode.

"I'm about to cum. You got to back up," I told him.

"Shhh," he responded, while he kept grinding.

Then he pulled out. I thought he was about to cum, too, but instead, he picked me up and backed me against the wall. I wrapped my legs around his waist, and he proceeded to bounce me up and down on his dick so slowly that I let out a sigh that only a pleased woman could do.

"Oh my God." I wrapped my arms around his neck and pulled my body as tightly to his as I could, burying my head in his neck. I licked one side, and he began to go faster with the bouncing.

"Please don't do that," he whispered.

I pulled my head back, looked him in his eyes, and gently kissed his lips. At that moment, he slowed down again. By then, I was dripping wet. He looked at me strangely when he realized I was now squeezing my pussy tight on his dick every time he pulled me down on him. He kept pulling, and I kept squeezing. He leaned me against the wall with his one hand still holding my waist and the other holding the wall.

"Damn, girl, what the fuck is that?"

I kept looking him in his eyes.

"Don't stop."

I could tell with every squeeze he was getting closer to cumming.

"Stop. Don't do that, Wendy."

"Fuck me, Deacon Mark Fredericks."

He dropped his head into my breast. I thought his reaction was in disappointment since I had called him Deacon in the midst of fucking him in the church's hospitality room. However, before I called his name again, he had taken my breast in his mouth and was moaning.

"Wendy, I'm sorry."

"What is it?"

"I'm so sorry."

"What's wrong?" I asked, as he continued to fuck me slowly.

"I'm about to cum," he said.

He sat me down, shoved his dick damn near down my throat, and kept pushing. Then he bent me over a nearby chair, grabbed my waist, and began pounding my pussy hard.

"Harder, please. Yeah, harder, please, Mark."

"Wendy…Wendy, I'm…"

"Mark, harder, please. Yeah. I want to cum with you,

please. Harder. Yeah, like that. Yeah…yeah! Fuck."

"Shit, Wendy! Ahhh…."

"I'm cumming! Don't stop, Mark! Fuck me! Yeah, yeah, yeah!"

"Wendy? Wendy?"

"Yeah?"

"Can you open your eyes and tell me how you locked yourself in the hospitality room?"

Slowly, I opened my eyes. "What?"

"I told you to pass me the sorter, but you bent down to get it and said it was not there. When I said it was more than likely in the hospitality room, you left but never came back."

"No, I bent down to get it and you were gone when I turned around."

"Yeah, but you said you would go and get it. You called my name in the hall, and I told you that I was in the restroom. Then the phone rang, and I took a call for the pastor. When I returned you still weren't back. So, I thought maybe you had gone to use the restroom, too. Then when I looked around and the sorter still wasn't in the counting room, I came to check on you. That's when I heard you banging on the wall. Are you okay?"

"I'm fine. Here's the sorter. We should get out of here and get finished so you can get on over to the church."

"Okay. It shouldn't take us long at all. You want to grab something to eat, or are you not going over to the other service?"

"I think I should go home and lie down before going to go see my mother this evening. Maybe next time we have a second service I'll attend."

"Okay, so now you owe me a dinner and a second service. And I'll be sure to tell Pastor, too. You know he'll hold you to it."

I was counting so fast that my fingers were starting to cramp up. *I have got to see someone about my mind. Hell, I'm in the house of the Lord, and I'm fantasizing about being screwed by a married deacon. A fine, sexy, chocolate, aged-to-perfection, married deacon. Yeah, I need to see someone.*

"That's it. We're done here. I'll write the totals as such, and if you sign here, we can leave. Thank you, ma'am."

"You are more than welcome, Deacon Fredericks. Have a good night."

I ran out the church so fast, I think I left smoke at the front door.

Chapter Eight
Why Today?

What in the hell could Mr. Wallace want to see me about? I'm the top performer in our office. I'm number one in the region in my department. What in the hell?

"Wendy, you don't know why he wants to see us?"

"No, Jessica. If I knew, I would've told you. I was going to call and ask you had you heard anything."

"What time is your meeting with him?"

"Ten o'clock, and yours?"

"Ten-thirty. You scared?"

"For what, Jessi? I mean, what I do for this company goes without recognition. If Mr. Wallace wants me to act up, let him say something I don't like."

"Wendy, I'm sorry about the way I acted the other night after Wes' party. Truth be told, I have been crushing on him for about three months now, and for him to just look past all my flirting and come at you, it kinda pissed me off."

"But, Jessi, I don't have any interest in Wes. You're my friend, and had you told me that you liked him, I would have been working overtime trying to hook you two up."

"I know that. I just wanted to try and do this one myself. I'm so tired of Travis that it's ridiculous. I guess I wanted out by any means necessary."

"Jessi, don't you know if you don't want to be with Travis, all you have to do is put his ass out. That's your mother's house. Hell, if for nothing more than you're tired of his bullshit. That's why I finally left Rashad's ass, and the fact that I caught him fucking the shit out of my neighbor. But, when you really get tired of his whack-ass shit, you'll walk away."

"I guess, girl. Well, good luck with your meeting. Stop by my desk first when you get out with Mr. Wallace."

"Okay. You know we're going to have to go to lunch outside of the building to really be able to talk about these meetings."

"I know."

"Well, I'm going to the restroom to say a prayer. Then I'm going in. I'll see you in a few. And, Jessi, you don't have to put up with Travis' shit."

"Good luck, Wendy."

"Thanks, girl."

*****

"Hi, Mr. Wallace. This is an unexpected meeting. Is everything okay?"

"Yes, Wendy. Have a seat. I have good news and bad news. What would you like first?"

"Give me the bad first so I can use the good to be lifted."

"Okay. The bad news is the corporate office called this morning about your job performance. The CEO of the company, Miles Boyd, is coming tomorrow for a meeting with you."

"What the hell? Excuse me, Mr. Wallace. I mean, he wants to see me?"

"Yes, ma'am, he does. And the good news is he's coming to offer you two job promotions."

"Oh my God, Mr. Wallace! Two promotions? That's great

news. I know you had something to do with this, didn't you? Well, let me thank you now."

"Wendy, you've earned every bit of the recognition you're about to receive. I am very proud of you."

"Thank you so much."

"I'll see you in the morning at nine o'clock."

"Thank you. Thank you. Thank you. Whatever these promotions consist of, I will not let you down. I promise."

I hugged him hard, like he was my dad giving me a car at my Sweet Sixteen birthday party. Then I walked out of his office with the confidence of a woman who had just fucked a room full of men and didn't even break a sweat!

I can't wait to tell Jessica. Damnit, she's gone in to her meeting. I don't have anyone to call other than Momma. Wait! Yes, I do.

"Deacon Fredricks? Hi, it's Wendy. How are you?"

"Good, Sister Wendy. This is a surprise. You okay?"

"Yeah, I just wanted to share my good news with my good deacon."

"What good news is this?"

"I'm about to get a great promotion on my job. The CEO of our company is coming down tomorrow, and I meet with him at nine o'clock to discuss the details surrounding the promotion."

"Wow, Wendy! That's great. We should celebrate. Let me take you to lunch."

"I made plans with my girlfriend Jessica to see how her meeting went. But, I can just take a break and chat with her, then meet you for lunch. Is that okay?"

"That's perfect. I have to take Pam's car to the detail shop, and then I will be ready. You want to try Henry's place again?"

"Yes, and this time, I will not put my foot in my mouth." I

wanted to say I would put his dick in my mouth, but instead, I said, "See you around noon."

He quickly replied, "I'll be there."

"Hey, Keith, is Jessica still in with Mr. Wallace?"

"No, she left right after her meeting."

"Did she say anything?"

"No. She just grabbed her purse and left."

"Did she take her computer?"

"Nope, just her purse."

"Thanks. I guess I'll just call her. Have you had your meeting yet?"

"No, mine is at eleven-thirty."

"Well, good luck to you, Keith."

"Thanks, Wendy, and congratulations."

"On what?"

"Being the best. At least that's what they say."

"Thank you, Keith."

"Are you that good at everything?"

I rolled my eyes and replied, "You'll never know."

If he wasn't so damn short, he might have a chance. But, I need a man that can hold this body up if I asked him to. He would never do.

*****

"Hey, Mr. Henry. You doing okay today?"

"Hey, Ms…Wendy? Yep, I remembered."

"I'm flattered."

"With that pretty face, who could forget your name? Are you dining alone today?"

"Actually, Deacon Fredricks is supposed to meet me here for lunch. I'm celebrating a promotion on my job."

"Congratulations, pretty girl. I'll get his table set up for you guys right away. Have a seat. Can I get you something to drink?"

"Sweet tea, please."

"Got it coming your way."

A few minutes later, a waitress came over to me.

"Ms. Wendy, your table is ready if you want to follow me."

"That was quick. Thank you, Tabitha…right?"

"You got it. Nice dress, too." She flashed a very inviting smile.

As soon as Deacon Fredricks arrived, I stood so we could hug. *Okay, hug him, but don't press your body all up against him. Here we go. Why did I feel his dick through his pants? This is so fucked up. Now how am I supposed to focus on lunch? Let me drink some tea and calm my body down before it gets too damn hot.*

"So, Deacon Fredricks, how has your day been so far?"

"Better now that I get to congratulate the lady of the day up close and personal. So how does it feel to be on top?"

"Damn good. Oops, I mean, it feels really great. I didn't expect it at all. I enjoy my job, and I work hard at it. I'm good at what I do."

"I bet you are, Ms. Wendy."

I wanted to tell him that I could show him just how good if he would let me, but for some reason, today, I had much control over what I was feeling. Still, I knew if I closed my eyes for one second, I would blow it. *Note to brain: stop staring at his fork going into his mouth. It's beginning to fuck with you. Let me try something else. One potato, two potato, three potato, four. Shit. I feel the heat rising from under my dress that I'm not wearing any panties underneath.*

"What are you going to do to celebrate? You know Marvin

Sapp says, 'Praise him in advance'."

"Fucking you would be a nice way to celebrate."

"Wendy?"

"Yeah?"

"Are you here?"

"Yes, baby. I'm right here."

"Wendy?"

"Shhh."

"But, Wendy..."

"Be quiet and fuck me. You want to help me celebrate? Stick your dick inside me now."

"Wendy, shhh. Open your eyes, please."

"Fuck me, Deacon Fredricks."

"Wendy..."

"Yeah, baby, right there. Don't stop."

"Wendy, please."

"What is it, baby?"

"Please, open your eyes."

"I'm about to cum. Wait. Right there. Right there. Yeah, baby. Fuck, Mark. Right there. Shit, I'm cumming. Oh, I'm cumming now."

"Wendy!"

I finally opened my eyes to find Deacon Fredricks now sitting right next to me with our menu standing up, obviously to cover my face and my hand that was under my dress. I had fucked myself at the table in public. I really can't tell you how loud I was. I just knew my pussy was wet and the look on his face said if he weren't married, he would've taken me outside to my car and fucked the shit out of me. He wanted me, and I wanted him again.

But, before I could get the words out of my mouth, he said,

"Let me guess. You have to go?"

"Please let me out of this booth. I'm so sorry. I'll pay you back for lunch. I'm going home to look for a new church online."

"Wendy, you weren't that loud, and I'm not letting you out of this booth until you tell me what happens when you do that. It's like you tune everybody and everything out. When I heard you in the hospitality room, I wanted to come in, but you sounded as if you were being pleased so well. When I opened the door, your eyes were closed tight, and when I finally got you to open your eyes, you acted as if you didn't know where you were or what you had said. Why does that happen? How do you get to that point?"

"Deacon Fredricks, please let me out of here. I have to go now. Please."

"You want me to take you home? I can. And we can come back later and get your car."

"No, just let me out. I'll call you later. Please."

"Wendy..."

"Now."

"Okay, but promise me you'll call me later."

"I will. I promise."

After hauling ass out of that place, I called work and told Mr. Wallace that I would be in the next day bright and early. I needed to take the rest of the day off to handle some personal business. I then turned my cell phone off, went in my house, got on my knees, and prayed, because what I did at that table only the Lord could fix.

*****

Now that was a much-needed nap, but what I don't understand is who could be ringing my doorbell like I owe them money.

"Who is it?"

"It's Deacon Fredricks. May I come in?"

What in the fuck is he doing at my house?

"Hey, Deacon Fredricks. Yeah, come on in."

"I know you said you would call me, but it's time we clear the air," he said after I let him in. "I called you several times to check on you, and when I didn't get an answer, I decided to just come over."

"Deacon Fredricks, I'm fine. Um, can I get you something to drink?"

"No, but I do want you to tell me what goes on with you so I won't feel like I've done something wrong when we're together."

"Deacon Fredricks, this is a personal issue that I'm going to get some counseling for. I know what happened today was inappropriate and may have caused you some embarrassment, but please don't judge me with this. Just know that I'm going to seek some type of help for myself. Some may say I'm sick."

"I say it's sexy for you to openly express how you feel. You just can't do it in public places like today. Your inner thoughts are what make you a woman. If you're doing things in your head and not all over town, it makes a world of difference."

This man just said me fucking him in my head is sexy. Please don't do this, Deacon Fredricks.

"Well, Deacon Fredricks, I was in a terrible relationship with Rashad for a while. After one abortion that he knows nothing about, a couple of STD's, and a few trips to the ER, my desire to be with him changed drastically. So, in my mind, if I have to fulfill my sexual desires, that's where I do it. It's safe, there's no co-pay, and no drunken breath in my face unless I

84

want it. I try to control it, but when it starts, it's hard to turn it off. Sometimes I feel dirty, nasty, even slutty, but then I cum so hard that the satisfaction takes me to another high and all those feelings of disgust leave. I don't know where it comes from. I close my eyes and try not to feel it, but once my eyes are closed, that's it."

"And once you open your eyes?"

"My body is usually exhausted. I just remember pieces of what I've said to the person I imagined I was with. It's so erotic that I want to control it, but not being able to turns me on even more."

"Well, do you ever want to have real sex again?"

"I actually had sex yesterday, but it was out of spite. I fucked Rashad because I could. Excuse my language, Deacon."

"Did you enjoy it at all?"

"I came. That's all that matters."

"Wendy, you do understand there's more to having sex or making love than just having an orgasm, right? And I can't believe I'm having this conversation with you, but I guess after today, I think I've earned the right to know what's going on with you."

"I mean, who are you going to tell? Your wife? I can hear you now. 'Hey, baby, you remember Wendy Brooks that has been working so well with the girls in Sunday school and that you sent to count money with me Sunday? Yeah, she fucks me mentally every time she sees me.'" I paused to look up at him since I didn't mean to tell him that part, but then went on to say, "You be sure to tell me how well that goes."

"You've had intimate thoughts of me? I'm who you've been fantasizing about?"

With the most embarrassing face ever, I replied, "Yes."

85

He sat up with interest. "Often?"

"Yes."

"When?"

"Details are not good, Deacon Fredricks. It only creates an atmosphere for this evening to turn into something bad."

He moved closer to me, looked me in the eyes, and asked me again. "When?"

"The first time you gave me a ride home."

"What happened?"

I sat there boldly with my legs crossed, hoping he could not hear the throbbing sound that began to ring from my pussy.

Taking a deep breath, I said, "After I saw your dick when you came out of the restroom. You left. I went upstairs and got in the shower."

"Then what happened?"

"I touched my pussy from the outside-in. I rubbed my clit fast, then faster. I took my fingers and pushed them inside my pussy as deep as I could. I pulled them out and rubbed my clit again and again."

He sat back on the couch and asked me to please finish. I could see his dick growing in his pants as I recalled that day. I wanted to squat down in front of him and take him in my mouth so bad, but I don't think he wanted to feel me physically. I think he wanted to feel what I feel when things are going through my head.

As he sat back with his eyes closed just listening to me talk, he said, "Go on, Wendy. What happened next? Did you cum right then?"

I closed my eyes to remember and answered, "No. I heard a voice calling my name. I thought it was Rashad, but it wasn't. As the voice called for me, I used it for something so lustful that it caused me to rub my clit faster because I wanted to cum with the thoughts of you still in my head."

"Did you cum then?"

"No. I got even wetter. Then I rubbed my clit even faster because the voice was so close to me that if it were Rashad, he would ruin my desire for you. I was almost there and the voice was right outside the door. I released so hard that the knock at the door sent chills down my spine."

"Was the knock Rashad?"

"No, it was you. The car wouldn't start, so you came back in to tell me."

"So you came for me?"

"Yes."

"Good. Now open your eyes."

I opened my eyes to find my legs spread and my hand in my pussy. It was wet and my legs were shaking. To my surprise, I looked over at Deacon Fredricks. His dick was in his hand and cum was all over it.

He looked at me and said, "Stop stealing your orgasms from me with fantasies and just ask me for them. Now, may I have a towel, please?"

I hesitated before moving because I wanted to lick that shit off him, which would have probably led to some serious fucking in my living room, but I finally got a word out. "Yes."

While going upstairs, I prayed he would follow me, because I was going to plant his fine-ass body in the middle of my bed and take his dick like Mrs. Pam *should've* been doing. Who knows? She could've been fucking him well. However, at that very moment, his dick was in his hand, at my house, holding cum that I made him do without even touching him.

Damn, my pussy is jumping again. Get him out of your

house now!

"Here you are," I said, returning with a washcloth. "I hope it's not too hot."

"It's fine."

"So I have a question for you, Deacon Fredricks. Do you consider what we just did cheating?"

"Depends on who's asking."

"I am."

"Do you think I just cheated on my wife?"

"No penetration, so maybe not. But did you lust for me? You know that's a sin, Deacon."

"I do. But, I didn't touch you."

"I saw your dick."

He said boldly, "That wasn't the first time. According to you, it's been several times."

"True."

"Tell me about the next time you were mentally with me."

"No, because then, I will want you physically, and you're here. Then you will have cheated, no question."

"How does it make you feel to know that mentally I can fuck you so well, and now that I'm in the same room with you, I can control myself and not physically take you?"

"It just tells me that you have great self-control."

"Was I with you in the hospitality room at the church?"

"Yes."

"Did you cum for me there, too?"

"Yes."

"Was it just as good as the first time?"

"Better."

"Was today good, as well?"

"Yes."

"Do you want to tell me why you think that is?"

"No."

"Why?"

"Because if we keep going like this, you will cheat on your wife past what we have done already."

"I cheated? I think the jury is still out on that one, but I will let you know once the verdict is in. I'll let myself out, Ms. Wendy, and let me know when you want to tell me more about you and this 'thing' you do. Goodnight."

I couldn't move. I felt like it had all been a dream. *I sat in the same room and masturbated side by side with this man based on what happened in my mind. I have to be crazy. There must be something wrong with me. Let me Google my symptoms and see what comes up.*

Better yet, let me just write my symptoms down and find a doctor for tomorrow after my meeting. I have got to get a hold on this shit. Okay, doctors in Chicago, Illinois. Wait. Do I look up a psychologist or a sex therapist? Well, if I look up a psychiatrist, maybe they can refer me to a sexual doctor if there is such a thing.

Let me see...psychiatrist. Damn, it's a lot of doctors in our area. Get the fuck out of here! Oh my God! Dr. Mark Fredricks, Psychiatrist. If I click on this link and this muthafucker's picture comes up, somebody is going to have to bury me tomorrow. I'll be damned. Dr. Mark Fredricks, PhD-eacon.

Chapter Nine
Congratulations to Me

Since I'm a VIP, what better way to celebrate my new promotion than to let Mr. Hamilton cater to me at his club? Should I call him and let him know I'm coming, or should I just show up? If I call him, he may think I like him just a little bit. Do I call Jessica to ride with me, or do I go alone so I can have my moment in the spotlight? I should wear this black dress. No, I'm wearing this red one. He'll like this one. Now, where did I put that business card of his?

"Hi, Mr. Hamilton. How are you?"

"This sounds like the beautiful Ms. Wendy Brooks, and if not, you have the wrong Mr. Hamilton. However, if you know Wendy Brooks, can you tell her to call me, please?"

"That's cute and very flattering. Thank you. Busy night for you?"

"Every night is busy for me, but I will shut this place down for you."

"I see you're in a good mood. Perhaps I should come see for myself."

"Don't tease me, Wendy Brooks. Would you give me that pleasure of seeing your beautiful face tonight?"

"I think I will. I received a very nice promotion on my job today, and I want to celebrate."

"And you thought enough of me to want to come here? Let me do you one better. I'm heading to my club in Miami for a big party tonight. Pack a bag and come with me."

"What? I'm not going to Miami with you."

"Why not? Let me take you there and help you celebrate. I'll get you your own suite, and we'll just have a good time. I'll take you to my club, and you can pretend like you don't even know me if you want to. Just come with me."

"I said I just got my promotion. The money reflecting that change doesn't kick in for another two weeks."

"Wendy, I only asked you to pack a bag. You can just put your toothbrush in it, if you want. I'm more than willing to fill it up when we get to Miami. Just show up at the club tonight, and I'll do the rest."

"I… Okay, I'll see you soon."

"Are you bringing Jessica or will you be alone?"

"I'm coming alone. Not to be selfish, but I got the promotion alone so I'll be celebrating alone."

"I can't wait to see you. Walter will be waiting for you downstairs."

"Bye, Mr. Hamilton."

What in the hell did I just do? I thought while quickly dialing my mother's number.

"Hey, Momma."

"Hey, baby. How are you?"

"I'm fine. Look, I'm going out of town tonight with a friend of mine. I'll be back on Sunday."

"Where you going?"

"To Miami."

"What friend is taking you to Miami, Wendy? Rashad?"

"Heck no! Rashad and I are over, Momma. There are no

getting-back-together trips for me and him. Look, you don't know them, but I will be back Sunday evening. I'll call you when I get there tonight."

"Y'all driving?"

"To Miami, Momma? Wait. I don't know how we're getting there. I just know I'm going."

"Sounds a little funny to me, but have a good time."

"I think I will. Oh yeah, I got a promotion on the job, Momma. I'm now Senior Vice President of Recruiting & Finance for our region. I will be doing a lot of traveling and training other people to do the job I use to do. The pay increase is insane. In addition, I received a bonus and a credit card for travel expenses. It's a blessing, Momma. Hard work really pays off."

"You've always worked hard, baby. I'm very proud of you. I got my bank statement from last month, too. I wonder who put a thousand dollars in my checking account again."

"I don't know, but I hope you go and get those shoes you saw at the mall."

"I got those and two more pairs today when Ethel and I went. I love you, baby. Have a great time, and be careful."

"I will, and I love you, too, Momma."

Well, he said to just show up. Maybe I should at least take panties. Okay, I'll pack a small bag with a toothbrush, makeup, and one pair of panties. That'll do it. Girl, you're crazy.

*****

"Hi, Walter!"

"Ms. Wendy, what a pleasure to see you this evening. Mr. Hamilton tipped me for taking your car. You have made him a very happy man by accepting his invitation. His tip says so."

"Well, I guess I'm glad I could help. My bag is in the back

seat. Should I bring it in?"

"No, ma'am, I'll make sure it gets in the limo. You guys should be ready to head to the airport in about thirty minutes or so."

"How did he know I would say yes to get me a plane ticket?"

"He didn't, but he has a well-respected reputation with the airlines. You are first class all the way."

"Wow! Thank you, Walter."

"The pleasure is mine, Ms. Wendy. Enjoy your trip and congratulations."

Smiling as big as the Joker, I replied, "Thank you."

*****

This has to be the biggest damn plane in the world. I can't believe I said yes to go with this man to Miami. I guess I'm developing the mentality that you only live once, and since I didn't already plan a trip to Miami in the near future, it worked out. What is his first name, Wendy? Oh, it's on his card. Let me see before he comes and sits down. Greg Hamilton.

"That's me," he said, catching me looking at his business card.

"Shit, you scared me. I was just saying to myself that I have gotten on this plane with you and don't even know your first name."

"You had my card; you've been to my home; you've been to my job. Yet, you've never even asked me. You insist on being so professional with the Mr. Hamilton thing that I just let you do what you do. I actually find it a turn-on for you to call me that."

"But, a lot of people call you that."

"True, but their eyes don't say what your eyes say when you

say it. Now, is there anything else you'd like to know before we take off to Miami that might keep you from having a good time?"

"Since you have all these things, why don't you have a wife or girlfriend or a friend-friend?"

"What in the hell is a friend-friend?"

"That's the lady you have an intimate relationship with. You take her to Miami, church, parade her around, but y'all are not officially a couple, if you're into titles."

"Oh, I see; a friend-friend. Well, Ms. Brooks, the reason I don't have a wife is because I'm waiting on God to send her to me. I don't have a girlfriend because women see these 'things' I've worked so hard for and think because they fuck well, it automatically qualifies them to receive 'things' and demand answers to questions I don't have to answer for them. Once I explain to them that I can get no-cost pussy from anywhere, without trips, shopping sprees, or dinners, I'm an arrogant asshole. Is it that I don't deserve love, respect, compassion, companionship, or to be just me? They think because I have money I don't need those things."

"Well, where have you been looking for women?"

"In my profession, you can imagine. I host pro-ball players and celebrity parties in my clubs all over. I have groupies just like they do. But, it's all about the choices you make."

"Well, I think you *should* have love, genuine love, demand respect, have buckets of compassion, and a companion who knows Greg underneath those suits."

"Why did you say yes to coming with me tonight?"

"Because the last time I was in Miami, I wanted to walk up to this man and kiss him because he was *so* fine. So, since you were going, I decided to use you to get to him."

95

"Wow! Your honesty is appreciated."

"I need some honesty in my life. The last few years have been full of lies. I've had tons of bullshit, and I'm tired of it. Now, why did you ask me to come?"

"Because when I looked out my window at the club to see how the line was moving one night, I saw this beautiful woman crossing the street. She walked with confidence from her ancestors, had a perfect body that women would pay to have, and her smile could send chills over your entire body. When I looked into her eyes, they said she needed to be loved past her pain and *I* wanted to do that."

"Mr. Hamilton, what makes you think I need love from you?"

"Oh, I wasn't talking about you. I was talking about this other girl, but she couldn't go tonight. So, I asked you."

He turned to the window casually, then turned back, and we both laughed hard because the look on my face said he was about to get cursed out. There was a slight pause, and we looked into each other's eyes before realizing we were both blushing. I knew then he meant the things he had said.

The plane landed, and we were picked up by another limousine and taken to the most beautiful hotel in Miami, as far as I knew. Like he said, I had my own suite, and on the bed were a box and a dress bag.

I saw the damn movie. This can't be happening to me. I didn't look in either one. I immediately called my mother and Jessica. As soon as I finished sharing everything with them, the phone rang in the room; it was Mr. Hamilton.

"Can you be ready in an hour?"

"Yes. I don't know what's in the box or the bag, but you didn't have to do that."

"Just take it as a token of my appreciation for coming and a gift for your hard work on your job. You deserve that and more."

"How do you know what I deserve?"

"You're a woman, and women deserve to be treated like queens."

"Who taught you that? Your mother or your father?"

"My grandmother. My parents died when I was fifteen on their way to one of my basketball games. My grandmother always talked about how my father treated my mother, and this was my mother's mother. Then when my father's mother confirmed it, I began to work hard on how I treated women. Now, can you be ready in one hour?"

"Yes."

"Great. I'll see you in the lobby."

"Okay."

Lord, if I'm dreaming, please don't wake me yet. If I'm fantasizing this entire thing and am really at home in my bed, please don't let me open my eyes until this night is over. I'm going to take my shower, open these gifts, get dressed, and have one hell of a night. So, please, don't wake me if I'm dreaming.

*****

I couldn't find Greg in the lobby until I turned towards the door, and there he stood.

"Wow, Wendy. You look absolutely beautiful."

"Thanks to you, Mr. Greg Hamilton, and I promise not to cramp your style tonight wherever we're going."

"It's a celebration. We've been up and running here for five years. No police, no drugs, no deaths, nothing for the city to question. I think it's well worth celebrating. Some of the local celebrities are coming for the five-year toast, and we're looking for a great crowd tonight."

"And you chose me for this celebration? I'm flattered."

"That's good, because I look forward to you joining me for many more celebrations."

"Be careful what you ask for, Mr. Hamilton."

*****

Oh my God, if I could call someone and brag, I would. Jessica is only going to talk shit because I didn't bring her. This party is the shit. Grown men and beautiful women. I have turned down so many men and women until it's beginning to be a game. One lady almost could have gotten it; she was hot. And Greg is holding on to me like a prize. He keeps introducing me to all these people as his lady friend. Is there such a thing as a lady friend? Who gives a damn? They all keep smiling and giving me business cards for all kinds of connections. I tell you this, when I get back to my hotel room, I'm going to invite him in and fuck him so good that he might change the name of this club here in Miami to Wendy's Place!

"Greg, I'm going to the restroom. I'll be right back."

"You okay?"

"Yes, I'm fine."

"I'll be over by the door by the time you get back, so just come that way. I'm waiting on the rose man. We have sold sixty-five dozens of roses, and people are still asking for them. So, I had to call the florist for the remaining thirty-five."

"You ordered one hundred dozens of roses?"

"Yes. We normally sell about fifty a night, but it looks like every man in here tonight is trying to get laid when he gets home."

As I laughed and walked away, he asked me if I needed anything. I almost blurted out that I didn't need anything else because the ass he would get that night was on the house. I remembered closing my eyes at his house and what I felt like when I woke up. Whether it was with him alone or him and his housekeeper, I wanted that feeling again.

I haven't had a drink all night because I've been too busy smiling at all these people.

I went to the bar, where a beautiful woman took my drink order.

"A shot of Patrón with a lime, please."

"Mr. Hamilton mentioned he would be bringing someone special tonight, and when we saw you, we knew it was for real."

"What do you mean for real?"

"He always tells us he's bringing someone special or a special guest, but then he shows up alone. We really want him to have someone in his life because he deserves it. He works hard and he treats us like family. So, whatever you did to get here, thank you."

"I didn't do anything but say yes."

"Good enough. He doesn't trust many women, and he has turned down so many that at one time, we began to question whether or not he wanted a woman. But, his drive keeps his mind focused on having better and doing better all the time. He comes down here through the week just to meet with us and motivate us past what comes on our checks. He's sent all of us to school for bartending and CPR. Three of the waitresses are in business school, and he paid for their first two years of attendance. They don't even have to come back to work for him if they don't want to when they graduate. We all have insurance and savings accounts that we only see the statements for. He opened them, and if anything happens to us, the money goes to our children. We take a trip every six months to somewhere we would probably never go had it not been for him. He's a giver, and we love him for that."

By this time, I had put back four more shots of Patrón and was very turned on by all the things I had just found out about this wonderful man.

"But why isn't he married?"

"His parents died a long time ago, and his focus has been on just living his life and helping others. He never misses church and always talks about the day he's going to get married and have children."

"Wait. He doesn't have any children either?"

"Nope. He said his wife is going to have his children."

Up to six shots now and I'm feeling good.

"Well, it was nice talking to you…"

"I'm Tonya, the number one bartender in the building."

I laughed and shook her hand. "Well, nice to meet you number one."

On the plane, I told him that cute little lie about coming back to Miami to kiss a man. I think I found him. I saw him still standing by the door and headed that way.

"Excuse me, sir?"

When he turned around, I kissed him like I *really* needed him.

"Ms. Wendy Brooks."

"I'm ready to go, if you don't mind."

Smiling with lust in my eyes, I licked my lips as if I could already taste him. He turned his head to the side as to read into what I was trying to say.

"Give me two seconds to say goodnight over the mic and thank everyone for coming, then we can leave. Ron, call for the limo, please."

"Yes, sir."

"Come on, baby. Come go on the stage with me."

"No, no, I can wait here."

"No, no, you can come with me. Please."

He's so damn fine. I rolled my eyes and followed suit.

"Ladies and gentlemen, thank you for helping me celebrate this wonderful occasion. Five years and we have not had one mishap, gunfight, police call, shut down, or failed inspection. I owe you all a lot. If it were not for you all, I would not be able to run this place the way I do. They said we couldn't have a nice club where you dress to impress and have a great time networking, mingling, and drinking respectfully." He raised his glass. "To five years!"

Oh shit. He just kissed me on stage right after his "I'm running for mayor" speech.

"Goodnight!"

My goodness, he's waving like Barack, and they won't stop clapping. Now this part I'm going to tell Jessica about.

*****

"Have a good night, Mr. Hamilton."

"You do the same, Ron. You guys know how to reach me if you need me. I'll be here until Sunday morning."

"Yes, sir. Ms. Wendy, enjoy your stay here in Miami."

"Thank you, Ron. Goodnight. What respect they have for you, you should be very proud. I'm blown away by the things I have heard about you tonight. You must have paid them well before I got here."

"No need to. I just know how important an education is and how important it is to be successful in life."

"Will you dance with me when we get back to the hotel? I mean, you walked and talked all night, but you never asked me to dance. So, I'm asking you. Dance with me."

"Jacob."

"Yes, sir?"

"Pull over, please."

I looked around to see what was going on. "What's wrong?"

As Jacob opened the door, he whispered to him, which made me scared.

"What's wrong, Greg?"

Just then, Teddy Pendergrass' "Come On and Go with Me" began blasting from the limo's speakers.

He reached out his hand and said, "Ma'am, may I have this dance?"

I know it sounds corny, but it was real. We were on the side of the street with music playing. The crazy thing is other couples started dancing around us, and I know he didn't pay them. They were smiling at us and each other. Some were kissing and singing out loud. I just buried my head in his chest and said to myself, *Lord, if I'm dreaming, I'm begging you again to please wait before you wake me up.*

After we made it back to the hotel, he escorted me to my room. He looked at me with the most passionate look in his eyes and said, "I'm so tired, Wendy."

"You can come in and lay down with me," I responded.

I wanted to say that all he would have to do is lay there because I would do the rest. I had my mind made up that I was going to start at the top of his head and not stop until I had his baby toe in my mouth. I was trying to be mindful of the fact that ever since we got off the plane all we did was run the streets. He should be tired, but I wanted him so bad.

I went into the bathroom, took off my dress, pulled my hair up, and got in the shower. I planned on taking a PTA (pussy, tits, and ass) shower, but I wanted to ensure my entire body had nothing related to Rashad. After washing the makeup off my face, I opened my eyes to find Greg standing behind me.

Now how did I miss this Negro getting in the shower behind me?

"Are you always this sneaky, sir?'

"So it's my fault your hearing is bad?"

"My hearing is fine, thank you."

"Give me your towel and turn around," he said.

He washed my neck and back, then down to my ass. He bent me over and cleaned my pussy from the front to the back like how my mother taught me to wipe as a little girl. *Damn, he's good.* He pulled me up and did the exact same thing again. Neck, back, bend over, front to back. He rinsed the towel, lathered it up again, and turned me around, pushing me back into the water that ran down the front of my body like a waterfall.

I didn't move. I watched him lather up the towel again, and gently, he washed the front of my neck, each one of my breasts, and then my stomach. Cute...he even cleaned my belly button.

"You're too much, Mr. Hamilton, too damn much."

I had no idea what he was going to do to me next, and I didn't give a damn. He sat me on the side of the tub that was fit for a king, opened my legs, sat on his ass, and cleaned my pussy, lip by lip, as if he were dissecting his first science project.

As the water ran over his head, he rinsed the towel and squeezed the water out over my pussy. When he stood up, I tried to, also, but he sat me back down. He cleaned his body without ever taking his eyes off me. I was mesmerized. All I could do was think of all the things I was going to do to him once I got his ass out of the shower.

He sat back down in front of me, put both my legs over his shoulders, and buried his head in my pussy as if he hadn't eaten in weeks. *Where did he get this damn tongue from? I swear it feels like it's touching my uterus.* He slid me closer to him, but I was about to cum already.

"Please stop," I begged. "You gonna make me cum. I don't want to cum yet."

He snatched the shower curtain down, laid it on the floor, put me on top of it, and stuck his dick in my mouth.

"Shhh, you talk too much."

It caught me off guard, but at the same time, I was like, *nigga, you so fucking bad.* I watched him lean back as I took his dick so deep in my throat that I could feel myself about to gag, but I wouldn't give his ass the satisfaction.

Then he said, "Shit, I don't want to cum yet."

So, I pulled his dick out of my mouth and pushed him back just enough to get up. Leaving him still on his knees in front of me, I got on the counter and pulled his face back to my pussy.

It was now my turn to say, "Shhh, *you* talk too much."

My cockiness must have pissed him off, because he locked my ass down on that counter and all I could feel was my clit growing and throbbing. The tingle I felt was about to show all over his face.

So, in the nicest way possible, I told him, "I'm about to cum in this muthafucker."

He slid my clit between his top lip and his tongue, and oh my goodness!

I grabbed his head so tight and moaned, "My pussy is about to explode. Please stop. Please. Shit, Greg, I'm cumming. Don't stop."

He kept on until I let out a scream so embarrassing that I couldn't look up at him, but I didn't have a choice because his strong ass picked me up and placed me on his dick, which commanded my full attention. I wrapped my legs around that yellow-ass man who had a dick the size of a ripe cucumber in early summertime. He slid me up and down with no regards to my saying, "Wait...wait...wait."

He pushed my body backwards onto the counter and had me laid out like a damn filleted piece of meat. Sad thing was I couldn't run from the dick because my head was pressed up against the mirror, so I had to take it. He was fucking me so good that I couldn't do anything but close my eyes. He had one of my breasts in his hand and his mouth on the other, but I wanted to taste my pussy on his lips. So, I pulled his face to mine and kissed him just to see how sweet I really was. That shit turned his ass on even more!

He began fucking me harder, while pressing his hands in the middle of my chest so I couldn't get up to resist in any way. He lifted one of my legs over his shoulder and turned my body to the side. Oh shit! He had me then. As he began to slow grind inside of me, I felt his dick right on my g-spot.

He bent his knees and rode back into my pussy with ease for about five good strokes. Then he started banging me just a little faster. He dipped down again, and when the muthafucker dipped, he managed to turn my ass over without his dick ever coming out. He fucked me from the back so slow that I could feel his dick throbbing inside of me. I winded my hips slowly, and when I popped my ass a little, he let me know he liked it.

"Damn, girl."

I whispered back to him, "You better not cum."

As I popped it again, he responded the exact same way, just

105

with a different word.

"Shit."

"You better not fucking cum, Greg."

He took my hair and rolled it up in his hand, jerked my head back, and told me, "You don't tell me what the fuck to do." Then he began fucking my pussy harder. I thought I could take it, but I begged him to stop.

"Greg, please…"

"I know. Don't make you cum, right? What? Don't stop? Don't worry, I won't."

His dick seemed to get harder and harder as it went deeper and deeper. I just knew he was going to shove that shit straight up through my stomach to my throat, but my pussy just got wetter with every word he said. He took both my arms, pulled them behind me, and rode me from the back like my arms were reins on a horse. I could feel my pussy building up, about to burst on the inside.

"I'm about to cum on your dick. Don't stop. Fuck me. Fuck me, please. Harder. Harder, please. Oh shit! Oh shit, Greg, wait. Fuck!!!"

But he wouldn't let me go. He kept fucking me, and I knew I was about to bust again.

"Greg, please let me go," I pleaded, but when I looked in the mirror at him, he shook his head and winked his eye at me.

That shit made me tighten my pussy on his dick like a baby holding its mother's hand in a room full of strangers. Now his facial expression was something totally different.

"What are you doing, Wendy?"

"Naw, bitch, keep fucking me. You better not stop, punk ass." I squeezed his dick again, and the nigga's knees buckled. When he let go of one hand, I told him, "Grab it back."

He looked at me in the mirror like I was a different woman, and I was. He got my arm back and tried to stay in the game, but I squeezed my pussy and bounced my ass like I was in the ATL and had trained every dancer in Magic City. His eyes got tight, and my pussy got even tighter. I knew that muthafucker was going to cum and make me cum again, too.

"Shit, Greg."

"Please cum for me again, Wendy, because I'm about to cum for you. Shit, girl. wait. Wait."

"Fuck, Greg. Oh shit. That's it, baby. Right there. Right there, Greg."

"Wendy. Fuck. My dick is cumming. Oh shit, baby, it's cumming! You're making me cum, baby. Fuck! Yeah, squeeze that pussy on my dick, baby. Fuck, yeah."

"Yeah?"

"Hell yeah, girl."

The only word I could get out of my mouth was, "Shit," then I caught my breath for the follow-up. "I need something to drink."

He came right behind me with, "Shit, I need a doctor."

"What's wrong?"

"Girl, that pussy can give a brother a heart attack. I need a doctor on my staff. Come on. Let me clean you up."

He picked me up, sat me on the counter, turned around, started the water, then turned back to me and put his face back in my pussy!

Light-skinned men are in again. I don't give a damn what they say.

Chapter Ten
Back to Bullshit

"Rashad, why are you at my house?"

"Where you been all weekend?"

"Why?"

"Because I've been here since Friday trying to give you this." He passed me a piece of paper.

"Okay, so you're not HIV positive. Yeah? Now move."

"Don't you get it? We're meant to be together."

"Rashad, the test only proves you won't be dying from having unprotected sex anytime soon. You may not have HIV, but trust, you've had enough other STDs to kill the both of us. So, move."

"Why you being like that? I love you, Wendy."

"When, Rashad? When did you start loving me? After the first black eye I had? No, wait. Was it after you cheated with my neighbor or the list of other tricks you've been with? Uh-uh. Maybe it was when you pushed me down the stairs and I was on crutches for a month? When, Negro? When did you start?"

"I told you…"

"I know. You told me you're sorry. Me, too. Now please get from in front of my door so I can go in and get ready for my workweek."

"Are you seeing someone else?"

"Yes, three or four people. Now what?"

"Wendy?" Greg's voice rang out behind me, causing me to turn around. "When you got out of the car, you left one of your bags, and I didn't know if you needed it."

"Thank you, Greg."

"Oh, so this is your new nigga? You don't even like light-skinned men. Nigga, she's playing you."

"If that's the case, we played all weekend." He walked closer to me. "You okay, baby?"

"She's fine."

"Shut up, Rashad. Don't even try it. Greg, this is my ex-boyfriend, Rashad Fields. Rashad, this is Greg Hamilton."

"Well, I guess a thank you is in order then for you, Mr. Fields."

"What you talking 'bout, man?"

"Because if you weren't the worst man she's ever had, I wouldn't have the opportunity to be the best man she's ever had. So, yes, player, thank you."

"Man, you better get the hell away from here before you get fucked up talking crazy."

Walter's voice startled me. "Mr. Hamilton, is everything okay?"

Then Rashad's stupid ass started yelling.

"Oh, so it's two of y'all? Ain't nothing."

Greg laughed before responding to Walter. "Yes, everything over here is fine. This guy was just leaving so Wendy can get settled. Right, Rashad?"

I jumped in before things got out of hand.

"Yes, he was just leaving. Rashad, don't do this. I asked you to leave way before Greg came anyway. Just go, please. I said it before, and I'll say it again. This relationship is over. I mean it.

So, no more unannounced visits, and if I ever want to talk to you again, I'll call you."

"You weren't saying that last week when you were riding my dick."

"Oh yes, I did. Then I told you the same thing, for you to get your shit and get out. Let's revisit the entire conversation if we're going to bring it up. Isn't that exactly what I said?"

"Man...girl."

"Man...that's what I thought, but you don't ever have to worry about that again. Greg, thanks for a great weekend, and Walter, thank you for bringing me home. Goodnight, gentlemen."

I went in the house and ran up the stairs to look out the window so I could see if anything was going to go down right in my front yard. I must admit, Greg got Rashad's ass with that "worst man-best man" line. I wanted to high-five his smooth ass. Okay, I'm lying. I really wanted to pull him in the house and let him bend me over my lounge chair, but Rashad dog ass would have gotten mad because he couldn't watch. *Selfish bastard.*

I know damn well this isn't Rashad's stupid ass ringing my doorbell or this will be the quickest pot of grits I have ever cooked in my life. I opened the door to a 5'9", jet-black hair, C-cup, stallion-legged, apple-bottomed senorita standing there.

"Hello, can I help you?" *And if she asks about Rashad, I swear...*

"Hola, neighbor. I saw you arrive at home, and I wanted to say hello. I moved in over the weekend and wanted to know who lived to the right and left of me."

"Well, directly across from you is the neighborhood skank, Chrissy Dawson, and if you have a señor, hide him, lock him in

111

the attic, or take him with you if you leave home."

"When I met her yesterday, she explained to me that you all had a little falling out, but she didn't care to mention over what."

"She fucked my boyfriend, in my bed, several times. Call it a little falling out if you'd like."

"Oh, I see. Okay, well, I wanted to invite you over for a glass of wine if you're not busy."

"Well..."

"Kali...my name is Kali Santiago."

She extended her hand for me to shake. I have a few friends for a reason, but I didn't want to be her friend. I wanted to touch her fine ass. I had never been with a woman before, but I swear I could feel my clit swelling up under my dress.

"I just got back in town, so give me a few minutes to get cleaned up and unpack. Then I'll be on over."

"Okay. Well, here is my card and my home number is on the back. So, give me a call when you're about to head over."

"Wait. Do you have a little angry Hispanic dog that will bark at the sight of a black woman?"

A huge smile came across her face. "No. So, there is nothing for you to be afraid of when you walk in the door, and by the way, nice dress."

After she left, I went upstairs and took a shower. *My pussy is still nice from the wax. Fuck that unpacking shit. Teeth and lips are done, and yes, no panties. To her place I go.*

"So what brings you to town, Ms. Kali Santiago?"

"Well, my mother died last year in my hometown, and I was trying to hold on to so many things there. So, I said to myself, 'You know what, Kali? Pack your shit and move now. Your momma is not coming back no matter how long you stay here.'

So, one Google search, phone call to the local realtor, U-haul truck, and a job transfer landed me here next door to the lovely Wendy Brooks."

"Who told you my last name? I know Chrissy called me Wendy, the Bitch. So where did you get Brooks from?"

"I accidently checked your mailbox, and your husband's name wasn't on anything jointly with you. So, I guessed you were single."

When she started singing the hook of "Single Ladies (Put a Ring on It)", we laughed out loud together.

"But, there has been a man sitting on your porch since Friday, so I was confused. Then you came home tonight with another man. So, if nothing else, I had to see up close and personal what all the commotion was about with my neighbor."

"And?"

"And I'll drink to the beautiful and sexy Wendy Brooks."

"Sounds like you're flirting with Wendy Brooks."

She smiled behind her glass.

"So do tell, Ms. Kali Santiago. Are you a lesbian or something?"

"Do I have to be?"

"To do what?"

"To drink to the beautiful and sexy Wendy Brooks."

"No, you just have to be honest to drink to the beautiful and sexy Wendy Brooks."

"Well then, honestly, Ms. Wendy Brooks, I'm not a lesbian. I love men, and I adore women. Have I been with a woman before? Yes. Did I like it? Yes. Would I do you? Yes. Anything else I can be honest about?"

"Yeah, where is your restroom?"

She smiled as if she knew I was gushing on the inside.

113

"Down the hall to the left."

"Thank you." I jumped up fast as hell.

I didn't have to use the restroom. Truth is, I was about to throw her on the floor and taste everything Hispanic about her. *Maybe if I sit here long enough I can get myself together.* I had never been with a woman before, but I had touched myself and had my pussy eaten enough to know exactly what to do to her. *Come on, Wendy. Shake it off. Deep breaths.*

"Wendy, are you okay?"

"Yeah, I'll be right out."

"Good, because you're two shots behind, ma'am."

I wiped my dripping pussy and looked in the mirror, trying to convince myself that no matter what, I would not trade my dick in for pussy. *I can rightfully call Greg if I want to get laid, right? Right. Here I go.*

"Kali, girl, that…"

No she is not bent over in the fridge without any panties on. So, I sat at the bar, took my two shots, closed my eyes, and swallowed. All I could see was her nice ass in my mind.

"Wendy?"

"Yeah?"

"Touch me."

"Where?"

"Right here."

"Damn, Kali, your pussy is so wet."

"I know. Shit. Oh, mami, yes."

"You want me to stop, Kali?"

"No. I want you to put your mouth on me."

"Where?"

"Everywhere."

How she got up on her counter so fast I don't know, but

when she laid back, I took one of her breasts in my mouth so gently that she exhaled like she had just sat down from an exhausting day of work. I kissed her other one and came down her body until I reached her perfectly shaved pussy. I started to put my finger in it right away, but my mind made my face go first. It smelled so good. She ran her fingers through my hair and began to squeeze my head and moan uncontrollably. I licked her slowly, then I pressed my entire opened mouth up against her clit while she called my name.

"Wendy."

I didn't stop. I couldn't stop. I put my finger in at the same time I was sucking her pussy, and she arched her back in delight. She began fucking my face like she was about to explode on my next move.

"Please don't stop, Wendy, please. I want to cum for you. Don't stop, mami."

She took my hands, placed them both on her breasts, and squeezed them.

"Yeah, Wendy, I'm about to cum."

I couldn't say a word because I wanted her to cum. I wanted her to cum harder than any man had ever made her cum. She pushed my head back and pulled me to the floor. Pulled my dress up, straddled my pussy, and began to ride me. Our enlarged clits were rubbing so hard together that before I could get the words out, she screamed, "Fuck, I'm cumming! I'm cumming, Wendy!"

I didn't want her to stop riding my pussy because I was about to cum, too. So, I grabbed her by the waist and rocked her body forward and backwards, faster and faster. I could feel my shit on the verge of busting. She moved my hands and began to grind down on my clit with her pussy. My pussy was so wet and hers was so hot that I could just about feel the heat from the inside.

"I'm about to cum, too, Kali. Fuck, girl, you riding my pussy."

"Yeah, mami. You like that?"

"Yeah."

"Tell me again, Wendy."

"I like your pussy on my pussy."

"Is it hot?"

"Yeah."

She moved faster, like a man giving me a good hand job.

"I'm cumming, Kali. Shit."

She stopped riding me and put her face on my pussy, sucking my clit until I came again. Then she rubbed it faster and shoved at least three fingers inside of me until her knuckles banged up against my ass. She went deeper and deeper, faster and faster. I let out a loud scream,

"Fuck! I'm cumming again. Shit, girl."

"Wendy? Wen...dy?" When I opened my eyes, she asked, "Are you okay?"

I was on her floor with my hand under my dress. She grabbed the tequila, took me to her bedroom, and the next morning, I woke up to her looking at me.

"What time do you have to be at work?"

"Oh shit, I'm still at your house?"

"Wendy, after all the drinking we did last night, you couldn't have walked home if you tried. Coffee?"

"What time is it?"

"Seven."

"Shit, I have my promotion confirmation meeting at nine o'clock."

"You have plenty of time."

"I see you're new to the area. If you don't get into traffic by 7:45, you may as well wait until 9:30 to head to work."

"Lucky for me, I don't go in until Wednesday."

"Um, Kali, where is my dress, and why am I naked?"

"Well, your dress is on the deck where you took it off, and you are definitely naked by choice. Please tell me that you remember something about last night."

"I do. I saw you bent over getting limes out of the refrigerator. I remember being two shots behind. I also remember opening my eyes to you asking if I was okay."

"You're pretty much on point, but you left out the part about you masturbating on my floor, which initiated the rest of the evening of us finishing a bottle of Patrón. Thus, explaining why your dress is on the balcony and you being naked in my bed."

"So, I'm assuming we fucked. And from the tingle I'm getting from your description of last night, I liked it."

"You liked it on my deck, on my floor, on my couch, on my table, up against my wall, and you really liked it in my bed."

"So that's why I can smell your pussy on my lips?"

"Wait. I didn't say you liked it by yourself. You made me like it on the bar, on my desk, bent over my chair, and in my shower."

"Bent over your chair? How did I make you do that?"

"With this." She pulled out a very well-endowed strap-on dick that looked like something I saw on a J. Slater video.

"I did not put that on."

"Yes, and you fucked me like you knew what you were doing. Now, is there anything you want to tell me?"

"No, but what are you doing with a strap-on dick?"

"I won it at a toy party in Atlanta. I asked you to put it on and fuck me."

"I got to go, because as shocked as I am that you're saying I came on numerous occasions last night, you're also saying I strapped on a dick and made you cum more times than I did. The thought is messing with my mind and making me a little hot, too. So, yeah, I'll call you later."

After dressing, I went home as fast as I could.

Chapter Eleven
It's Official-HBIC (Head Bitch in Charge)

"Momma, you're not going to believe what they offered me in my promotion. I now have my own office, an assistant, a company credit card for travel, and my salary? Oh my God, it doubled."

"Baby, what did you do down there for them to be so good to you?"

"Momma, I have saved that company more money in the past two years than they have saved in the past eight years. I deserve every bit of what they are giving me and more. I'm so happy."

"Well, you make sure you give God the praise, and go to church on Sunday to give your testimony."

"Really, Momma, that's not necessary. How about I shout right around my room and let the Lord know it's all good?"

"Don't play with me, Wendy Pauline Brooks."

"Fine, Momma. I'm going to church, but it won't be no putting my promotion on blast. Momma, the doorbell is ringing. I'll call you tomorrow."

"Is it the gentleman who took you out of town over the weekend?"

"Momma, who told you I was with a man? I could have gone with Jessica to celebrate."

"Well, if you must know how I know, Jackie's niece, Maria, works at the airport in security, and her boyfriend works in maintenance. He saw you walking with a tall, light-skinned man to the counter for check-in."

"A mess, Momma, and I don't know who's at the door. So, bye. I'll tell you later who it was."

"Love you, honey."

"Love you, too, Momma."

She's so nosey.

"Deacon Fredricks? I mean, Dr. Fredricks."

"No need to be formal, and who told you I was a doctor?"

"Don't worry about how I know."

"May I come in?"

"Deacon Fredricks, I don't know what's going on with you, but a phone call usually works when people want to stop by for a visit. So, I'll just assume this is very important."

"Yes, it is. Two things. First, I received a phone call today in my office. There seems to be a woman saying you and I are having an affair, and that if I don't get it together, she will make it her business to tell my wife. Now, of course, I know you had nothing to do with this, but why is there a mystery woman threatening to tell my wife anything?"

"Deacon Fredricks, you know damn well...I mean, excuse me. You know I would never do anything like that, and I don't play games. So, it's obviously someone with too much time on their hands. And the only person who has even seen you at my house is my nasty-ass...excuse me, my dirty neighbor, Chrissy."

"But I haven't done anything to lead her to believe that there is anything going on between us. I've been over here in broad daylight. It's not like I was creeping."

"Deacon Fredricks, remember, this girl fucked my...damn it. Excuse me again."

I took a deep breath because I was really trying to be respectful by not using profanity in front of the deacon, regardless of what I had said to him in the past.

"She slept with my boyfriend at seven o'clock in the morning. Time of day doesn't matter with her. Anything she can do to get back at me, she'll try it. She's upset because even with all the free pussy... Look, I'ma say excuse me one more time and that should cover all the profanity I'll use until you leave. Now, she's mad because even after all the free pussy she gave Rashad, he's still beating down my door to be with me."

"Well, I told the person I don't play games. I love my wife, and she loves and trusts me. So, she can take her chances and see how far she gets with the lie she is about to tell."

"I know that, Deacon Fredricks. Calm down."

"I don't care how weak my flesh may be at times, I do love my wife."

"Well, we have one of the two things out of the way. Chrissy is a lying whore, just in case you're taking notes. Now what's the second thing you wanted to talk about?"

"I want you to consider coming to my office so we can talk more about your problem."

"What problem?"

"Your sexual actions when you visualize them, how they make you have a complete orgasm regardless of the time and place."

"You think it's a problem? I may well be normal."

"Wendy, there is nothing normal about you masturbating in a public restaurant and not even knowing it. That's against the law, too. Had we not been in my favorite corner on a slow day, you may have been put out. Now mind you, it's a turn-on for a woman to touch herself when a man is present, but over lunch with a group of senior citizens in the next room is a bit much."

"I can control myself, Deacon Fredricks."

"If that were true, I wouldn't be here. Now, I've been doing some research and talking with a few of my colleagues about what may be happening in your head, and I really want to help you."

"Like I said, there is nothing wrong with me. So, I'm going to have to decline."

"When was the last time you had an episode?"

"An episode? I'm about to be offended."

"It must have been yesterday."

"Why would you say that?"

"Because if it were more than three days or so ago, you wouldn't be saying you're about to be offended'."

"Deacon Dr. Fredricks, thank you for your concern, but I think I'll take my chances with healing myself. I can't say I will give Chrissy the satisfaction of thinking she has ruffled any feathers with her little phone call, because then, it will make it look like we're guilty of something. I've learned to pay her ass no attention, and that pisses her off even more. If you're not worried, I won't either."

"Changing the subject won't help either, Wendy. I just don't want you to be somewhere and someone take advantage of what you may be going through mentally. They may think you want them in a way that you really don't. Does that make sense?"

"It does. And thank you again, but I'll be fine."

"Is it insurance? Because I won't charge you if you just agree to come."

"Mark Fredricks, I have damn good insurance, okay? And I

don't need a fucking doctor."

"Are you pissed off now?"

"Nope. I just enjoy the free pass of cursing in front of the deacon."

He laughed and walked up to me. "Think about it, please."

I looked him in the eyes and took a deep breath. "It was yesterday, okay? And it was with a woman. After eating her pussy and letting her ride my pussy until I came, I opened my eyes and my hand was under my dress. We got drunk, and later on, she said I fucked her with a strap-on dick. That part I don't remember, but she said we both enjoyed it. Now, goodnight."

I reached for the door as he turned around slowly. I tried not to react to the fact that his dick was hard as hell and pressing up against his pants.

"See, you can't handle me as a patient. You want to fuck me too bad. But, I'll take a reference, though."

I smirked because yes, he loved his wife, but just the words out of my mouth could get his dick ready for me. He looked back at me, and I closed the door in his face. *Yeah, I'm that bitch, and I don't know where she came from, but I'm her. Rashad freed me and I love it. But do I really need a doctor?* I laughed to myself. *Dr. Feel Good! I'll take his ass! Damnit,* I thought, hearing my cell phone ring. *It would be upstairs.*

"Hello?"

"Hola, señorita."

"Hey, Kali. What's up, girl?"

"Nothing, 'bout to take a shower. You want in?"

"Kali, Kali, Kali. What a nice invitation, but let me say this. I like men, a lot. What happened with us last night was good, I'm almost sure, but us fucking on a regular is not something I plan on doing."

123

"I didn't ask you to come fuck me, Wendy. I asked if you wanted to take a shower with me."

"Which will probably lead to us fucking again, right? So, I think I'll pass, but if I feel like getting my pussy eaten, I'll call you back."

"What if I want my pussy eaten?"

"Then call who was eating it before you moved into Bridges Cove."

"You are so selfish, Wendy. And you know your pussy is good. That's why you can get away with saying that."

"Yeah, I do. So, be a good little girl and touch it for me, then go to bed."

"You cocky bitch."

"Actually, if you think about it, I was last night. It's a metaphor." She laughed as my other line beeped. "I got another call. Goodnight. Hello, Mr. Greg Hamilton," I said after clicking over.

"Hey, pretty lady. How are you?"

"Horny, and you?"

He laughed.

"Why is that so funny?"

"You are so bold and very beautiful and I love it."

"I turned down some pussy in hopes that you would call me."

"Wow! I didn't know you enjoyed pussy nor had that as an option."

"Well, I don't think I need it on a regular. That's why it was so easy for me to turn it down. I do want to see you, though."

"You want me to send Walter to pick you up?"

"Yes."

"Can you stay all night?"

"Yes…I mean, no. I have to work tomorrow, so I'll have to come back here to get my car for work."

"You can take one of my cars. Just be ready in an hour. As a matter of fact, bring your clothes for the week, if you want to. If not, we can go and buy you some."

"I don't want to go shopping. I just want to see you."

"Then Walter will be there in an hour."

"Thank you, Greg."

"Yep."

I hung up the phone only to question why I openly told him I have bi-sexual tendencies. *Maybe I do need to see Dr. Somebody. I was never this way before. Maybe I need to just stay away from Greg until I see a doctor. Why is he calling back?*

"Hello?"

"Stop second-guessing yourself and get your shit together. Walter is on the way."

No he did not hang up on me. He is too good to be true. A grown man. How I get that shit in my life? Whatever the flaw is, Lord, let it show up sooner than later.

*****

I know damn well that's not Walter already. It hasn't been an hour.

"Hey, Walter. Come on in."

"No, ma'am, I just wanted to let you to know I was here. I'll wait out here to get your bags."

"That's crazy. Just come in and have a seat. I'll only be a few more minutes. Can I get you something to drink?"

"No, I'm okay."

I ran back upstairs since one of my bags was still in my room along with my computer bag.

"Okay, I think I'm ready now. I had to grab my laptop and work for tomorrow."

"Ms. Wendy, thank you for changing Mr. Hamilton's life. He really likes you."

"Walter, I didn't change Greg's life. He's actually changing mine. But, there has to be something else to him. Men like him just don't come to me like this."

"He's been through a lot and has made a lot of mistakes and changes in his life. When I started working for him, he trusted no one. I earned his trust; so much so that he trusts me with you."

"Trust you with me? What do you mean?"

"He's expressed to everyone that you are off limits."

"What does that mean? He doesn't own me."

"He's never declared a woman to be off limits to any of us. You must be special is all I'm saying, Ms. Wendy. So, I'll take your bags to the car so you can lock up."

"Off limits? Do you all share women or something?"

"No, ma'am. Not off limits like that."

"Walter, is he sick or something? Like going to die in a year or so?"

"No, ma'am. Mr. Hamilton is very healthy, and we all pray he'll be around for a long time. Ask him questions you're not sure about when it comes to him. He's a very honest man and he likes you, so you have an open door. Take advantage."

"Thank you, Walter, and I'm glad he has you."

We pulled up at a house that was almost three times the size of the one I was brought to before by Greg.

"Walter, who lives here?"

"This is Mr. Hamilton's family home."

"What do you mean family home?"

"This is where he and his family spend all the holidays and special gatherings."

"And he wants me here?"

"Yes, ma'am. This is where he will be this week, and he wanted you here with him."

"His family is not in there, are they?"

"No, ma'am, just the two of you and his staff."

"Don't lie to me, Walter. I hate surprises. Well, sometimes I do like them."

"I wouldn't lie to you, Ms. Wendy. He's in there alone waiting on you."

He stopped the car and got out to open the door, but I was frozen. The house looked like something out of a magazine.

"Ms. Wendy? Ms. Wendy, you gonna get out?"

I couldn't move. Then my cell phone rang.

"Hello."

"Baby, you okay?"

"Greg, this is not the same house."

"I know, but does that matter?"

"No, but have you seen this house?"

"Yes, I built this house for my family and friends. Look up."

When I looked up, he was standing on the top balcony beckoning for me to come to him.

"Okay, I'm getting out."

"Wendy, I'm not going to do anything to hurt you. I promise."

Walter extended his hand to me, and I eased out of the car.

"Ms. Wendy, he likes you. It's okay."

With Walter behind me carrying my bags, I took a deep breath and began walking up the stairs that led to the front door. When Greg opened the door looking so damn good, any worries

I had left my body instantly.

"Hey, baby."

"Hello, Greg. Thank you, Walter, for everything."

"Walter, can you get Elizabeth to take Ms. Wendy's bags upstairs and have her unpack them for her?"

"I can unpack my own bags. That's not necessary."

"Yes, it is. All you need to do while you're here is relax. White wine?"

"No, I need vodka, please."

"Walter, tell Rosa to fix Ms. Wendy a vodka and cranberry, please."

"Yes, sir. Ms. Wendy, enjoy your evening, and I'll see you in the morning."

"In the morning?" I asked.

"Yes. Walter will be taking you to work this week."

"Greg, I don't need a limo escort to work. My co-workers will think I'm taking my promotion a bit far."

"Do you care what your co-workers think?"

"No, but I thought I was going to drive."

"Do you have to drive? No. Can you drive? Sure, but only if you want to. I want you to be treated like a queen, so let me do that. Please."

"I'll think about it."

"I'll call you, Walter, and let you know what she decides."

Walter looked at me and smiled. "Goodnight again, Ms. Wendy. Call me if you need me, Mr. Hamilton."

I started to wander around the house, and by the time Greg found me with my drink in his hand, I was up to room six.

"Greg, do you really need this much house?"

"Yes. I love it when my family comes in town. I have a niece and three nephews that need their own space when they come here. After my parents died, I found out I had a sister and a brother. That's the only family I have now. I mean, I have cousins and whatnot, but immediate family, that's it. And I love them. There is a library, indoor pool, game room, a movie theater room, fitness center, and two kitchens. There is also a basketball court and tennis court for my cousin who swears she is almost ready for Serena. There is a lake and a field for racing dirt bikes and 4-wheelers for the boys."

"Why so much?"

"Why not? When I say we lived in the projects, we did on the outside, but on the inside of our house, we passed for middle class. No one was allowed in our house unless Mom or Dad approved it. We moved stuff in late at night when we got it. We never opened our blinds or door wide enough for people to see in. It was a secret that we had anything better than our neighbors. I dressed okay, and we ate good and had clean clothes. We lived on the third floor, and that was only because Momma said roaches normally didn't want to go up; they liked to go down. So, with no one living above us, we didn't get any bugs, which made my dad and me really happy."

"Wow. How often do you see your family?"

"My extended family, mainly on holidays, but I fly down to see my brother and sister every other Wednesday, if I can. Sometimes I go with them to Bible Study, but I always take them and the kids to dinner when I'm there. Then I fly out the next morning.

In the middle of our conversation, in comes this beautiful woman carrying two drinks on a tray. Now when I say beautiful, I mean from head to toe. She had skin the color of toffee and was about 5'7". Her long, jet-black hair was pulled up to show a set of diamond earrings that dazzled in the light as she got closer. She had on a black dress that was lace, flowed all the way to the ground, and fitted every curve of her body. The black bra underneath accented her breast enough for me to take a gulp of my drink immediately. Her panties were a boy-cut fit that covered her ass, but it was a perfect apple-bottomed ass. She was fine as hell, and I couldn't stop looking and drinking.

"Thank you, Rosa. Oh and, Rosa, this is Ms. Wendy Brooks. She will be staying with us this week."

She smiled in delight. "Hi, Ms. Brooks. Pleased to have you."

Not like I would be pleased to have you.

"Thank you."

"If you need anything, please don't hesitate to let me know."

"Thank you, Rosa."

"Mr. Hamilton, what would you like for dinner? Elizabeth is ready to begin preparation."

"I forgot to ask Wendy when she got here. Baby, what would you like to eat?"

I was looking at Rosa so hard that he had to call my name to get my attention.

"Wendy?"

"I'm sorry. Whatever you choose will be perfect."

"Tell her to decide, and we'll be out here until it's ready."

"Yes, sir."

He watched me watch her walk away. When I turned up the rest of my drink, to my surprise, he was handing me another one simultaneously.

"Does she make you uncomfortable?"

"Excuse me?"

"Does it bother you that Rosa is here?"

"Does all of your staff look like that?"

"Yes. I have a male and female masseuse on staff, too. So pick the days this week you want a massage and invite Jessica over for one, as well."

"Why? Why is she so beautiful?"

"No one wants ugly help around the house. What if I have a bad day? Then I would have to come home and look at some ugly-ass woman or man cooking my dinner. Hell no. That would just piss me off even more."

"So you have men and women here cooking and cleaning?"

"Yes, and serving drinks, cutting grass, or whatever needs to be done around the house."

"This is too much, Greg."

"Wendy, I work hard for everything I have. My circle of friends is very small because people tend to try and take advantage of you if you're well off and they are half stepping. They always need a favor or have run into hard times, or they promise to pay you back when they get their taxes. I help those who are really trying to help themselves. Make me your last resort, not your first option."

"I understand that. Have you slept with Rosa?"

He gave me the strangest look. "No. Rosa works for me. And so does Elizabeth, Mark, Hector, Roberto, Tawny, Tim, and Janice. They all are easy on the eyes, but they are here to work for me, and when I have more guests, I pull staff from my other homes to come here. None of which I have had any intimate relationships with."

"It's just hard to imagine. I mean, Rosa is half naked."

"She is in uniform, and she is covered in the areas that need to be covered. When I have events here like Super Bowl parties and New Year's parties, whatever the event, she is in uniform.

131

She gets to keep all the tips she may earn from being in uniform, on top of the nice salary I give her. She's also in medical school, and I pay half her tuition. She can quit here anytime. After that, I will only pay half her next semester of school, and then she is on her own."

"So you are something like a pimp then?"

"No, ma'am, I'm very much the opposite of a pimp. I don't hit my staff members, and they don't sleep with my guests for money. I'm a very professional man. With her body, she can easily be a dancer in somebody's club and be talked about because she is on the grind to go to school by any means necessary. But, I gave her a job that only requires her to stay in school, look pretty, and do minor household chores. I gave her a basic bartending class at the club for a couple of weeks to maintain the bar here. She drives a Mercedes that she bought with her own money. She has a condo downtown that she pays for with her own money. I sign her check just like I do everyone else's, and she's an honor student. I'm a giver, Wendy. I don't have to take anything from anybody."

The more he talked, the more I wanted to go down and suck his dick until he came right there on that balcony. I felt so free there, and all his giving made me want to give it to him.

"Tell me something else I don't know about you, Greg."

"I use to be bi-sexual."

"Excuse me?"

"I use to be bi-sexual."

"You mean you use to sleep with men and women?"

"That's what the term bi-sexual meant last time I checked."

"What the fuck is use to be? Oh my God, you've slept with a man? What kind of pleasure did you get from that? Oh my God. You get Walter's ass here and get my shit. I'm leaving.

How in the hell did you *use to be* gay?"

"I didn't say gay, and please calm down."

"Fuck you. You've been with a man before, probably several men. Oh my God. I think I'm going to be sick."

"Wendy..."

"Don't you fucking touch me! I knew it. I knew you were too good to be true. Is this where you have your little gay parties, too? Up here high in the sky so no one can see you. Well, newsflash, asshole! You are closer to God way up here, and he sees that shit."

"Wendy, if you just calm down and let me talk."

"And say what, Greg? What else did you *use* to do? Were you a woman before, too? Do you sleep with animals? Oh my God! Are you HIV positive or something? Get Walter here now!"

"Wendy, I'll call Walter, but I need you to just listen to me, please."

"I need another drink. Where the fuck is Rose?"

"I'll get *Rosa* to fix you another drink, but you have to calm down."

"Oh, so they don't know you use to be a fucking fag?"

"I will not be disrespected. Now you need to calm down."

"Disrespected? You have lied to me over and over again, and you want to talk about respect?"

"I haven't lied to you about anything." He pushed a button on the wall.

"Yes, sir?"

"Can you bring Ms. Wendy another drink, please? A double."

"Yes, sir."

"Greg, do you have any disease that may cause the both of

us to die in the near future?"

"No, I don't. I can show you my last six HIV test results. When I say use to be, this was like right after my parents passed away. And no…no one but my grandmother, my pastor back home, and one other person knows that about me. Will you please let me tell you what happened, and then you can decide if you want to stay or leave. Just don't walk away without knowing. Please?"

When Rosa came in with my drink, I couldn't even focus on her.

"Thank you, Rosa," he said, as she smiled and walked away.

Even though he was wearing an all-white linen suit, he got on his knees in front of me. "I have never felt the way I feel about you with any woman I have tried to date. I've never even come this close with telling anyone what I'm about to tell you."

"Is Walter the other person that knows any of what you are about to tell me?"

"Yes. I will not lie. The evening Walter and I shared together changed my life. He gained my trust many years ago. I don't know why I told him what I told him, but he sat there and listened. He was a Godsend that night, because I had already planned to kill myself when I left the bar I met him in."

I looked him in his eyes and gave him all my attention because whatever he said next was going to determine if I stayed or if I turned away and never looked at him again. *I have a new job, no Rashad in my life, and a new attitude. I'll be fine.*

"The next morning, I woke up in the Marriott in a suite. I sat up, and on the table directly in front of me was a Bible with an envelope on it, a full bottle of the same liquor I drank the night before with Walter, and the loaded gun I had on me at the bar. I opened the envelope and the note read, 'Try reading this book before you open that bottle or pick up that gun. The room is paid for until Monday morning. Take your time.' There was a knock at the door. It was room service with breakfast and coffee, but I didn't put the Bible down. I took a shower with the Bible in the bathroom with me. I got dressed and ate breakfast with the Bible next to me. Then God spoke to me and said, 'Now read.' I read until there was another knock at the door. It was room service with lunch. I ate with the Bible right there. Then God spoke to me again and said, 'Read on,' and I did. Walter paid for that suite for me for three days with a full breakfast, lunch, and dinner; three days for me, a stranger. I don't even remember all of what I told him that night, and he won't tell me. He said it doesn't matter. He said if I look back, I'll never move forward.

"Three years after my parents died, I turned to men, women, anybody who would hold me. I was twisted and torn for two years after that. It wasn't until I almost gave my grandmother a heart attack when she caught a man giving me head in her house that I changed. That was the day I said before I kill her, I'll just kill myself. But, God wouldn't let me do it. He knew what he wanted me to do for the people I have around me right now. He knew I would need to see Walter again; He knew I needed to see my grandmother again. He knew I needed to meet my brother and sister.

"So, yes, I use to be bi-sexual, or I guess you can say I use to be anybody-sexual. I needed love, the love I knew I was missing from my mother and father. But, God told me that He had all the love I needed. I read it in His word. So, I began to rebuild my life. After I checked out of the hotel, I went to my church with that same Bible in my hands. I had folded all the pages that confused me and told my pastor that I needed him to help me understand why my parents were no longer alive and to help me get the devil out of my head, or else I wasn't going to make it one more day. And he did. We spent the next twelve hours eating pizza and drinking Coca-Colas. I walked to my grandmother's house with that same Bible still in my hands and told her that I was sorry. She hugged me tight like it was her last time to see me. She said, 'You feel like you've been born again'. Now how that feels through another person, I don't know, but I dried her tears, and that night, I got in her bed. When I turned over to tell her goodnight, I saw my father's face in her face, and I closed my eyes and went to sleep. My life started over from that day to now."

"And all of that made you the man you are today?"

"Yes. So, I've been there, baby. Beaten, battered, and torn to pieces by this ole world. Still, I didn't let it kill me. Almost, but it didn't. And if you still want to leave, you can, but I wouldn't trade that part of my life for anything in this world. I don't desire men; I don't think I did at that time. I just did it to do it. Like I said, I needed anybody who needed me. I used men and women for my own selfish reasons. I don't have to anymore, though. I was young, dumb, and going through a grieving process all by myself, and I didn't know that I didn't have to. I just didn't go to God; I chose man. I love my life now. I love helping people because someone helped me. You asked me to tell you something you didn't know. Well, I told you how God sent Walter to save my life. Now, I'll call him so he can take you home."

Rosa and another woman who I assumed was Elizabeth came on the balcony with two trays. Elizabeth was a white girl, but the chick was bad.

"Dinner is served, Mr. Hamilton."

"Thanks, Liz, and when you get back to the kitchen, can you ring Walter for me and transfer the call up here?"

"Yes, sir. Ms. Wendy, I hope dinner is to your liking. Enjoy."

I said thank you and tried not to drool while looking at her.

"I'm going to the restroom. I'll be right back," he said. He looked back at me like he knew as soon as he got out of my sight I was going to hightail it out of there.

The phone rang, and by impulse, I answered it.

"Hello."

"Ms. Wendy?"

"Yes, Walter, it's me."

"You okay?"

"Yes. Thank you, Walter."

"For what, Ms. Wendy?"

"For not leaving Greg in the bar the night he met you."

"I told you he liked you. Liz said he needed to speak with me. Is he around?"

"It was because of me. I thought I wanted to leave, but now, I think I want to stay."

"Are you sure? If he told you everything, I know that's a lot to take in, but Mr. Hamilton is a great man. I know everybody has a story to tell, but he really is a changed man."

"I know that now. I'll see you at seven-thirty."

"See you then, Ms. Wendy. Goodnight."

"Goodnight, Walter."

Chapter Twelve
Is It a Man's World?

"We were very impressed yet again, Wendy, when the numbers came in this month and our department was in the number two spot in the region. I don't know what you are doing, young lady, but we greatly appreciate it."

"Thank you, Mr. Nelson. I was very pleased with my promotion you sent down by Mr. Boyd, and I plan on working very hard to get us in the number one spot again next quarter and keeping us there."

"As long as we are never in the bottom twenty like we were before you came aboard, I'm happy. There are two additions to your team that will be joining us at the ten o'clock meeting this morning. Michael Jenkins is a transfer from Texas, and Robin Nash is from Florida. I think they both will give you the cushion you need to delegate more responsibilities in order to start some traveling and training in other offices that has been requested."

"I've been requested to go and train people?"

"Yes, ma'am. That's why corporate approved the company credit cards for you and gave you an assistant. You have become a hot commodity, and people want to be where we are. At the same time, you will have to maintain this office's status. We are confident you will, and that's why we paid you your worth. We look forward to compensating you for your efforts in getting the others on our level."

"Thank you for your vote of confidence, Mr. Nelson. I won't let you all down."

"We know. You guys take a break, and when we return, I'll introduce Michael and Robin to Wendy. Then I'll let Wendy give them a tour and spend some one-on-one time with them and maybe get Mr. Wallace's assistant to make reservations for dinner. Just tell them what you expect of them in the positions they will be filling."

"Yes, sir. I'll get Nancy to get us reservations somewhere. Will you be going us?"

"Oh no, tonight's my anniversary. I'm flying my wife to Miami for the week. You are on your own once introductions are done."

"Well, congratulations, Mr. Nelson, and I wish you many more!" I smiled as he headed out the door, then said to myself, "It's a man's world my ass!"

*****

"Michael and Robin, this is your new manager, Ms. Wendy Brooks."

They both stood, and to my pleasure and surprise, right in front of me stood one of the finest brothas my eyes have seen and a sistah wearing a bad-ass suit and a pair of pumps that made me green with envy.

"Pleased to meet you, Robin, Michael," I said, while shaking their hands.

Mr. Nelson then gave a ten-minute speech about the company and my promotion/new position. Then he said, "Wendy, they are all yours, but don't worry, guys, you're in great hands."

"Thank you, Mr. Nelson." Trying not to blush, I smiled and then began my short meeting with thanking them for wanting to be a part of my department and expressing that I looked forward to hearing about the skills they each possessed.

"Will you two be available for dinner tonight?"

"I apologize, but I have the movers scheduled to be at my house at six o'clock. Well, actually, what time are you planning to go?" Robin asked.

"I had Nancy make reservations for seven o'clock. What about you, Michael?"

"Well, I'm staying at the Marriott downtown this week, and my things will be here this weekend."

"Okay, what about this? Robin, you and I will have lunch, and Michael, you and I will have dinner."

After they both agreed, I gave them a tour of the building, showed them their offices, and before I knew it, it was time to go out for lunch. My phone rang, and it was Walter. At that very moment, I remembered I didn't have my car.

"Hi, Walter."

"Ms. Wendy, Mr. Hamilton asked me to check on you to see if you needed a ride for lunch?"

"Actually, Walter, I do. I have a new employee that I need to take to lunch and one I am taking to dinner this evening at seven. Can you check with Mr. Hamilton to see if this is okay?"

"No need. He told me that he would get Carl to drive him when you needed me. So, I'm on my way to pick you up right now."

"Okay, I'll be down in about ten minutes."

I immediately thought of what Robin would say when she saw a limo there to pick us up for lunch, but I waited until she asked.

"I don't mean to pry, Ms. Brooks, but…"

"Call me Wendy, and this is my boyfriend's limo. This is Walter."

"Hello, Ms. Wendy, and…"

"Walter, this is Ms. Robin Nash, the new Director of Budgeting for our company."

"Pleased to meet you, Ms. Nash."

"You, too, Walter."

Once she got in the limo, Walter winked at me as if to say, 'You better do it, girl'. We rode for a minute before she said anything, as if she were afraid to speak.

Then Walter called back to me and asked, "Ms. Wendy, where would you all like to go?"

"Just pick some place nice, please, that you'd like, and we can all enjoy lunch today."

"Yes, ma'am."

"Okay, Wendy, spill it. What does your boyfriend do for a living, and does he have a brother?"

I laughed. "He owns his own company, several of them."

"Damn, girl. And please excuse my language."

"It's okay. I forgot I didn't have my car right as Walter was calling me. I didn't want to give you the wrong impression about the limo, but if Walter didn't come, we were going to have to walk up the block and get some pizza or something, and I really wanted to sit down and talk about the job."

"Truthfully, all I really thought was, damn, I'm going to enjoy working for this company."

"I drive a nice car, too, but it doesn't have a Walter attached to it."

"Well, your man must think you're something special to send his limo to take you wherever."

"It's all pretty new. I not too long ago got out of a messed up relationship, and when I wasn't looking, God put this man in front of me."

"Excuse me one second." She closed her eyes and put her hands together in a praying position. "Lord, if you're still in the putting business. Can you please *put* me a man something like Wendy's right in front of me, too? Amen."

"Robin, you are crazy."

We both laughed.

Over lunch, I was very impressed with her goals and her commitment to making sure our company stays ranked. Then she asked me sort of a personal question.

"Wendy, are those your real breasts?"

"Yes! Why you ask me that, Robin?"

"Because the minute most women in Corporate America get a bonus they get an *added* bonus, if you know what I mean. Yours look so nice that I just had to ask."

"Well, yes, these are my breasts, and thanks to Victoria, it's our secret how they sit up to have people wondering, much like you, on whether or not they are real."

"Well, they are nice breasts, Wendy Brooks."

Before I started to get excited and blush, I looked up at her. She was wearing a look on her face that suggested she could pull them out and put them in her mouth right there at the table. I picked up my glass and tried to shake off what I felt coming on. My breathing picked up and my eyes began to close.

She touched my arm and asked, "Are you okay?"

"Yes, I'm fine. Why?"

"Your chest began to move like you had just finished running a marathon."

"We need to get back to the office. Let me call Walter and

get the car."

"I'm running to the ladies' room. I'll be right back."

"Okay," I said, while dialing Walter's number. "Hey, Walter, it's Wendy. We're ready. Okay, thank you."

Don't be scared, Wendy. Call him. I picked my phone back up and dialed.

"Hey, I need to see you. I have a seven o'clock dinner engagement tonight, so can you come to my house around four-thirty?"

*****

I was pacing the floor of my house while talking to myself, until the doorbell rang. *'Bout time.*

"Are you okay?"

"Look, Deacon Dr. Fredricks, I almost fucked my new hire at the table in my mind today. Her first four hours on the job and I almost fucked her."

"Wendy, calm down."

"No, you tell me there's a pill or something I can take for this shit, because right now, my job is going great, my social life is going great, and I have a great man. Well, I think he's my man. Regardless, I don't want to go around fucking all these people in my head or at the table or in the bathroom or wherever and lose him, my good job, or people I really care about."

"Then you have to come to my office and see me. Be a regular patient and let me get you the therapy you need."

"No office visits. I'm not coming there so people can think I'm crazy. You come here. I'll pay extra for the house call, but I'm not coming to your office. No way."

"Wendy, I can't come here and see you. It's not the right atmosphere for us to work on what you may be going through."

"Then forget it. I'll risk it all. I'll either deal with it myself, or I'll finger the Yellow Pages and find someone to come here and treat me. Never mind. Goodnight."

He walked right up to my face and got close enough to where his lips were outlining mine. "I can't treat you here."

He took his hands and went down the sides of my body until he reached the length of my dress. Then he ran his hands back up my body, feeling my legs up to my thigh until he reached my breasts.

"This is why I can't treat you here."

I felt my pussy begin to throb. I exhaled, and he closed his eyes as to catch the lust from my breath in his mouth.

"I can't treat you here."

I took his right hand and rubbed it down my stomach to the top of my pussy, then put his left hand on my ass.

"Can you treat me here?" I moved his hand down further on my pussy. "Can you treat me there?"

"Wendy, please don't."

"Shhh." I moved it again to right on top of my clit. "What about there? Can you treat me there?" I took his hand and rubbed it more in my wet pussy. "I can't hear you, Doctor. Can you treat me there?"

He squeezed my ass and pulled me closer to him.

"Wendy, please don't do this."

I moved his hand more and more over my clit until I felt his dick harden and press up against my leg.

"I want you to treat me, Dr. Fredricks. I want you to help heal my body. Can you do that? Can you heal me?"

His hand was so deep in my pussy that the juices began to run down my leg. He picked me up, sat me on the couch, and got on his knees in front of me.

"I can't treat you here. Call my office if you want to make

an appointment," he told me, then got up and left.

I wanted to go after him because he had me right where he wanted me, yet he couldn't do me. I don't know if that pissed me off or turned me on. *Now, I guess I have to finish this shit myself.* I laid back on the couch, put one leg up and the other on the floor, and envisioned the dick that just left my house inside my pussy. Soon, I came hard. Twice! *Shame on you, Deacon Dr. Fredricks, for leaving my pussy like this. Now I'm tired and hungry. Shit, Walter will be back in fifteen minutes, and I still have to shower. Damnit!*

*****

Damn, Walter is here already. Now get yourself together right this minute. No matter how fine Michael Jenkins is, you just had two orgasms, you're riding in your boyfriend's limo, and your man gives it to you real good. So, there's no need for flirting or giving him the impression that you are single. Okay, 1...2...3...break.

"Hi, Walter."

"Ms. Wendy, don't you look beautiful."

"Thank you. Did you get the address for Mr. Jenkins' house that I texted to you?"

"Yes, ma'am. He's actually at the Marriot that is only a few blocks away from you."

"Wow, I didn't know that. Well, I guess I wouldn't. We didn't talk much about it in our brief meeting today."

"Is he excited about his new position?"

"Yeah, Walter, he acted as if he were. A young black man, too."

"How does he feel about reporting to a woman?"

"I guess it really doesn't matter how he feels. That's the job."

"Some men are very intimated by a woman being in a position of power."

"Well, he doesn't appear to be one that will challenge my authority, but most people send their representative to their first meeting with others. The real person doesn't come out until later on."

"Very few people are who they really are when you meet them the first time. But, I hope he does well."

"He's a black man, so I hope he does, too. I'll call him and let him know we are down here."

With Michael being as fine as he is and living this close to my house, I don't know if that's a good thing or a bad thing. He better not ever show up trying to borrow sugar, because I might just give him some. Some of my sugar, that is.

"Come on down, Michael. We're here in the front.

"All this for little ole me?" Michael said as he got in the limo. "You shouldn't have, Ms. Brooks."

"Good evening, Mr. Jenkins."

"So I guess your promotion really worked out in your favor. Now I'm going to have to really do my thing and take your job so I can get me a limo, too."

"If that is what you came here to do, perhaps you should renegotiate your contract, because my position won't be available for a very long time."

"So you like being on top?"

"I can do what I do from anywhere, Mr. Jenkins."

"Ouch."

"Truth hurts."

"Where to, Ms. Wendy?"

"Castillio's, please."

"Downtown it is."

"And, Mr. Jenkins, this car belongs to my boyfriend, Mr. Greg Hamilton."

"Not the Greg Hamilton that owns The Waterfall in Dallas, is it?"

"Um, Walter, does Greg own a club named The Waterfall in Dallas?"

"Yes, ma'am, and The Overtime Sports Bar."

"Thank you. Then, yes, that would be the Greg Hamilton."

"My boys are not going to believe this. We go to The Waterfall all the time. Mr. Hamilton gets plenty of my money during the professional football and basketball seasons, and he's using it to ride my beautiful boss around in a limo. It's a small world. I've seen tons of pictures of him, but we always miss him on the nights he's in town."

"Well, I'm glad to see you appreciate the fact that he has those establishments for you to relax after work. You'll have to enjoy a couple of his spots here, as well."

"So how did you bag Greg Hamilton? I just knew he had like ten women per state, per club."

"To my knowledge, he has one woman and still tons of clubs. Mr. Hamilton is a well-respected man, and he treats me like a queen."

"Well, you have to be good to have Greg Hamilton. That's all I'm saying."

"Once you get off his dick, maybe we can talk about you, Mr. Michael Jenkins?"

"Wow! Do you kiss Greg with that potty mouth?"

"All over, I sure do."

"I might be jealous."

"That's okay. Plenty of men and women are. Now, if you don't mind, tell me about you, Michael."

Dinner was going great until Michael's phone rang and a woman started screaming from the phone.

"I'm having dinner with my boss. I said I'ma call you back." He hung up the phone and extended an apology, but no sooner than he got it out of his mouth, a woman walked up to the table.

"Negro, please, this ain't yo' damn boss! Bitch, who the fuck are you?"

Now mind you, I was looking at her like she was crazy, because I was sitting there with his résumé on the table.

"Oh bitch, don't sit there like you can't hear me. I bet if I slap the shit out of you, you'll hear me then."

"Tracy, chill the fuck out! What is wrong with you? This is my damn boss. And when the fuck did you get here?"

"None of that shit matters. I've been calling your damn phone for an hour. You told me there wasn't another woman and your move here was for business, but as soon as you get your black ass off the plane, you out grinning in some bitch's face?"

I tried to let him handle the crazy-ass woman, but I couldn't take it anymore.

So I politely said to him, "Michael, thank you for taking time out of your evening to sit down with me and go over your experience. I look forward to working with you and Robin. I guess your girlfriend will be taking you home, and I won't let this evening effect your position. But, moving forward, if you would, please let her know my name is Ms. Wendy Brooks, Senior VP of Budget Consolidation for the company that now employs you. And if she interrupts another meeting or calls me a bitch ever again, my Senior VP ass is going to jail. Goodnight."

I shook his hand and walked past her with so much class that the white people in the restaurant were smiling like they had just seen Elvis. To top that shit off, Walter pulled the limo in front of the window, by the table we were sitting at, and opened my door on cue.

"Thank you, Walter. I'm ready to see my man now."

"Right away, Ms. Brooks."

*****

"Hi, Ms. Wendy."

"Hey, Rosa. How are you, dear?"

"Good as you look."

"Why, thank you."

"Can I get you a drink?"

"Yes, please, and I'm guessing Mr. Hamilton is on the balcony?"

"Actually, I think he's in his office. I'll bring your drink there."

"Thank you, Rosa, and by the way, white looks very nice on you."

She boldly replied, "I can only imagine what it looks like on you."

Oh shit, I'm flirting with Rosa, and she's flirting back. I better get my ass up these stairs before I start my night over with another appetizer.

"Gregory Hamilton. Good evening to you."

"Damn, you look beautiful. Is that how you went on your business dinner?"

"Yes. Why? Do you have a problem with my attire?"

He put his pen down and stood up to approach me. "Yeah, I do."

"And that is?"

"You've been in here thirty seconds, and you still have it on." He leaned in to kiss me.

When I closed my eyes to enjoy the feel of his lips, he ripped my damn shirt open.

"Wait a damn minute! Do you know how much I paid for this shirt?"

He ran his hands down the sides of my skirt, got to the bottom, grabbed it at the split in the front, and ripped it up to where my panties were exposed.

"How much for the skirt, too?" he said.

Then he picked me up and laid me in the middle of the floor on the softest, purest Persian rug money could buy. Not that I have even walked on many rugs, but this one felt like a bed of feathers. Go figure.

"Now, you lay there and calculate the panties and bra in, too. Then after you cum, tell me how much I owe you."

He went down and put his warm mouth right on my clit. I felt his hands on my breasts, but then I felt hands rubbing up my thighs. I was lifted up underneath my ass, and it felt like he was trying to eat my entire body. He was pressed so hard against my pussy, I felt like I could cum at any second. He was still taking me in his mouth, when I felt warm lips and hands again on my breasts.

When I felt a finger slide inside my pussy, it caught me off guard because both his hands were on my breasts, while my ass was still in the air and now a finger was inside of me. But, I couldn't open my eyes. I felt something else go inside of my pussy. It wasn't the finger this time. Something warm and wet. So, I began fucking Greg's face with my pussy because I wanted to cum for him so bad with everything that was going on all over my body.

Then there came a hard dick making its way into my mouth. *When the fuck did he reposition himself to put his dick in my mouth?* I didn't think twice about it after it was there, though. As I felt a tongue or whatever pushing inside my pussy, I stroked his dick with my wet, juicy mouth. He began to moan in pleasure, and so did I.

However, I knew Greg's mouth, and that was not his tongue inside of me. *Maybe it feels different because he's upside down or something, but I don't want him to stop.* I began using my hand to stoke his dick. It got harder, and he moaned louder, but this time, I didn't feel the vibration of his moans on my pussy. I could actually hear him moaning and calling my name out loud. He started fucking my face so intensely that I had to really hold his dick because he was going deeper in my throat.

The deeper he got caused me to gag, and he fucked my face even harder. There was a hand now rubbing my clit faster, just the way I liked it, and I was about to cum on his nice-ass rug.

"Fuck, Wendy, I'm gonna cum in your mouth if you keep sucking my dick like that."

All I could do was moan as he bounced his dick faster and faster in my mouth, while his hands were all over my pussy.

"I'm 'bout to cum Wendy!" he shouted.

I was, too, but I couldn't say it because his dick had my mouth full. I had spit everywhere, and I wanted to taste him so bad. I rubbed his balls and stroked his dick faster. He got louder, and I sucked harder. I felt his body stretch all the way out on top of me. The hand was gone from my pussy, and his tongue was sucking my clit so fast that I was about to explode from the inside-out. I moaned louder, but it was useless because his dick overpowered my mouth like a caged animal that wanted to be free.

"I'm cumming, Wendy. Baby, shit, take this dick. Fuck! Oh shit, baby. Yeah, yeah, yeah."

I couldn't verbally express that I was cumming all over his rug and down my ass. So, the shaking of my body would have to speak for me.

"Damn, baby, you okay? Wendy? Baby, open your eyes."

I heard Greg talking, but my eyes were shut so tight that I could almost feel tears forming.

"Wendy? Baby, open our eyes, please."

When I did open them, he was standing right in front of me, and Rosa was standing behind him holding my drink.

"Baby, are you okay?"

I looked at him and whispered, "Greg, what did you do to me?"

"Nothing. Are you okay?"

I looked around the room, and then I looked down at my clothes, which were still intact.

"Wendy, look at me. Are you okay?"

"I need to lie down, please."

"Okay, I'll take you to bed, baby."

"Wait, Greg. Tell me what happened when I came in the room, please."

"Well, you spoke to me. I told you about your outfit and that you had been in it too long to be standing in front of me. I got up from my desk, came around the front to kiss you, and you closed your eyes. Your breathing changed. So, I sat you down on the couch and called for Rosa. I've been trying to get you to open your eyes for about ten minutes. Baby, are you okay? Do you need a doctor?"

"A friend of mine seems to think I do."

Chapter Thirteen
Decisions, Decisions

I just got in the door. Who could be ringing my doorbell?

"Chrissy?"

"Hi, Wendy. I know I'm not on the top of your friends list right now, but can I come in? I really need to talk to you."

"Chrissy, look, I just got in. I've had a long week, and I'm really not in the mood for any company."

"I promise not to bother you long. Please?"

"Come on in."

Why, Wendy? Why are you listening to this shit?

"Wendy, I'm so sorry for disrespecting you and your house by sleeping with Rashad. I mean, the first time it happened I told him it wouldn't happen again. But then, he called again and again, and it just turned into something we both began to enjoy. We never thought about you or the consequences of you finding out, and I apologize for that."

"What kind of woman sleeps with another woman's boyfriend and comes over to apologize like nothing big really happened? I could have killed you and Rashad that day, but I didn't do anything to either of you. Instead, I let you leave and dealt with Rashad in my own way. You're a slut and can't help it, and so is Rashad. I loved him, while you only loved fucking him. There is a difference. And it wasn't that your pussy was better than mine. His ass was just greedy. You were an easy, next-door fuck that he couldn't turn down. You got his dick, and I kept his money. So, I guess you got what you wanted. I've learned not to hold grudges against people who seem to not know any better. That's what I'm saying about you *and* Rashad's ass. So now, if you'll excuse yourself, I have to unpack."

"Wendy..."

"Chrissy, let it go. Just leave please. We're still not friends, and you are who you are."

She walked right up to me and kissed me in the mouth.

"What the fuck are you doing?" I shouted, stepping back.

"Trying to see if I can make it up to you. Let me taste you, please?"

"Chrissy, if you don't get the fuck out of my house, I'ma give you the ass whipping you missed months ago."

"You don't want to fight me. You probably want to fuck me, too, just like Rashad did. So, let me apologize to you the way I really want to."

"You think I'm playing with you?"

She dropped to her knees, put her hand up my skirt, rubbed it across my pussy, and then stuck her finger in her mouth. My mind said, *You ought to let her eat your pussy. She owes you that much.* Then I thought, *Maybe I should taste her to see what is so good about her pussy that my man just had to have it.* However, since I really wasn't in the mood at the moment, I decided some other time.

"Chrissy, get your ass up and out of my house. I don't give a damn how easy it was for you to drop to your knees and get what you wanted from Rashad. I am not him. Goodbye and goodnight."

I turned to go upstairs, and when I looked back, her ass was sitting there like she had lost her best friend. *There is no sympathy pussy in this house. But, I will give it to her. She is fine as hell in that outfit, but I will not stoop to her level. She fucked my man. They fucked up, not me. Damn, who am I trying to convince?*

She finally got the picture and left. I could only laugh to myself.

Now who could be calling while I'm basking in the memory of what Chrissy looked liked on her knees in front of me?

"Hi, Kali. No, I'm not going out tonight. You? Oh, my friend works at the club on Main Street. Yeah, that's it. Well, have a good time. I'll call and have you put on the VIP list if you promise to wear something nice to show off those nice-ass ta-tas. You so crazy, girl. Okay, bye."

It's so nice to have pull. Should I? Naw, I don't even feel like getting dressed. I just want to sleep in my own bed, then wake up tomorrow and treat myself to a little shopping.

"Hey, baby. My neighbor is coming to the club tonight. Can you put her on the VIP list and treat her real nice? Kali Santiago. Yeah, you can come over afterwards if you'd like. Well, just call me and let me know. Okay, bye."

I wonder if we're in an official relationship now. Maybe I should ask him if he comes over tonight. I pulled clothes out my bag that smelled just like him. *Perhaps I will ask him.*

*****

Damnit. Where is my cell phone? Hiding in all these damn pillows.

"Hello."

"Hey, baby, you sleeping?"

"Not if you're on the way."

"I am. Do you need anything?"

"Just for you to get here as soon as possible."

"I'm coming, baby."

"Not yet, Gregory, but you will be very soon." I could tell he was smiling through his chuckle. "Hey, did my friend Kali make it to the club?"

"Yeah, and I told her that we were dating and that I didn't want her easy pussy. I just finished my rounds, and now I'm on my way to see you."

"She tried to holla at you?"

"No, baby. She tried to *fuck* me; offered me her pussy more than once right there in the VIP booth I put her in."

"Wow! I'm sorry, baby. I just wanted her to have a good time. I had no idea she didn't understand the meaning of *my friend.*"

"Next time, call me your man so we won't have these problems."

"We're not going to have these problems anymore anyway. I'll see you in a few." It didn't dawn on me what he said until I was just about to hang up. "Wait. My man? So you're my man now?"

"I'll answer that when I see you."

"Bye, Greg."

This will only take a minute. By the time he makes it through downtown, I'll have showered and be back in the bed. Tennis shoes? Check. Ponytail? Check. 'Don't fuck with my shit' attitude? Check!

"Who is it?"

"Open the fucking door, Kali!"

"Why the attitude and profanity, Wendy? It's only two o'clock in the morning."

"Let me say this so you will understand it. I can be the sweetest person to have around or I can be a fucking nightmare. Greg Hamilton, owner of the club you visited tonight, is off limits to you. I said he was my friend, translation my BOYFRIEND. He does not want your time or your pussy. I give him EVERYTHING he needs. Now, as your neighbor, I'm *asking* you to please respect my relationship with Greg. But, as his girlfriend and a woman scorned, I am *telling* you to stay the fuck out of his face." I put a huge smile on my face. "Hope you had a great time at the club, girl. Goodnight."

Shit, Walter must have put the damn car in overdrive. I am so busted.

"Wendy, why are you coming across the yard with sneakers, a sweat suit, and a very elevated ponytail? The last time I saw someone dressed like you at this time of morning, my cousin's wife found out he had two girlfriends and a baby on the way. So, were you jogging or were you being bad?"

"Baby, I just wanted to make sure Kali understood from a female's point of view how important it is not to throw your pussy at someone else's man. That's just disrespectful, and in order for us to live here and be all neighborly, I needed to make sure there was clarity amongst the two of us. Her behavior towards you tonight, she got that one for free. The next time she crosses the line with you, it's gonna cost her ass. Goodnight, Walter. I'll bring him home tomorrow."

"Goodnight, Ms. Wendy, Sir."

Greg waved Walter on, and we went inside laughing.

"Baby, I put towels in the bathroom for you. Are you hungry?"

"Yes," he replied, and before I knew it, his head was between my legs.

159

"Baby, wait. Shit, Greg. I meant hungry for food. Damn, baby. Shit. Yeah, right there. Right there, baby. Oh my God, yes. Don't stop, baby. Shit. Yeah, yeah, yeah, baby. Fuck, baby, you gonna make me cum. Yeah, yeah, Greg. Yeah! I'm cumming, baby. Damnit. Uh, fuck me. Please fuck me."

Instead of him keep going, though, he stopped. "So, officially, will you be my lady?"

"What?"

"Will you be my lady?"

"If I say no, are you not going to finish this?"

"If you say no, I'm going to fuck you so good you'll reconsider."

"It gets better than what I've already had?"

"*I* get better than what you've ever had. The stuff we've done together, Wendy, is just the beginning. I don't want to date you to just date you. I want to date you to keep you."

"Why, Greg?"

"Why not?"

"I can give you a number of reasons."

"And none of them would change the fact that I want to be with you, exclusively. I want to make you understand that your last relationship was not the way life and love is supposed to be. You have made me see and understand that honesty and trust are a must to live again from a past that was full of pain. Now, Wendy Pauline Brooks, will you please be my lady, because I want to be your man?"

I didn't know any other way to tell him yes other than to take his dick and put it in my mouth, and when I swallowed his juices, hopefully the look in my eyes made him understand my pussy was his and his dick was now all mine.

However, just for clarity, when I came up and laid next to

him, I told him, "Yes, I will be your lady."

After he turned over and kissed me, we fell asleep naked. Sex without penetration, and we were both satisfied. *Hell yeah, I want to be his lady.*

The phone ringing scared me so bad that I hit Greg in the face on accident. He was so tired, he barely even moved.

"Hello. Good morning, Momma. No, I didn't go out last night. I stayed in and did laundry. Why you up so early? You okay? Yes, I'm going to church. Momma, what's wrong? No, I'm not alone. Why? Are you on your way over? Yes, it's Mr. Miami, Ma, and his real name is Greg, Greg Hamilton. Why? Yes, ma'am, I trust him. Yes, I do like him. Momma, what's wrong? Yes. Yes, ma'am. So what did he say? What? Cancer? Wha-What do you mean cancer? No Momma, you don't have cancer. I'll make you an appointment tomorrow with a different doctor; one downtown with more experience. SO WHAT IF YOU HAVE BEEN GOING TO HIM FOR YEARS!"

I woke Greg up when I began yelling.

"Momma, I'm getting dressed and coming over there. I'm sure this is a big mistake. You just need me to read the paper for you because you don't understand what it really says. Why not? Well, I can pick you up from church. Well, I can come when you and Ms. Ethel come from lunch. Momma, please don't do this to me. Don't tell me something like this and try to push me away like it's nothing. I'll be over there this afternoon. Yes, Momma, right after I go to church. Okay, I promise not to come by until I go to church first. Mom…Momma, I love you."

When I hung up the phone, Greg took it out of my hand.

"Baby, look at me. I need you to talk to me. Look at me. What did your mother say?"

"Why? You don't care. You don't even know me. Don't ask

161

me about my mother. You think because we sleep together on a regular basis that entitles you to be in my personal business? You can get dressed and get the fuck out for all I care."

"Wendy, it's not going to work. You can say whatever you want to say to try and push me away right now, but I'm not going anywhere. Now, tell me exactly what you mother said."

"Fuck you, Greg. You're not my counselor. I don't even know why you're still here. I asked you to leave. Why can't you just leave me alone? I want to be left alone."

"Why, so you can go through whatever this is by yourself like I did when my parents passed away? You think it's by chance I am here right now? God put me here for this very moment. He knew you would need someone, and I'm here. Now, what did your mother say?"

I looked at him with tears in my eyes. "She...she said she has cancer...breast cancer, and she may have to have one of her breasts removed. But, Momma is healthy. She is so healthy. She can't have cancer. I've only heard her cough like three times in my entire life. *My* mother doesn't get sick."

"Do you want me to drive you over there?"

"No. She told me not to come over until I have gone to church."

"You want me to call Walter to come and take you?"

"No, I'm going to drive, but can you call him to come and pick you up. That way, I can go ahead and get dressed so I can go and see her right after church is over."

"Yeah, I'll tell him to come and get me, but as hard as it's going to be, please respect your mother's wishes and go to church *first*. Then go and see her. It has to be a reason for her to make that request. So, do that for her, okay?" He kissed my forehead. "I'll start the shower for you."

He got up, but I couldn't move. My legs were stiff, and my heart was beating so hard it sounded like the drum line of someone's marching band. I started sweating like I had run a marathon. I couldn't move.

"Wendy, come on, baby. Get up."

"Please just go, Greg. I'll call you later today after I see Momma. I…I just need to be alone."

"Promise you will call me. Please?"

"I will."

I kissed him goodbye, I think. I was like a zombie. I took my shower, got dressed, and drove myself to church, but I don't remember doing any of it. What I do remember is walking up to the altar for prayer and falling to my knees. I was crying so hard my head felt like it was about to pop.

Someone picked me up from behind, and I just turned to lay my head on their chest. My heart told me it was Deacon Fredricks, but when I looked up, to my surprise, it was Rashad. After church, he walked me to my car. Everyone wanted to know what was wrong, but the hesitation of them asking showed on all of their faces. Even Deacon Fredricks looked my way, but I guess he was just as confused as I was to see Rashad consoling me.

"You want to talk about it?"

"No, but I'm glad to see you at church, Rashad."

"Well, I'm trying to clean up my act so I can get my lady back."

I rolled my eyes and told him, "Keep praying, brother."

"Wendy, we've been through a lot of things together, and there's nothing you have to keep from me. What's wrong? I mean, what had you on bended knee at the altar crying the way you were crying? Are you sick?"

"Are you in the obituary column?"

"Funny. Come on now. If anybody knows you, I know you. We may not be together right now, but I will always care about what happens to you."

"Rashad, that's very sweet of you, but I'll be fine."

"Ms. Wendy, are you okay?"

I turned around thinking, *It's about time.*

"Deacon Fredricks, yes, I'm fine. Thank you for asking. Um, this is Rashad."

"Mr. Rashad, I've heard so much about you. Looks like you made it to the right place today at the right time. Look how the Lord works. Wendy, if you need anything, just let me know. Rashad, nice meeting you," he said with a big-ass smile.

"Same to you, Deacon Fredricks, and I will see you again soon. I kind of enjoyed the sermon today."

"Great. Then please do come back." He looked at me as if to say, *Please call me later and let me know that you're really okay.* Instead, he only said, "Bye."

"That's cute, Rashad. Thanks for making sure I got to the car. I'll see you around."

"Around what time? You know I'll be there."

"I'm going to see my mother. Then my man will more than likely take me to dinner."

"Wendy, the Lord is not pleased with your decision to call yourself dating this man."

"Coming from Satan himself, yeah, that sounds about right."

"You don't love him. And right here on these church grounds I'ma tell you face to face, I'm coming back to get what's mine. You can tell Mr. Hamilton I said so."

"Awww, you remembered his name. Funny the things you

pay attention to. I have to go. See you."

I got in my car and pulled away. *Lord, why did you send Rashad of all people to get me up off the floor during altar prayer? You sure do work in mysterious ways.*

*****

"It's me, Momma. Open the door. I know you're in there. I have a key. I'm only going to ring this bell one more time before I come busting in."

"I was in the bathroom, ole crazy girl."

I reached out and hugged my mother like we hadn't seen each other in at least fifteen years.

"Wendy, baby…you're choking me."

"Sorry, Momma. Sit down. You should be resting."

"Wendy, I have cancer. I'm not having a baby."

"I know. Sorry. Speaking of, can I take a look at the results on what your doctor thinks he saw?"

"Wendy, I trust what Dr. Morgan said. He's been my doctor since before you were born. It's cancer, baby. Good thing it's treatable and has not spread too much. That's why we're going to start immediately with my treatments."

"What's immediately, Momma?"

"Tuesday."

"Okay, I'll take off so I can take you and make sure you get home and get you some dinner. Do I need to look into having someone here at the house with you daily?"

"First of all, you will not be taking off your job. You just got that promotion, and you have people to train and things to do. Ethel is going with me. I already confirmed it with the doctor."

"Momma, how could you? You know I'm not going for that. I will call Ms. Ethel myself and tell her to enjoy her

Tuesday because I'm taking you to the doctor."

"You will do no such thing. Wendy, look at me." She grabbed my face and looked me dead in my eyes. "Baby, I'm not going to die. I'm going to be fine. You still owe me a wedding day and at least two grandbabies. Death right now is not an option. I already talked to the Lord about it, and He agrees. Now stop worrying and tell me more about Mr. Miami."

"Momma, now is not the time to talk about Greg. Now, do I need to send someone over to clean and run errands for you?"

"No. Does Greg have any kids? Has he ever been married? Where do his parents live?"

"Ma, stop it! Stop pretending you're not sick. I don't want to talk about Greg!"

"Well, you may as well, because I don't want to talk about CANCER! I will not let the devil make me think I can't get better. Now, if you don't want to talk about Greg, I suggest you talk about something else, because if you mention cancer, sick, or trying to help me handicap myself, I'm going to put your ass out of my house." With tears running down her face, she asked, "Now, damnit, does he have any kids?"

I answered slowly, trying to fight back my own tears. "No, ma'am, he doesn't. He owns several clubs and is a perfect gentleman. His parents passed away in a car accident when he was younger, and he asked me to be his girlfriend."

"Well, what did you say?"

I wiped her tears away. "Yes. I said yes."

"That's good. So when do I get to meet him?"

"If you let me take you and Ms. Ethel to the appointment on Tuesday, you can meet him then."

"Deal. 'Cause, chile, had you told Ethel she couldn't take me or go with me, you'd had a lil' war on your hands." She laughed, got up, and went into the kitchen. "You want some tea?"

"No, ma'am." I went in after her and took another look at her. That was my momma, so bold and beautiful; ready to fight for her life. "Momma...I love you."

"Awww, baby, I love you, too. I hate to rush you off, but me and Ethel are meeting Jackson Perry and Timothy Newsome for wine and cheese at the art gallery at three o'clock. So, I have to change clothes. I can call you later when I get back."

"Momma, are you going on a date? Please tell me you're seeing Mr. Newsome, because last time I saw Mr. Perry, he didn't look like he had many teeth in his mouth."

She laughed loudly and remarked, "Ethel said she didn't need his teeth anyway for what she wanted him for."

In disgust, I replied, "Momma, that's nasty. You and Ms. Ethel are being fast going on dates and what not. Unbelievable."

"Like I told you, I have cancer, baby, but I ain't dead."

She kissed me and told me to lock the door behind me because she was jumping in the shower. After taking a deep breath, I went and got in the car. *Maybe she is in the denial stage of her condition. I watched that on Oprah one time. I wonder should I call the doctor on Monday myself before taking her in on Tuesday. That might piss her off, but what the hell. She only has* cancer. *I'm a nervous mess, and she's going on a double date. Get it together, Wendy Brooks.*

"Hey, baby. Yeah, I just left Momma's. Oh hell, according to her, fine. As a matter of fact, she and her hot-ass, old-ass friend Ms. Ethel are going on a wine and cheese date with two men from her church. Yes, I'm starving. Okay, see you soon."

As I was driving to Greg's, I couldn't help but to smell Rashad all over my clothes from when he was holding me at the church. I refused to question God, but really? *Rashad?* If I called and told him that I'm proud of his actions, he would look at it as a possibility for a comeback, which was not the case. I cared for Greg and wanted to see where our relationship was going. He was nothing like I have ever had before, and it felt good to be treated the right way.

Am I ready to settle down now that I have been freed from Rashad's little prison? Is there anything else I want to do before I really let Greg in? Well, hell, it's too late now because I said yes. You have a man now, girl. Enjoy it. You've had enough bumps and bruises from Shad. Let Greg heal all your wounds.

"Hey, Walter."

"Hey, Ms. Wendy. You look beautiful today."

"Thank you, Walter."

"Hey, man, you pushing up on my lady?"

"No, sir, but you have to admit she's looking mighty pretty today."

"She sure is, Walter. Hey, pretty lady."

He greeted me with a kiss so tender and so genuine that I almost melted right there at the door.

"I cooked for you."

"You did not. Where's Rosa?"

"She's on vacation for two weeks. I sent her to Mexico to visit her family."

"You sent her?"

"Yes."

"Okay, she works for you and gets paid and…"

"And as a bonus, I paid for her travel to and from Mexico to see her family."

"You are such a great man."

"I have my flaws, but giving is what I do. I'm a giver. And if you let me, I plan to give you everything you want and need."

Sounding irritated, I replied, "Okay, you said that already."

"Then just stay tuned, pretty lady, and you'll see."

"Hi, Ms. Wendy."

"Hi, Elizabeth. It's good to see you again."

"You, too. Let me know if you need anything."

While looking up at Greg, I said, "I think I have everything I need right now."

"Mr. Hamilton, the table is all set for dinner. Please let me know if you need anything for the rest of the evening."

"Thank you, Liz. As a matter of fact, I think we will be okay for the rest of the night. If you could just tell Walter to alarm the house, you guys are free to take the rest of the night off."

"Are you sure, sir?"

"Yes, ma'am."

He escorted me into the kitchen, and I looked back at Liz, wearing a smile of approval. They loved him so much. The appreciation showed on their faces all the time.

"So how was church?"

I didn't want to talk about church because then I would have to share that Rashad came to church and the whole altar thing.

"It was good," I simply replied.

"Well, what man's cologne are you wearing? It better be the Lord's." He laughed and passed me my plate.

I took a big sip of my wine and just said it. "Rashad's."

He looked up at me and waited for the rest of the story.

"Out of the blue today, he came to church. I was at the altar crying about Momma, and when someone picked me up off my knees, I just hugged them. I thought it was my favorite deacon, but when I looked up, it was Rashad. He walked me to the car and hugged me again, then said if I needed anything to let him know. I told him I didn't. I didn't even tell him about Momma. I just got in the car and went on to Momma's house. I was shocked that he was there. I mean, I could never get him to go to church when we were together."

"Are you okay, though? I mean, now that you have seen your mother?"

"Not really. I plan on calling her doctor tomorrow to get more details on her cancer because she is scheduled to start chemotherapy Tuesday. I wanted to know if you will go with me to take her. I mean, she has Ms. Ethel going, too, but I need someone to go with *me*."

"You know I will. I'll have Walter drive us. You know, take her to chemo in style."

"You're so silly. This tastes great, baby. So, tell me. If you can cook this well, why do you have someone else cooking for you?"

"Because I did my share of cooking when I was growing up. My grandmother made me cook all the time so when I moved out, if I ever needed to cook for myself, I could. Then I said when I was in a position to not have to cook, I wouldn't. I have been to almost every restaurant in this city, and eating out all the time is not good for me. So, now, Rosa takes care of that for me. I cooked for you tonight to let you know that if I lost everything and you had to work while I stayed home with the kids, I could have your dinner waiting when you got off work."

I almost spit my drink on the table. "Kids? You want kids?"

"Don't you?"

"I never thought about it until my mother brought it up today. I mean, I have plenty of time to have kids. I just got this promotion at work and I just got you. So, I don't want to rush anything."

"I'm not trying to rush you, baby. It was just a question."

The doorbell rang, but the look on Greg's face said he wasn't expecting anyone.

"Excuse me, baby."

He's fine and he can cook his ass off. Damn, Wendy! You're lucky, girl.

I heard Greg's voice elevate. "No, you can't come in. What the hell are you doing here? You know I don't play that shit."

A woman's voice yelled back, "All I asked you to do is call me back. I really needed to talk to you and explain what happened."

"I don't give a fuck what happened. Some things should never happen, and doing what you did was one of them. Now, I'm going to close this door, and if you ring my fucking doorbell again, I'm going to call the police on your stupid ass. Stay the fuck away from me, my house, my clubs, all of it. You don't exist in my world anymore. You were here and didn't want to be here. You let another motherfucker make you think the grass was greener on the other side. So, take yo' ass back over there on his shit."

He slammed the door so hard that it scared me. Whoever it was started beating on the door. I ran to the front where he was still standing.

"Baby, come on. Let's go upstairs and finish dinner on the balcony," I said to get him to move.

Hell, I was scared I'd get tossed off that bitch, so I was very hesitant about suggesting that at first. By then, whoever was outside was now kicking the door.

"I swear I'ma shoot this crazy bitch. I'm a count to five."

"Baby, calm down. Let me talk to her. Maybe she'll leave if

171

I talk to her. Or she said she wanted to explain. Why not just let her explain?"

"Fuck that bitch. And I would never call a woman out of her name unless they deserved it. So, that BITCH can beat it. She ain't got shit to say to me. She has from the time I get upstairs and back to be gone."

I've never heard him use improper English or swear this much, so I know he's mad as hell.

I opened the door.

"Can you please tell Greg to come here? I'm not leaving until I talk to him."

"Ma'am, Greg doesn't want to speak to you right now. Maybe some other time, but not now. He's going to have you arrested, and I really don't know if it's worth going to jail for tonight."

"Wait. You're not Rosa or Liz."

I didn't even see Greg come up behind me.

"It ain't none of your fucking business who she is. I tried to tell you to get the fuck on, but you don't get it, do you?"

I heard sirens like someone had started a war on the next street. Then four police cars swarmed his front entrance.

One officer yelled, "Ma'am, put your hands behind your head and turn around."

She started screaming at Greg. "You called the police. You weak bitch! I loved you! I made a mistake, and I came over here to apologize to you and called the police on me? Fuck you, Greg! Fuck you, you weak bitch!"

Greg stepped in front of me and yelled back at her, "Weak? Bitch, I'm stronger than any man you'll ever have. I could have gone upside your motherfucking head, but I'm trying to have pity on your stupid ass."

The officer yelled as he approached the woman. "Ma'am, close your mouth, put your hands behind your head, and turn around."

Before turning around, she spit in Greg's face. I grabbed him because he immediately lunged for her.

"Greg, please. Please let them handle it."

"You gonna spit on me, bitch? You know that shit is going to cost you. Spit, hoe? I got you. I was better to you than your raggedy-ass mammy was to you. Better than your crackhead daddy who tried to fuck you every day, and you spit in my face? That's your ass, bitch."

I tried hard to hold him back, but he was dragging me until another officer grabbed him.

"Greg, please calm down, man."

I ran to the kitchen and got a towel to clean his face for him, while the officer brought him in and closed the door.

"Man, that bitch spit in my face."

"I know, man. I was hoping you didn't hit her."

"I wasn't going to hit her. I was going to push her ass down those steps and swear it was an accident."

"You know we'd fixed that shit in the report, too."

"Hey, Richard, this is my lady, Wendy Brooks. Wendy, this is Officer Richard Starks."

"Hi, Officer Starks. Thank you for getting him back in the house before it got ugly out there."

"I got him, and now, we have her. Man, look into getting a restraining order against her tomorrow. That way, the next time she even thinks about coming around, we can arrest her ass again."

"I will. Thanks, man."

After the officer left, I opened my arms to give him a hug,

but the doorbell rang again.

"What's up, Rich?"

"Hey, man, can I speak to you right quick? Alone."

"Yeah."

"I'll start the shower for you, Greg."

"Thanks, baby. What's up?" he said, turning back toward Officer Starks as I went up the stairs.

When Greg finally joined me, I could tell he was distracted. All that cussing and fussing, slamming doors, and yelling had me hot and bothered. So I stood naked in the bathroom ready to do him in the shower. However, he came in, sat on the counter, pulled me to him, and held me like he was about to be shipped off to fight in the next war.

"What's wrong, baby? Look at me. I don't care about her or her reasons for showing up here tonight. So, don't worry about that. Please don't let her ruin our evening."

"She has HIV," he blurted out. "Well, at least that's what she told the other officer to tell Richard to tell me."

"Okay? Did you ever sleep with her without protection?"

"Maybe a few times, but after I found out she was cheating with this dude named Jamel, we didn't sleep together anymore. Then this bitch comes over here and spits on me? And the fucked up thing is I don't know how long she had been sleeping with him before I found out. That's what she wanted to explain, but I meant there was nothing else to explain. Cheating is cheating. And we've been over."

"Well, when was the last time you were checked, Greg?"

"Six months ago, but I'm going to get checked again tomorrow just to be sure. I want you to get checked, too."

"Baby, I'm not worried about you having HIV. God didn't give you to me to take you away like that. So, like I said, let's not let her ruin our evening. For all we know, she could be lying because you wouldn't talk to her. So, don't go getting all down about that. Come on. If you wash my back, I'll wash yours."

He looked up at me and smiled. Then he kissed me like I was flawless. I tried not to rip his clothes off, but there was something about the way his lips touched mine at that very moment that instantly sent my body into a burning blaze. I normally had a problem with getting my hair wet on Sunday before I go to work, but to hell with *good hair*, especially when Greg Hamilton was in my face. *Fuck this hair!*

Chapter Fourteen
Laughing, Trying Not to Cry

"Jessi, are you going to be okay?"

"Yeah, I'll be fine. I can't believe his punk ass did this to my face."

"What happened?"

"I told him to get the hell on and leave me alone. I was tired of his shit. He needed a job and a damn clue. Some bitch named Shelby called when he was in the shower. Then his bitch ass hit me in the fucking face because I answered his phone."

"Damn. I can't believe you came to work like this."

"This might be the safest place for me right now. I sprayed his ass in the face with Clorox bleach."

"You didn't call the police?"

She looked away.

"Jessi, please tell me you called the police?"

"No, I dropped the bleach, grabbed a wet towel and my makeup bag, and left."

"Well, I'm calling them for you."

"No. Please, don't. I'm going to be okay. I just want it to be over with. I think he left the house, so I'll be fine."

"Number one, you can't stay here hiding in the bathroom all day piling makeup in this one spot. Number two, you *will* press charges on his black ass, or more than your face will be fucked up next time. Your mind will be fucked up, because you will take him back and he'll do this again and again and again. He'll have you thinking you did something wrong. Your body will be fucked up, because you will be hiding bruises not only on your face but all over your body. And your spirit will be fucked up, because you will question what's wrong with you, and the answer is nothing. Now, do I need to drive you to the police station?"

"No. Really, I'm fine."

"You know what Rashad put me through. His abuse started out verbal, moved to mental, then physical, and then there was a combination of all of them. My mother had me grounded in church, and I let him make me stray. I had a house that I let him come and go as he pleased in, but that still wasn't enough. I cooked, cleaned, gave him sex how and when he wanted it, and it still wasn't enough to make him the man he promised he would be. I still have the bruises to show you how this can only lead to something very bad if you don't stop it now. Please, press charges on Travis."

"Wendy, you don't understand. I'm not you. I don't have any of the things you have. I have only enough to get by. If it weren't for you, I wouldn't even have this job. My entire family lives with my mother. I don't go to church. I don't do anything."

"But that's by choice, Jessi. With your new promotion, you will be making enough money to move out and have anything you want. And you can start by getting rid of Travis' ass for good. One wrong smack upside your head and you could be dead. Trust me. Come on, you know the nights I've spent in the ER with CAT scans, under observation, wrapped in tons of bandages, and I still took Rashad back. Please don't live my life all over again. You've been there already with me."

"Fine, but I need you to help me, Wendy. I need you to help me make sure he doesn't ease his way back into my life."

"First thing you need to do is take today off, go to your mother's house, and get all your stuff."

"Where am I going?"

"You're coming to stay at my house until we find you a condo of your own. You're going to drop off his funky-ass car, and I'm going to call Greg and get one of his cars. You can drive mine until we get you your own car. This is a new day, Jessi. Everything stops and starts today."

"I love you, Wendy."

"I know! Now put these fly-ass Gucci shades on compliments of Mr. Greg Hamilton, and go get started packing up. I'll get someone to take your calls for today. Here's the key to my house. Sign on to your computer and check your email when you get to the house for anything I may send for you to clear up on your accounts that I don't work on for you. You know what? Better yet, take my car and I will have Greg pick me up. We will drop Travis' car off at his mother's house, and he won't even have to come back to your mother's house at all. Text him and tell him anything he left at your mother's house will be in his car at his mother's house by six o'clock tonight. It's a new day, Ms. Jessica Reins. Now, go."

After giving me a high-five, she took off.

"Mr. Wallace, here are the projections for next quarter, and I received the numbers from last quarter. If you pay close attention, we're not in the red anywhere."

"Wendy, they want you to fly to New York to train three people in their revenue office. You will be there for approximately three weeks, spending one week training each person."

"Wow. What a way to change the subject. You ready for me to train already?"

"Wendy, you're the best in our region. Who else did you think they would ask for? These people are in the bottom rankings, and if you can equip them with just a piece of what makes you and our company so productive, this could mean something very big for you."

"And what if I train them and they still don't perform at the level they are expecting?"

"I don't doubt your skills. They will make the necessary changes, and either way, this will not affect your position. It can only enhance it for an even better future here. So what do you say?"

"I mean, you're saying it now as if I have a choice. Do I?"

"Not really. Your plane leaves Wednesday afternoon at three o'clock."

I laughed and shook my head. "Good ole Mr. Wallace. I'm taking the rest of the day off. Jessica's desk is being covered by Mallorie, and I will email you before I leave on Wednesday. I'm assuming Ms. Nancy has my itinerary?"

"No, your new assistant Candace has it."

"My new assistant? Why didn't you tell me? I walked past that young lady at least four times today and didn't say anything but hello and nice shoes. I'ma kill you."

"I have something else for you, too."

"What, Mr. Wallace? Because it seems as if you are full of surprises today."

"First, your company credit card for your first trip of many. Your hotel is already booked, and your car is reserved."

He hands me another envelope.

"Secondly, this is a little something extra for you for being such a great asset to our company."

"What is this?"

"Don't open it right now. Open it when you get on the plane."

"Mr. Wallace, I'm a woman. If you tell me NOT to do something, I'm only going to wait until you turn your back and do it anyway."

He smiled, hugged me, told me to do a great job, and left me standing there in his office. I was all bubbly on the inside. After doing my "you better do the damn thing" dance, I headed out to meet my new assistant.

"Hello, Candace. Can I see you in my office for a few minutes, please? And bring my itinerary with you, please."

I really didn't pay any attention to her past her pretty smile because I had been so busy all day with clearing Jessi's desk, but when she stepped foot into my office, she almost took my breath away.

"Why have you not mentioned to me all day that you were my new assistant?"

"The people around here said you were a very busy woman, and when and if you needed me, you would let me know. So, I just waited."

"Well, have a seat and let me get you up to speed on a few things. Number one, don't listen to these people around here. If you need me, say so. I am very laid back, but when I'm working, I'm working. This trip to New York comes as a surprise to me because I had a ton of meetings to schedule this week. So, I will be doing them, but they will all be calls. Therefore, I will send you that list tonight, but don't begin scheduling until Monday after I find out what my days will be like with the people in New York. Decline any outside meetings that come in unless they are from Mr. Wallace, because I am sure he will want to check in and see how things are going. I have a mailbox on the 2nd floor that you will need to check daily. Anything from corporate, open it and scan it to me. Here is my card, *call me* if things come up in the office that I should know about, which is everything. Now, let me see this hotel and car. Nice hotel, even nicer car. Did you book this?"

"Yes, ma'am."

"No need for the ma'am, but thanks for the awesome hotel accommodations and the nice car. I'll be out for the rest of the day since it looks like I have to pack for this trip. If you need me, call my cell, please."

Once she finished writing down all my instructions, she headed back to her desk. *Now I'm sitting here at my desk waiting on Greg and holding this envelope that Mr. Wallace asked me not to open, but thinking about how I'm going to tell Greg I'll be gone for almost a month. Well, Lord, you know what I need to do, and you know how I need to do it. Guide me, please.*

In an uncertain tone, Candace stuck her head in my door and said, "Ms. Brooks, I think your ride is here."

"Thank you, Candace. Do you need anything from me before I head out?"

"No, ma'am…I mean, no. I think you gave me everything I need, and if I have any questions, I won't hesitate to call you."

"Thank you."

A man's voice radiated through the room. "Baby, you ready?"

"Hey, handsome. Yes, I am, and this is my new assistant, Candace Miller. Candace, this is my boyfriend, Greg

Hamilton."

"It's a pleasure meeting you, Mr. Hamilton."

"You, too, Ms. Miller. Baby, give me that bag. You just walk. You know Walter would have a fit if you came out carrying anything other than your purse."

I laughed because I knew it was the truth.

"Okay, Candace, I'll see you when I get back."

"Back? Where are you going?"

"Come on. We'll talk about it in the car."

Mr. Wallace poked his head out of his office along with all the others that were being nosey as hell because they saw a clean limousine in front of our building with a well-dressed Walter standing by the door. I waved at Mr. Wallace and smirked as the haters watched Greg and I walk hand in hand out of the building.

"So where are you going that's going to make me sad for days?"

"I have to go to New York and train three people for three weeks. I leave Wednesday."

"Did you just find out today?"

"Of course, I did. You think I would keep something like this from you? I can barely be away from you for more than three or four hours these days. Are you serious? Their revenue department is suffering, and before they fire these people, Mr. Wallace wants me to see what I can do to keep them employed."

"I understand. Will you be able to leave on the weekends?"

"Baby, it's training, not jail. I can do whatever I want to do as long as these people get trained. I'm leaving on Wednesday so I can go into their offices on Thursday and Friday to observe what they are doing wrong. Then I will spend the weekend setting up a plan for them to implement. This could mean something really big for me. I've never trained before, but they must see something in me. So, I said yes. Well, I really didn't have a choice with Mr. Wallace."

"I'm proud of you, baby. You're smart, courageous, fine, and you're not afraid of a challenge; my kind of lady."

When I looked up, we were stopping at a doctor's office.

"You have a doctor's appointment today?"

"WE do."

"We? Greg, what are you talking about?"

"We do. So we can take our HIV test, remember?"

"Yes, but I didn't know we were going today. Are you really that concerned?"

"Not concerned, but I want to make sure *we* are okay."

"Greg I haven't even thought about that since she left. I know I'm not HIV positive, and I know you're not either. But, if this will make you feel better, then let's go."

He looked me in the eyes like a guilty man does before they confess to a crime, then he kissed me.

"Thank you."

I hesitated to get out of the car because at that very moment I was afraid. I closed my eyes and all I could think was, *Lord,* before Walter reached for my hand.

*****

The drive to my house was very quiet. I was nauseated and had a headache. I talked to Greg about getting someone to take Travis' car to his mother's house for Jessica, I think. My mind was still a blur. Walter let me out, and I went in without waiting on Greg. Jessica was there with shit everywhere.

"Jessi, what the hell is all of this crap? I can barely get in the damn door."

"Sorry, girl, but that's as far as I could get with doing it all by myself."

I heard Greg call for Walter to help, I guess. I immediately began running boxes upstairs to the extra bedroom. I was throwing boxes and bags everywhere. Greg grabbed my hand, took me into my bedroom, and sat me down.

"What is wrong with you?"

"Greg, are you HIV positive? You already know the results of the test, don't you? You only took me down there to confirm I didn't have it. Why couldn't you just tell me?"

"I didn't have it six months ago, and the only reason I wanted to go with you is because I love you and don't want anything to take you away from me. Have I had that many partners? Yes. Did I always practice safe sex? No. But now, I am in a relationship with a woman that I want to give my all to, and I want to make sure my past won't kill our future. So, I am praying I do not have HIV. I will continue to get tested EVERY six months. It was time for my checkup, and with that ole crazy-ass girl coming over and me knowing she and I had been together, I didn't want to take any chances. I love you, Wendy. It's been a long time since I have loved anyone. But, I love you. That was my only motive for getting the test done today."

"You don't love me, Greg. You're just enjoying being in the moment with me. So, please don't confuse that with love."

"And you please don't try and tell me how I feel. You regulate your feelings, and I'll deal with mine. Now, I'm going out there to help Jessi get some of her clutter from in your living room because it looks like you have a roommate for now. If you need me, I'll be downstairs helping Walter."

Once he walked out of the room, I felt like someone had lifted a brick wall off my entire body. Just as I lay back on my bed, here comes Jessica climbing on top of me.

"I guess he told you!"

"Get off me, ole crazy girl."

She rolled over, and we laid there looking up at the ceiling.

"He really loves you, Wendy. I've never heard a man pour it out like that. He can have any woman in the world, I'm sure. But, for some reason, God gave him you. Why you trying to mess it up? Do you know what I would have given for Travis to look at me the way Greg looked at you the night you met him? He's down there picking up my shit, not yours, but mine. Why? Not because he gives a damn about me. It's because he gives a damn about you. Don't mess this up because you're scared. Rashad fucked you up. Let Greg fix you up. Come on...I've never been in a wedding before."

I looked over at her with a "wait a damn minute" expression.

"Look, Jessi, you're moving faster than I am about the whole thing. I will stop acting like a jerk if you promise not to take Travis back. You know he's gonna come by talking all slick once he finds out where you are, or blow your phone up begging. Don't fall for it, please. If I agree to give Greg all of me, then you have to give all of you to you! You deserve a break today."

She held up her pinky like we did when she went with me to the abortion clinic and we made our very first friend promise. So, I knew she was serious about moving on.

"Oh, and you will be here at the house for about a month alone."

"What? Why?"

"Mr. Wallace is sending me to New York to train some people. I leave Wednesday, and I will more than likely spend the day tomorrow with Greg after we take Momma to chemotherapy."

"Chemotherapy?"

"Shit. I'm sorry, Jess. I forgot to tell you. Momma has breast cancer. It's in the early stages, so we have to start treatment now."

"How are you?"

"I'm scared for her, but she's being so damn tough that it only makes me worry more."

"Well, you know if anyone has a direct connection with God, it's your momma."

"Yeah, but it's still Momma, Jessi."

"I know, but you have to know she'll be fine."

There was a knock on my door.

"Come in."

"Baby, we have everything upstairs now. Let's go and get dinner. Me, you, Jessi, and Walter can celebrate your greatness in the company, Jessi's greatness in whatever this move means, and…"

I interrupt him. "And the greatness in you. Yeah, let's celebrate."

Chapter Fifteen
A Good Day

I sat holding Greg's hand like we were waiting on results from a paternity test. They hadn't called Momma back yet to start her process, but she was sitting with Ms. Ethel looking at pictures from their wine and cheese date. *Fast asses.* I looked out the window and saw Deacon Fredricks heading into an office across the street. I couldn't help but wonder what he was doing out so early in the morning. The office only said *Care Specialist* on the outside.

"Momma, you okay?"

She looked up while finishing a laugh with Ms. Ethel.

"Yes, baby, nothing has changed since you asked me two minutes ago."

"Greg, I need some air. You want some coffee?"

"No, I'll take some water, though. You want me to walk with you?"

"No, but call me if they call Momma back before I return."

I headed out the door with no intention of coffee, but to see if Deacon Fredricks was okay. There was a woman at the desk, but I didn't know if I should ask where he went.

"Hi, ma'am. There was a gentleman that just came in the door. Can you tell me where he went to?"

Just as she began to say his name, guess who showed up in

the lobby.

"Deacon Fredricks."

"Dr. Fredricks is fine here. Come on back."

"Oh no, I'm not here to see you. I was just stopping by to check on you. I mean, I didn't know this was your doctor's office. I just thought you weren't feeling well, and I wanted to check on you."

"Well, since you're here, you might as well come on back. Julie, if Mr. Simmons is on time, tell him I will be right with him."

I followed him to an immaculate office Furnished with white chairs, tea table, white rugs. I mean, it was like a pure vision of heaven.

"Is this where the journey begins for healing?"

"You can say that. This is where I listen to people and try to work out their inner issues. You may call it heaven, but some of them consider it hell. Have a seat."

"No, I can't. I was across the street with my mother. She starts chemo today, and I need to get back."

"So that explains Sunday. I'm sorry I didn't get a chance to come and check on you. I wanted to, but I got tied up with Pastor, and when I got home, it was late."

"No need to apologize. I'm fine. I know she's going to be okay."

"Do you want to make an appointment to talk about anything else? Maybe at a later date?"

"No, nothing else is wrong. I haven't had an episode in a while. I'm dating someone now, and I just feel different."

"Different?"

"Yeah, like I really don't have a need for anyone else. He gives me all those other things that I use to fantasize about."

"How does that make you feel to know one man has that kind of power?"

"Well, I wouldn't call it power. However, I like knowing that all the pleasure I get comes from one person and he's real."

"The people you fantasize about are real. I'm real."

"It's been a long time since I have thought about you in that way."

"Why do you think that is?"

"Because I don't need you. I have what I've been missing."

"But you were with Rashad when you masturbated about me."

"Was I really with Rashad? I mean, come on. Think about it. Or was he just there?"

"Good question."

"Look, I didn't come over here for a minute clinic analysis from you. I thought I'd say hi."

"Well, thank you for coming, and if you need me, Wendy, I'm here for you."

"If that's an invitation to finally fuck you, I don't think so. I'm with a man that fucks me so well that the thought of another man around my pussy makes me sick to my stomach. His dick is just that good to me. So, Dr. Fredricks…have a good day."

I walked out of his office and grabbed a bottle of water off his tea table for Greg. I didn't know what in the world came over me. He was standing his ass there in that suit, and oh my goodness, I wanted to put him on that couch, straddle his lap, and slide up and down on his dick until he made my pussy cum. But, my mind was slow, and my mouth began spitting words out like some damn dominatrix from a bestselling porn movie.

Damn, he almost had me. Fuck! Shake it off, stupid.

I damn near ran back across the street.

"Here you go, baby."

"Hey, you. You feel better?"

"Yeah, I do."

"They just called your mother back. She took Ms. Ethel, of course. The nurse said it will take about thirty minutes to get her prepped and ready."

"Really?"

Knowing this, I took him by his hand, and we went outside to the limo. I asked Walter to give us a minute, and he got out of the car.

"What's wrong, baby? Your mother said you were going to be okay with Ms. Ethel going back to be with her while they set everything up."

I reached down, unzipped his pants, pulled his dick out, and sat on it.

"What the fuck? Your pussy is so wet. Shit."

"Shhh. Just fuck me, please." I leaned back, and he pulled me back and forth on his dick with ease. "Yeah, baby, just like that."

"Wendy, baby, shit. Don't squeeze my dick like that, baby. Shit, girl. Don't make me cum yet. Please, baby."

"Tell me you like this pussy, Greg."

"I love your pussy, baby."

He bounced me harder and harder while looking into my eyes. I knew the car was moving, but poor Walter just stood there like he was the lookout man. Moaning louder, my man was about to make me cum all over his dick.

"Give it to me, Greg. Make me cum, baby. Yeah, like that. Just like that, baby. Fuck me! Yeah! Yeah! Fuck yo' pussy, baby. Just like that!"

He wrapped his arms around my waist and threw me down

on his dick for one last stroke before I felt his dick jerking inside of me. We looked at each other, took a deep breath, and smiled.

He kissed me and asked, "Who did you go to see across the street? I watched as you stopped traffic while crossing as if you own the block."

"No one," I replied with a devilish smile.

Once we cleaned up in the back of the limo, he tapped on the window for Walter to open the door. We were walking back in the door just as the nurse called my name.

"Wendy Brooks?"

"Right here."

"Your mother is ready. You can come on back now."

I looked back at Greg, took his hand, and we went and sat with Momma and Ms. Ethel. We played cards, watched a movie, and had lunch; all right there in the doctor's office. I didn't think about work, Jessi and her drama, Momma being sick, Rashad, or Greg. I thought about nothing except what time Deacon Fredricks would get off so I could apologize for not fucking him in his office earlier. *Damn, I gave his nut to my man. Now I owe him one.* I laughed to myself. *Bad girl.*

*****

I was packed and waiting on Greg, who would be picking me up in half an hour.

"Jessi, are you sure you're gonna be okay here by yourself for a month?"

"Yes. Besides, you said three weeks. I know how to get to New York if I get lonely."

"You just make sure you call me instead of Travis."

"I promise. Plus, Greg said he had someone he wanted me to meet, so I might be as lucky as you are by the time you get back."

"Not a chance, honey. Because whoever it is may come close to Greg Hamilton, but he won't be *my* Greg Hamilton."

"Have you seen Greg, Wendy? Anything close, I am fine."

We laughed and hugged each other goodbye.

"Thank you, Wendy. Thank you for being my friend. Thank you for letting me crash here, and thank you for letting me know that loving myself is so important."

"It took me a long time to learn that for myself. So, don't get lost in having a man around. If he ain't acting right, then you might as well be by yourself. Now don't go getting all mushy on me either. This makeup has to last until Greg and I come from dinner. All the bills are paid for this month, so you are straight with that. If you happen to need some money, here."

I handed her an envelope.

"No, I don't need money from you."

"You may want to get groceries. I have nothing in there. So, take it. If you use it, fine; if you don't, fine."

The doorbell rang.

"Damn. Why does he always tell me Walter is thirty minutes away when he really means three? Rashad?" I said, shocked when I opened the door and saw him standing there. "What are you doing here? And I know I told you to stop showing up to my house unannounced. Damn."

"I just wanted to check on you."

"I'm fine."

"But Chrissy said you were moving."

"Why is your nosey-ass bitch all in my business?"

Jessica came downstairs when she heard me raising my voice.

"What's up, Jessica?"

"Not you, Rashad."

I quickly chimed in before Jessica cursed him out.

"Rashad, look, I'm not moving. If I were, I wouldn't tell you anyway. You lost your right to know anything about me and my life when we broke up. You do understand that we're broken up, right?"

"That's fine, but where are you going? Why you got all these bags packed?"

Jessica couldn't refrain anymore. "Damn, Rashad, you just don't get it."

"Shut up, Jessica. And why are you even here?"

"Actually, smart ass, I live here."

"So you moving out and giving Jessica your house? That's fucked up, Wendy, that you wouldn't tell me you're leaving."

In frustration, I stopped him from talking.

"Rashad, shut up and listen. I'm going to New York to train some people for my job. Yes, Jessi is living with me temporarily. She left her lowlife boyfriend, just like I did. Now, go tell your bitch next door to mind her own damn business, and you stop showing up at my damn house without calling."

Walter walked up to us just as I was ending the conversation with Rashad.

"Ms. Wendy, everything okay?"

"Hey, Walter. Yes, sweetie, everything is fine. Can you grab my large suitcase, please?"

"Yes, ma'am, I sure can." He walks past Rashad and said, "Well, brother, since you're here, do you mind grabbing that other suitcase for me?"

Rashad rolled his eyes, but he picked up the suitcase and took it outside.

"So you still riding in limousines, huh, Wendy?"

"Yeah, my man wouldn't have it any other way. You know, when I think back to all the days I had to walk to where I wanted to go because your stupid ass took my car and left me stranded, riding in a limo ain't that bad. Jessi, I'll call you before I board tomorrow."

"Bye, girl! Have fun and bring me something good back!"

"I will!"

As Walter closed my door, I sat back, looked at Rashad, and laughed. *Damn, I love me some Greg Hamilton. I just wish I knew how to tell him, especially with all the stuff that goes on in my head.*

Chapter Sixteen
Welcome to New York, W.B.

"Hey, Momma, I just landed. You feeling okay? Good. I'll call you tonight after I get back to my room, okay? Love you, too. Oh and, Momma, Greg is going to come by and check on you while I'm gone, so be nice. Okay, love you."

This was the part of flying that I hated, waiting on luggage.

"Hey, baby, I'm here. Yeah, I'm waiting on my luggage. No, I haven't picked up my car yet. Yes, I called her first so she wouldn't worry, and I told her that you were coming by to check on her while I'm gone. Okay. Look, I'll call you when I get to the hotel. Be good. Bye."

Hell, I might as well call Jessi, too, and get it over with.

"Hey, hoochie, you at work?"

"Yep, I'm sitting at my new desk, which is now your old desk."

"Cute. Well, I made it to the Big Apple, and I'm about to pick up my car and head to the hotel. I'll probably grab some lunch, then sneak into the office and see what these folks are really doing. You know they don't expect me in until tomorrow. So, surprise, surprise."

"Well, we know what you can do. So, do it and represent for this office!"

"You know I will. I love you, girl, and no Travis. Enjoy

some time by yourself."

"I will. Talk to you later."

*****

I looked around my room. *Nice hotel, Candace, very nice hotel. Hell, I might have to take a nap before going to the office. That damn Greg acted like a teenager last night, and now I'm tired as hell. No, I better go now. That way, when I come back, I'll be in for the evening.*

I pulled up to a ten-story building according to the address I was given. *This is a nice office building.*

"Hi. Can I help you?"

"Yes, I am looking for Mr. Peter Blake."

"May I tell him who's asking?"

"Sure. Wendy Brooks."

She stood up. "Oh, Ms. Brooks, we weren't expecting you until tomorrow. Mr. Blake is actually out of the office right now. I can call him for you."

"No need. Is there a conference room you can put me in and get Alicia Dallas, Stephon Tate, and Yarvis Alley together for a short meeting?"

"Yes, ma'am."

"No need for the ma'am, but thank you."

I could hear people whispering nearby, "She's here." Phones began ringing all over the floor. People were peeking out of their cubby holes to see me. They were walking by smiling and nodding, then running off like little kids. *What the hell,* I thought.

"Right this way, Ms. Brooks."

"Why is everyone whispering?"

"Mr. Blake talks about you all the time. You're like Oprah in this office. We always know when the quarterly report comes back and you're number one. So, it's an honor to have you here to help our staff."

"I'm just a woman who works hard. No celebrity status, just hard work. So, tell everyone to take a chill pill. I'm here to help, not hurt."

"Yes, ma'am, thank you. Oh, this is Alicia and Stephon, Yarvis should be right down. He works on the 4th floor."

"Thank you…"

"Madison. I'm Madison Greene."

"Thank you, Madison Greene, and may I have a bottle of water, please?"

"Sure, I'll be right back."

I turned to Alicia and Stephon. "Have a seat please."

Alicia was the first one to speak. Now mind you, she's about 5'2" with a short Fantasia *American Idol* haircut. She had the most beautiful set of dimples and her breasts? Oh my goodness! They accented that Apple Bottom ass she was carrying so well. Her legs were well defined like she had been training for the Olympics for months. She had on a black suit and a fuchsia camisole that also enhanced those D's, too.

Then there was Stephon, who looked to be mixed with maybe black and Italian. His skin was flawless and perfectly tanned. He had to be every bit of 6'3". His facial hair was lined to perfection around his face, and he had the most beautiful set of teeth since Lance Gross, who played Calvin on *The House of Payne*. *Damn, he's fine. Okay, please stay focused, Wendy.*

"Your water, Ms. Brooks."

That is NOT Madison's voice. Yarvis must have made it.

He placed the water in front of me and walked past the others to take a seat. I couldn't wait for him to turn around. Hell, from the back, he was 6'5" at least, chocolate from the skin showing on his hands, had broad shoulders, and a nice ass hiding under his suit jacket.

"Thank you, Mr. Alley."

"You're welcome, Ms. Brooks."

"All of you can call me Wendy, please. I know I'm not supposed to be here until tomorrow, but I wanted to make sure we have a clear understanding of why I'm here before we get started."

They all sat up at attention as if I had the last number of the lotto.

"I'm here to help. All of you work in the same department, which is revenue, and this company is losing it. We need to find out why, and then work on how to get it back and keep it coming." I paused to yell for Madison to bring me three pens and three pieces of paper.

"Now, if each of you will put your names on your sheet of paper, please. Okay, now write these words – The old way."

Stephon looked at me with concern, as if confused.

"Go on. Write it. The old way."

After looking at each other, they all do it. I then put a trash can on the table.

"Now, rip it up and throw it away. The old way doesn't exist anymore. I don't want to hear about the old way after today. If the old way worked, I wouldn't be here. I have three weeks to work with you to turn your office around and give you all the tools to keep it going in the right direction. I'm not the boss. I'm not the beast. I just know what works. I'll see you all tonight at seven-thirty for dinner and cocktails at the Peking Duck House. It was a pleasure meeting each of you."

I walked out the door and thanked Madison for her time. Before leaving, I told her to book that conference room for me for the next three weeks and request a projector along with plenty of water and coffee. *Now, let the games begin.*

"Hey, baby, whatcha doing? No, I just got out of the shower. I went by the office and introduced myself to the people I'll be training. I came back, took a good nap, and now I'm getting ready to meet them for dinner. Yeah, it's a woman named Alicia and two guys, Yarvis and Stephon. Yeah, they're all black, so you know that made me proud. But, I will be even more excited if I can get that revenue department back where it needs to be. No, I'm not worried about them trying to keep me. Unless you have a club here in New York, I'll be back in three weeks. Okay, I'll call you later. Be good. Bye."

I hung up with Greg and got ready to tease them just a little bit over dinner.

So what do you want to give them tonight, Wendy? That bad-girl shit or just casual cuteness? You're right. Bad is always good. I'll go early so I can get us a good table, order some appetizers, and have champagne on the table. We need to celebrate and get it out of the way so we can get to work.

Alicia is so pretty, and that damn Yarvis, his chocolate ass, I would do him in minute, if I didn't have Greg of course. I wonder what color Stephon's dick is? I mean, is it light like he is? He's mixed, so it must be mixed, right? He can keep the nice grade of hair from the Italian side of his family, but the black side needs to show in his dick.

I chuckled to myself as I slid into a very sexy dress, compliments of Greg Hamilton.

Okay, panties or no panties? Come on, Wendy, you just got here. You're right. No panties.

*****

"Table for four, please."

"Right this way, ma'am."

Damn, even the hostesses are fine as hell in New York. I know I can't live here. My pussy would stay out.

"Thank you."

"My pleasure, ma'am."

If he smiles at me one more time, I'll know where he lives. I should check on that crybaby Jessi before they get here. She's so scary.

"Hey, Jessi, what are you doing?"

"If I told you lying in your bed, would you be mad?"

"No, scaredy cat, because I figured you would be. How was work today?"

"Good. Your new admin was upset that she didn't hear from her boss today. I told her that you made it in and was tied up, but would probably chat with her tomorrow. So, don't forget to check in with her tomorrow."

"Hell, I forgot I had a damn admin. Hey, here come the guys that I'm working with. I'm treating them to drinks and dinner. A little meet and greet out of the office."

"Cool. Have fun, I have to go. Somebody is at your door. Wait! What you mean guys? They are not women that you're training? Hell no."

"One woman, two men. I love this job. Answer the door. Bye."

I hung up so she wouldn't encourage me to stop thinking what I had already been thinking. *Well, let's get this evening started.*

"Hey, Alicia, you look beautiful, girl."

"Thank you, and that's a beautiful dress you're wearing, as well."

"She's right. Very nice dress."

"Thank you, Yarvis. You all have a seat. Is Stephon going to make it?"

"Yes. He's parking the car. We decided to carpool over since we all stay within minutes of each other."

"How convenient is that, Mr. Alley?"

"Very. Where are you staying?"

"At the Embassy."

"Nice."

"I'm sure he was only asking to make sure you didn't need transportation into the office tomorrow."

"I rented a car, girl. There's no way I can be here for almost a month and not have some type of transportation for myself. There's Stephon." I waved him in, and as I sat back down, I caught Yarvis admiring my dress, again.

"Ms. Brooks, nice dress."

"Thanks, Stephon, and please call me Wendy. All of you, Wendy works just fine."

After getting the attention of the young man who would be our waiter, we placed our food and drink orders. Then the small talk began.

"So, Yarvis, tell me. How long have you been with the company?"

"Four years. I started in sales, but they finally recognized my skills and put me where I needed to be."

"So you have skills?"

"You should see them."

Alicia cleared her throat. "We all started about a week apart. The journey for each of us has made us really close."

"What about you, Stephon? Has the journey been a hard one for you?"

"I like it hard. If anything is too easy for me, I don't want it."

"Wow, a man who likes a challenge. I like it."

Three drinks and a round of shots later, the waiter comes up and asks if we'd like another round.

"We might as well. Work starts for us tomorrow, so why not enjoy the night. Right, Yarvis?" I said.

"I wouldn't have it any other way. Enjoy the good shit while you can."

"So they do use profanity. They are human after all."

Alicia immediately chimed in, "I told them not to bring their potty mouths to the table. It's obvious that Yarvis has had too much to drink, because he's getting too loose."

"And it's obvious Alicia hasn't had enough to drink, because she's still too tight."

When Alicia smacked Yarvis on the shoulder, it took everything inside of me not to reach over and touch her breasts. They looked real, and if they were, oh my goodness. She could get it.

"So, Wendy, what was your climb to the top like? I mean, you are like the First Lady in the company."

"It was easy. I like money, girl. I like making it multiply. I like the look on people's faces when they see I'm an educated black woman running this company side by side with a white man. Noting against my boss, but my numbers make him happy and my check makes me happy. We are a team. I'm not after his job, and he can't do mine. So, we know our lanes."

"Yeah, but me being a woman myself, how do I even get a spot on the road?"

"Well, Alicia, where a lot of women go wrong is they try to use their assets first to climb the ladder. Some fuck and suck their way to the top and get no real benefits. They walk around the office with their titties out and skirts so short that if they sneeze their pussy will pop out. So then, no one pays attention to the brains you have because they can't get past wanting to fuck you on sight. So, keeping you bound until you give them 'a reason' to promote you is what they wait on. Now, I didn't walk around like a damn nun, but I didn't give them anything to imagine until I was at the top. At this point for me, they all can look under my skirt and keep imagining.

"Now, Yarvis, I'm sure you're great at what you do, but you're black, my brother, which means you *have to* put in the extra work and think past your white counterpart. Where he stops thinking, you have to think past that. You can't fuck and suck your boss, which is normally a man, unless that's your thing?"

He looked at me with an expression that said, *Bitch, I'd fuck you right now, and you'll never question my sexuality again.* I smiled back as if to say, *Do it then, with your bad ass.*

"I was just saying, staying ahead means staying focused. Stephon, even though you look mixed, just like Yarvis, they ain't giving your ass shit either. You're not pure, baby. Cute, but not pure. You have to work harder than your counterparts and Yarvis' ass because he's not giving a fuck that you have some black in you. You're still given an 'easier road' than him because of the way you look."

When the waiter returned, I immediately ordered another round.

"Did I lose you all?"

Alicia sounded off, "Will you teach me? Teach me how to be like you. I don't want to be you, because that would be impossible. But, as a black woman, I have to go back and fix the perception they have now, and then slaughter their asses."

"Yes, ma'am, I can. I will. And you will be the baddest bitch in New York City. And, Yarvis, I will teach you how to work as a team and excel past those who really don't want you to be successful. Also, how to turn down some of the best pussy in town and have those whores begging you to fuck them but settle for sucking your dick *if* you have time. You think you fucking now? Wait until I'm done with you. Stephon, baby, you cute, but in this business, cute will only get you but so far. I know you're smart as hell. I saw your college transcript. You're not doing half the shit you can do. You stopped climbing because you have Yarvis and Alicia on the team. Unless you're fucking them, they are the enemy. Get on top and pull their asses up there with you, or stay your ass on the bottom and look under Alicia's skirt while Yarvis pisses on your head. The choice is yours. Cheers."

I took my last shot, slammed my glass upside down on the table, and got up to leave. *Welcome to New York City, Ms. Wendy Brooks. I think I like this place.*

*****

"Hey, baby, I'm back in my room. What are you doing?"

"Thinking about you."

"Thinking about me how? I mean, am I on top or bottom?"

"You are such bad girl."

"I know. I miss you already."

"I miss you, too, baby. How was dinner?"

"Nice. We had drinks and dinner and more drinks. Now I'm beat and drunk and ready to go to sleep so I can be ready to do what I came to do tomorrow. They are going to be fine if they learn to separate their personal relationships from business. I don't think they know how to compete as friends. You think I wouldn't try and make myself shine if Jessi and I were on the same level in my department? Shit! I'd spank that ass and take her out for drinks afterwards with my bonus money, much like I do now. They'll get it after it's all said and done."

"You're a beast, Ms. Wendy Brooks."

"I wish you were here so I could be a beast all over you."

"Me, too, but I'll see you soon. This time will fly."

"Who was that?"

"Who was what?"

"Are you out? I thought I heard a lady's voice."

"No, baby, that's the TV. I'm already in bed."

"Already in bed with who, Greg?"

"Yo' momma! Now go to bed and don't let your drunken state cause an unnecessary night of restlessness. I told you, I love you. So, no one is on your side of the bed. And if there were, you'd know about it. Now, goodnight, baby."

"Goodnight. I'll call you in the morning. And that bitch better not drool on my pillow."

"Bye, ole crazy girl."

I hung up and closed my eyes long enough to remember that somebody rang my doorbell when I was on the phone with Jessica. *Since I wasn't expecting anybody, let me see if this heffa let Travis' ass in my house.*

"What you doing, Jess?"

"Hey, girl. Nothing. How was dinner?"

"We had a good time. Can't wait to get started with them tomorrow. Who was at the door?"

"At the door?"

"The doorbell rang as we were getting off the phone earlier."

"Oh, that was the pizza man. I had ordered a pizza."

"When did you start eating pizza?"

"I had wings."

"But you just said you ordered a pizza. Have you been drinking my good vodka?"

"Hell yeah! You didn't say I couldn't. Look, I'm tired and it's late. I'll call you in the morning."

"Okay. Love you, Jessi-boo! And I'm so proud of you."

"Love you, too, girl. Bye."

*****

"Madison, thank you for setting up the conference room today. Tomorrow, no snacks. I am taking them out for lunch, so we should be fine."

"Yes, ma'am, Ms. Brooks."

"You can call me Wendy. Where did Mr. Blake sneak off to?"

"He's in his office. You going up?"

"Yes. Can you let him know, please?"

"Yes, ma'am…I mean, sure."

I chuckled at her, but I loved the respect.

"Mr. Blake, got a minute?"

"Sure do. Anything for Ms. Wendy Brooks. What can I do for you?"

"Mr. Blake, I need a copy of your numbers from the last three years, each quarter printed separately. Who can have that ready for me before I leave today?"

"I can get my assistant to pull and print them right now."

"That would be great."

"Wendy, thank you so much for coming. I don't think you know what it means to me personally. My job was at stake, and Mr. Wallace said if anyone could turn things around, you could. Not to add any more pressure to what you may have already, but thank you."

"Mr. Blake, you don't have to thank me for anything. It's my pleasure to come and help your team. It's a company as a whole, and we should help each other stay on top of the outside competition. So, I'll do whatever it takes to make sure you all get out of this hole and stay out."

"Thanks, Wendy. I'll get Cheryl to print what you need and bring it down. How long before you leaving?"

"Next thirty minutes or so, but I'll wait on her."

"Okay, I'll get her on it. See you tomorrow."

"You sure will."

I smiled with the assurance that I would keep my word and work hard to get his company up and running like it should be. After leaving his office, I met with Alicia, Yarvis, and Stephon to schedule one-on-one time with them.

"Alicia, can you come by my hotel tonight around seven o'clock? I want to spend some time preparing you for some individual work for tomorrow. Mr. Blake is bringing me some documents, and we will go over those to see what happened, how to fix it, and how to keep it from happening again. I'll do the same with you guys, too. You'll get paid overtime for the hours we work afterhours. So, whatever you may have to do once you get off, go and take care of that and then come on by room 6122.

"Stephon, I'll see you tomorrow at seven o'clock, and then Yarvis, you on Wednesday. Once I show you all the steps Thursday, we will collectively make a plan, practice with it, and on Friday, maybe we'll take off since your brains will be fried by then. Next week, we will work on last year's numbers. Then the following week, we'll focus on this year's and up until now. Then during my last week here, we will work on next year's goals and how to finish this year with a steady push to the top and what tools to use in order to stay there. Got it?"

"Got it!" they replied unison.

I was excited for them, and I was excited for me.

*****

"Hey, baby. I can't believe it's been three weeks already. I have missed you so much! And when I see you, boy…"

"Wendy, do you know how hard it's been not to jump on the first plane up there? I'm talking like after the first week, Walter was worried about me."

"Awww, baby. I tell you what. When I get there, I want you naked and ready."

"Shit…I planned on being in the car naked and ready."

"Baby, you would not believe the progress they have made. I'm so proud of them. I got them each a Visa check card with a thousand dollars on it. We're going to do dinner tonight, and I will see you in the morning."

"You talk to your mother today?"

"Yeah, she sounds so good. She said therapy is going really well. She was nauseated for a couple of days last week, but she said she is much better this week. I bought her a nice suit for church and some shoes. I bought Ms. Ethel a new purse. She loves purses."

"You are so sweet, Wendy."

"How would you know, Greg Hamilton?"

"I tasted, remember?"

"You so crazy. I-I love you, Greg."

"Excuse me?"

"I said I love you, boy."

"Do you?"

"Yes."

"Will you show me?"

"Yes, I will."

"I'll see you tomorrow."

There was a pause on the phone. I don't know what I was waiting on to hang up, but then he said the words that made my body tingle all over.

"And I'ma fuck the shit out of you when I see you!"

"I look forward to it, Mr. Hamilton."

"Bye, baby."

"Bye."

I got in the shower, feeling like I needed to put out the fire that had begun to blaze on the inside of me. I had managed not to mentally or physically fuck Alicia, Stephon, or Yarvis' fine asses. I guess there was so much work to do that it was hard to think about anything else. Although, there was one day I knew Alicia didn't have any panties on, and Stephon walked past me and brushed his dick across my ass, and that Yarvis, his lips stay moisturized because he licked them every time we made eye contact. I'd fuck him and call him LL the entire time.

I think Mr. Wallace will be very pleased with what I have done here. Shoot, my phone must be buried under my clothes. Hold on.

"Hello?"

"Hey, Wendy. It's Chrissy."

"Chrissy?"

"Yes, Chrissy."

"Chrissy, how in hell did you get my cell number?"

"I've always had your cell number. I stole it out of Rashad's phone months ago."

"What do you want?"

"I thought you should know that every day since you've been gone, Rashad has been at your house."

211

"Rashad doesn't have a key to my house anymore. That's my best friend Jessica that's over there, if you must know."

"Yeah, she's there, and so is Rashad. He's stayed over at least three nights each week since you've been gone."

"Well, there must be a reason he's there, but thank you for the notice. Funny, all the time you spent over my house no one ever told me about that."

"Some best friend she's turned out to be."

"And some friendly neighbor you turned out to be. Thank you again and have a good night."

"You know he's fucking her right?"

"You jealous?"

"Why would I be jealous, Wendy? I've had Rashad, in more ways than one. But, he being in your house fucking your best friend while you're trying to be nice to her obviously homeless ass is way lower than what I did. Hell, I was a stranger. I'm assuming you've known her for how long? My point exactly. Hope you enjoyed your trip. Bye, bitch."

I will not even begin to believe that's true. I know Jessica. If Rashad was there, he was there to get his little stash of clothes he hides, like I don't clean the damn house, and that's it. I took a deep breath and continued getting dressed. *That bitch is crazy. First, she tries to pull that shit threatening Deacon Fredricks about telling his wife, and now she thinks she can just tell me that my best friend is fucking my ex. This ain't Jerry Springer, bitch. Ugh! Wendy, do NOT let this get into your head. Do NOT let her make you believe everyone is as trifling as she is. Don't even call Jessi and entertain that shit.*

"Hey, Jess. What's up with you?"

"Nothing. What's going on with you?"

"Getting dressed for dinner with the team. I just wanted to

tell you that I may have to stay here another week. Mr. Wallace sent me an email requesting a week in the office to oversee them applying the skills learned; some crazy stuff their manager requested."

"Oh, wow. Well, I guess I'll see you next week then. I wanted us to go out and party. I mean, of course, after you come up for some air from Greg."

"Whatever. I have to tell him about staying another week, too. Have you been okay at the house by yourself?"

"Yeah, I've been fine. I'm going to owe you some money on the light bill, because I have to leave the TV on to fall asleep at night."

"You sure everything is okay?"

"Wendy, what's wrong?"

"Nothing. I was just checking on you. I know I haven't been able to talk to you that much since I've been gone. I know starting over is hard, that's all. And I love you!"

"I love you, too. Have a good time, girl. I'm fine."

"Okay, see you soon."

I knew better than that. Chrissy needs to get a damn life. Well, hell, it's my last night in the city. Let's make it good.

*****

"Reservations for Wendy Brooks."

"Right this way, ma'am. You look beautiful this evening, Ms. Brooks."

"Thank you. I see you're smiling, as usual."

"I can't help it. You're so fine I just smile to keep from saying what I'm really thinking when I see you."

"And that is?"

"If I tell you, I'd have to follow you home."

"Home is Chicago. Do you have that kind of vacation

213

time?"

"I'd quit to come see you."

I blush as the bartender brought over my favorite drink. Yes, I became a regular. Hey, what can I say? They had the best seafood in town. I gave him a nod, and he gave me the same flirtatious smile that he always did.

"I take it this is your last night here?"

"Yes, and I wanted to bring the gang back to where we had our first meeting. So, here I am, and there they are. It was very nice talking to you. If you are ever in Chicago, give me call."

I handed him my business card as Yarvis, Alicia, and Stephon made their way to the table, each looking edible.

"I already ordered your drinks. Please have a seat and relax."

Alicia spoke first. "Wendy, we really wish you could stay. It's so scary now to step out on what you told us and just go forward."

"Yeah, Alicia is right. What if it doesn't go according to plan?"

"Stephon, you guys got this. I mean, you've practiced so much that you guys can do this stuff in your sleep now."

"I hope you're right."

"Alicia, you know what we talked about in my room. Get that money. Nothing else matters."

I was surprised Yarvis was so quiet. He took his first drink straight to the head. While Alicia, Stephon, and I talked through most of dinner, all he did was drink. We all had reached a limit to where EVERYTHING was funny as hell. Then, all of a sudden, he spoke.

"Wendy, I want to fuck you...tonight. Before you get on the plane to go back to your man, I want to fuck you. We all want to fuck you."

I looked at him with a very confused face. After finishing my drink, I looked him dead in the eyes and asked, "Why?"

"Do you really have to ask that question?"

"Yes, Yarvis, I do. We've worked side by side for three weeks straight, and some days on the weekend, and none of you past the mild flirting have let on to sexual desires at all. So why now? Why tonight?"

Before he could say another word, Alicia said, "It happened the first day you came into the office. We had an open conversation about you. The guys...well, Yarvis expressed his desire then. Stephon later told me how sexually attracted to you he was, and then Yarvis caught me staring at your ass one day. Then he knew I had the same desires they had."

Stephon spoke, addressing Alicia. "And that day, I thought we all agreed we would leave our private thoughts private and not talk about them until Wendy left. I see that shit went right out the window after round five of shots. Damn, Alicia."

"Each of you had the opportunity to do whatever you wanted to do to me in my hotel room. You were all there. I set it up for each of you. Each of you knew I had a man and that I was going back home to him in a few weeks. Now one day before I'm to depart, everybody wants to fuck? Tsk, tsk, tsk. Maybe the next time you guys fuck up things around here and they demand I come back, we can get together. But, now, I have to go home and take this tight, good, hot pussy back to my man. It was a pleasure meeting and working with each of you."

I got up from the table, kissed Alicia on her forehead, and laid her envelope on the table. I kissed Stephon gently on his lips, gave him his envelope, and Yarvis, I tried to kiss gently, but he held the back of my head and pushed his tongue inside of my mouth, taking what he must have thought of on several occasions.

Once I pulled away, I looked him in his eyes, laid his envelope down, and said, "Goodnight and good luck."

I could feel them watching me walk away. I stopped at the hostess stand to get my credit card, and when I looked back, I could almost see the steam coming from each of their laps. I smiled and walked to my car, thinking, *Please, either let them show up all at one time or Alicia, Yarvis, and then Stephon, because he has something inside of him that I want to bring all the way out.*

No sooner than I showered and got into something a little more comfortable, which would be me naked, there was a knock at my door.

Who could it be? Heads, it's Yarvis; tails, it's Alicia. No. Heads, it's Alicia; tails, it's Stephon. Shit. Fuck this coin.

"Greg? Oh my God, baby! Wha-what are you doing here?"

"Jessi called me and said you had to stay another week. What I didn't understand is why you didn't tell me? And why am I still standing in your doorway?"

"Baby, I'm sorry. Come in. I'm just surprised to see you, that's all."

"Were you expecting someone else?"

"No, I wasn't expecting you or anyone else. I was about to get in bed and call you."

"You took another shower?"

"Yeah, Greg, but we went to a bar and had more drinks. There was music and smoking, and you know how I hate smoke in my hair and sheets when I sleep. Are you okay, baby?"

Fuck, someone is knocking at the door.

"I thought you weren't expecting anyone?"

"I'm not."

"Then who's at the door, Wendy?"

"I'm about to answer it, Greg, and then we'll both know. Alicia." I took a deep breath.

"Wendy, I had to see you before you left."

"Well, come on in. My sweetie showed up tonight to surprise me. So, you get to meet the man I have been talking about for weeks."

"Greg is here?"

He came to the door. "Hi, Alicia."

"What a pleasure to meet you. He *is* fine, Wendy."

I smiled as if to say, *Thank you.*

"Well, I won't stay long. I just wanted to tell you thank you again. The guys and I have learned so much, and we hope we don't let you down."

"I'm not worried about that, girl. You all will do fine. Just remember to call me if you need me. Tell Yarvis and Mr. Stephon to just work it like we practiced, and everything will be fine."

She hugged my neck and kissed the side of my face. But, it wasn't a goodbye kiss. It was more like a "you owe me one" kiss, and I planned on collecting.

"I guess you did what you came here to do, pretty lady."

"I don't appreciate you insinuating that I had other plans tonight, Greg. I know you're not pulling the trust card on me, are you?"

"Why didn't you tell me you had to stay here another week?"

"I don't. Sit down. Chrissy called me tonight."

"Chrissy?"

"My neighbor, the one Rashad slept with. Anyway, she told

me that Rashad has been staying over at my house. I know I left Jessi in my house so Rashad has no business being there, right? Especially not three days a week since I've been gone. I don't want to believe it because of the source, but I told her I had to stay here another week so I could come home and catch Jessi and Rashad, if that's really the case. I was going to fly home, stay at your house, and just wait. Because if my friend, the person I promoted on the job so she could have the income to get away from the same bullshit you helped me get over, was living in my house and fucking my ex, I was going to kick her ass and kick her out. I'm sorry I didn't tell you the lie I told her. But, can you imagine how I felt to hear one trifling bitch tell me that I might have another trifling bitch in my life?"

"Baby, I went by the house a few times, but Jessica was there alone."

"Did you call before you went over there?"

"Of course, I did. I do even when you're there."

"So that means he could have been there, left, and just come back after you leave."

"Baby, you don't believe that, do you?"

"I don't know what I believe."

"You know Jessi."

"I guess. What I do know is my man jumped the first plane here to come see about this 'stay another week' shit. That makes me happy."

"How happy?"

"Can I show you?"

He smiled while untying my robe. There I stood naked, face to face with my man. He picked me up and laid me on the bed. He smelled my pussy for slight confirmation that it had not been touched. Then he buried his face in it and began making love to my pussy with his mouth like his life depended on it.

My moans turned into light screams of passion as he pressed his tongue against my clit. Then he placed it between his top lip and his tongue, sucking it until the arch in my back leaned me into a damn near straight up position. I grabbed the side of his face and tried to pull him up because I was going to cum and scream at the same time if he didn't come up right then, and he knew that. He pushed my hands off, wrapped his arms around my legs, and pulled me back to him. I pushed up on my legs and began to fuck his face in a slow wind.

I moaned louder. He came up and plunged his dick inside my pussy. I was so fucking wet that his dick was gliding in my pussy. When I closed my eyes from the pleasure, I saw Alicia sucking my right breast and caressing the left one. I saw Stephon's dick going in and out of my mouth, and Yarvis' dick was thrusting into my pussy while Greg held my legs.

"Uh huh. Come on."

I could feel my body moving faster. I guess Greg knew he was about to make me bust, because he flipped me over and rammed his dick in my pussy from the back. All I could do was scream.

"Fuck!"

His voice rang out, "I told you I was gonna fuck you. Come on. Fuck me like you talked about."

At that moment, I was fucking the four people that were consuming my immediate thoughts.

"Come on, girl. Yeah. Just like that. Throw that ass on this dick."

"Like this?"

"Shit, just like that."

"You like that, daddy?"

"I like that. This is my fucking pussy."

"Yeah, baby, this pussy is your pussy tonight."

I still had everyone doing something to me in my mind. Alicia was kissing me in the mouth; Yarvis was sucking my titties; Stephon was running his dick inside of me; and I was stroking Greg with my hand. I was responding to Stephon's voice. He wanted my pussy, and I was giving it to him.

"I'm about to cum, baby," his voice said.

"Is that what you want to do? You want to cum?"

"Yes. Make me cum, please."

"That's what I came here for."

His dick went in stronger, and he began to bang up against my ass harder. That made me fuck him back, because just like he was going to make me cum, I was about to get one out of him, too.

"Fuck, girl. Don't do that. Don't do that."

"Shut the fuck up. You wanted it. Now fuck me like you mean it. That's what you came for."

I was being fucked so well. My body was on fire with pleasure from every area that could have been pleasured.

"Shit, your pussy is so tight on my dick. Yeah…yeah, back that pussy up on my dick."

"You like that shit? Fuck me, baby. Rub my clit. Please, rub my clit."

A hand was on my clit now, just as I requested.

"Yeah, yeah, baby. Fuck me. Right there. Fuck my pussy like you mean it, baby. You don't mean that shit."

I begged for harder and deeper, and I got harder and deeper.

It's too much; I'm about to cum now.

"Fuck yeah. I'm cumming now, baby. Shit. Yeah, right fucking there."

"I'm cumming, too, Wendy. Shit, I'm cumming."

He pulled and banged my ass on his dick as hard as he could, like he was trying to ram that motherfucker up through my throat.

"I'm still cumming, baby. Fuck, Greg Shit. Awww, fuck. Yeah, yeah. Shit, baby. Bring me your dick. Let me suck the rest of that shit out. Yeah, give it to me."

"Fuck, girl. Oh shit. Shit. Ahhh…I love that shit, girl."

"You love me?"

"Hell fucking yeah."

"Your mouth is so nasty, young man."

"I love you, Wendy."

"I love you, too, Greg."

"You love me? Then tell me who else you were fucking along with me just now."

"What?"

"Come on, baby. You know me. I pay attention to detail. I have to. In the business I'm in, all I do is pay attention. I've made you have orgasms in a number of ways. You have never fucked me the way you fucked me tonight. Tell me about it. Was it Alicia? Or was it the guys? Hell, maybe it was all three of them. Talk to me. What happened to you tonight, Wendy?"

"Baby, honesty has been our thing from day one, right?"

"Right."

"Greg, I love you, and tonight, I made love to you. No one else, or nothing else on my mind. I made love to you. I feel different on the inside about you, and I guess you could feel it."

"I could. Your body was warmer than before. Your touch set a burning fire for me tonight, baby. Your kiss instantly made my dick harder than ever before. If this is what making love to you is going to be like from now on since love is involved, hell,

I guess I should have loved you long before now."

"It would have been fake for me prior to this point, so it wouldn't have worked this way."

"What else do I need to know about you before we head back home?"

"I missed you."

He blushed as I told my first lie to the man I loved. I would never tell him that I made love to him, another woman, and two men in the same night and blamed it on love. He wouldn't understand. Could any man understand? I didn't need the others to enhance my night with Greg. He was due the good fucking I put on him. But I *wanted* the others. There's a difference.

Now look at him...sleeping like a baby. That's so cliché, Wendy. I laugh to myself and shake my head. *I'll be back to New York...and Alicia, Yarvis, and yes, Stephon. I owe them another trip.*

Chapter Seventeen
Lies and Deceit

I hate to say it, but I'm so glad to be home, sleeping in my own bed. Well, Greg's bed. No, I was right, my bed, with my man. Look at him with his fine self.

"Morning, baby."

"Good morning, beautiful. Did you rest well?"

"I did. It feels so good to be in your bed."

"This is *our* bed." He leaned in to kiss me. "What you got planned for today other than playing CSI Chicago?"

"Shut up. Baby, I'm serious. If Jessi is in my house sleeping with Rashad, it's going to be some shit."

"Wendy, you can't believe she is that kind of person. Now, you know what kind of person your neighbor is, but Jessica is your friend."

"We're about to see."

"Well, don't get your ass locked up."

"How? Hell, that's my house."

"It doesn't have to be."

"What?"

"If you move in with me, Jessica can have that house. Then she and Rashad can live there happily ever after. I mean, do you really care?"

"First of all, yes, I do care. That's my house, and she is

supposed to be my friend. Well, that's pending until further investigation, but I worked hard to get my house and the things in it. So, no, I will not just give it away."

"Is there a number two? You know black women love to count a brother down when they think they're going off."

I looked at him and laughed as I tried to pull "secondly" out the hat.

"And secondly, Mr. Greg Hamilton…you don't want me to move in with you. You're just talking after all that good loving I put on you."

"Your loving is the bomb, baby, but it has nothing to do with why I want you here with me. When I said I love you, I meant that. I want you close to me. I want to wake up with you; I want to go to sleep with you. I-I want to spend all of my next days loving you."

"Greg, go to work."

"So is that a no?"

"That is a 'go to work and I'll think about it'. My mother doesn't believe in shacking up, so until you're ready to get married, how about I stay at my place and you stay here. Then we can just spend a couple of nights here and there until we're ready. How about that?"

"How about we just get married?"

"Now you really need to get out of here and go to work."

I kissed him again, got out of the bed, and damn near ran into the bathroom. I started the water immediately in the event he said something else I needed to avoid. Then I could pretend I didn't hear him.

Damn, I need to send Mr. Wallace an email to let him know that if anyone asks, I'm still in New York, but just as sure as I go out there, he will be sitting on the bed waiting for answers to questions I refuse to answer. I'm going to go and see my momma, then have a cab drop me off at my house and just go and hide out until Jessi gets off. Then, this evening, I can really determine if I will have a criminal record or not.

"Hey, Momma, what are you doing?"

"Hey, baby, you back?"

"Kind of; sort of."

"What does that mean, Wendy? You're either back or you're not."

"I'm home, Momma, but I'm over at Greg's for now. I'm going home for a little while, then I will be back over here. I just need to check on Jessi, but I want to surprise her."

"Well, you know Marguerite's niece Keisha that goes with Antoine, who stays next door to Monique that works with Diane's youngest daughter Vanessa, said she saw Jessica at the mall with Rashad. She said they were just walking, but Jessica was smiling and so was he. But, maybe they just ended up there at the same time and shared a joke. I don't know. What I do know is Greg's sweet self came over here every other day while you were gone. He made sure I had dinner, the laundry was done, and he even treated me and Ethel to the nail salon and spa. He had some guys come over and cut my grass and everything, girl. He's a keeper."

"I'm glad you like him, Momma."

"I hope you do."

"I do. I could love him after a while."

"Well, you know I loved your father and he loved me, and when Greg stopped by, he made me feel like I wouldn't ever have to worry about you because he would take care of you just like he was taking care of me. I know you didn't ask him to do all that, but he went on and did it. That's a good thing to know."

"You're right, Momma. Do you need anything before I head over there?"

"Nope. Greg picked up groceries for me on Friday for this week."

I smiled big, and even though we couldn't see each other, I knew she was smiling, too.

"Bye, Momma."

"Bye, baby."

I looked around his enormous bedroom and shook my head.

He has to be flawed. I mean, past what he has told me. There has to be something I'm missing about him. Now why is Mr. Wallace calling me?

"Hey, Mr. Wallace. You okay?"

"Yeah, I was just making sure you were. I got your email marked confidential that said you were leaving New York but not coming in and that you would call me."

"Yeah, I had some personal things I needed to take care of at my house."

"Oh. Well, Jessica told us how nice you were to let her crash there until she found her a new place. She's out sick today, so when you see her, tell her I hope she gets to feeling better."

"I sure will."

No time like the present to check on the sick and shut in. You have got to be kidding me. Why is Rashad's car in my driveway? Lord, please don't set me up to spend the rest of my life in prison. I love Greg, and he wants to marry me. Don't let me go to jail today, please.

So, here I am again, tipping in my own damn house. Oh, now the bastard wants to leave his boots at the front door by the couch, when I use to trip over them when walking in the door.

I heard Jessica yelling at him from downstairs so loudly that it scared me.

"Rashad, you think this is a damn joke? I'm pregnant, stupid."

"No, listen, baby. I don't think it's a joke. I'm just excited."

"Number one, I'm not your damn baby, okay? Number two, don't be excited. This baby might not even be yours. It could be Travis'. So, wipe that fucking smile off your face."

"Yeah, but when was the last time you slept with him? We've been fucking what, everyday for the past three weeks? Come on now. You know that's my baby."

I sat down on the bottom step because my stomach sank to my feet.

"Rashad, you were a mistake. This whole thing was a mistake. Your ass is lucky Wendy had to stay in New York another week so I can get to the clinic, get rid of this baby, and pretend this whole thing didn't happen."

"What clinic? You're not having no abortion with my fucking baby."

"This ain't your damn baby, okay? Get that out of your head."

"You don't know that. It's a 50/50 chance between me and ole dude. And the way I put it down, it's more like 80/20. So, you're not killing my baby."

"Do you hear yourself? Better yet, do you hear me? I'M NOT HAVING YOUR/HIS...WHOMEVER'S FUCKING BABY!"

"Let me tell you something. All the time I spent with Wendy's ass trying to make a damn baby and she couldn't get pregnant, you think I'ma let you terminate my seed? You're crazy as hell. If you don't want the baby, just have it and give it to me."

"Rashad, I'm not having this baby. You think I'm going to let the only person I have in my life leave me because I fucked up? Hell no."

"You didn't fuck up. You fucked me, but call it what you want to."

His laughter made me ball up even more. I couldn't believe what I was hearing, and I couldn't stop the tears from running down my face. I tried to get up and walk upstairs, but my feet felt like they were bound with cement.

"Look, Wendy fucked me every way a man could think of, and she didn't get pregnant. You're giving me a chance to be something I never had, a father. Please don't take that from me."

"This child was not conceived out of love, Rashad. This was never supposed to happen. Whether this baby is yours or Travis', neither of you deserve to ruin its life. So, I'm not keeping it. And FYI, Wendy knew you would suck as a father. So, I went with her to have an abortion when you got her pregnant last year. See, we both know better than to let you fuck up another person's life."

Shit! Who could be ringing the doorbell?

When I stood up to answer the door, Jessica was at the top of the stairs.

"Oh my God! Wendy?"

I opened the door, and it was Chrissy.

"I told you that bitch was fucking your man."

"Wendy, how long have you been here? I mean, I thought you were still in New York?"

Before I could speak, Chrissy blurted out, "No, bitch, she ain't still in New York. I told her how your dog ass was over here fucking her ex, and she came home to bust your nasty, trifling ass."

Jessica immediately jumped on the defensive. "Shut the fuck up, Chrissy. I know you ain't talking."

Then Chrissy yelled at Rashad, "And, Rashad, you were better off fucking me. How could you fuck your ex's best friend?"

"Get out, bitch!" he yelled, as if he still lived here.

"Fuck you! You just mad I showed Wendy how trifling yo' ass is yet again. I hope she whoops the both of y'all asses."

Jessica came charging down the stairs in a rage. "I'ma do what Wendy should have done when she caught your ass over here in her bed since you can't seem to mind your own fucking business, bitch."

"I wish yo' ass would hit me, bitch!"

Rashad reached for Jessica. "Jessica, come here. Y'all quit."

That's the last thing I heard when I walked out the door. I remembered dialing 911 and sitting down on the curb. I could see people gathering by my house. People were calling my name, but I couldn't look up. I couldn't move.

Greg called, but I couldn't answer the phone. I heard the sirens and saw the police cars rushing past me, but I still couldn't move.

A man tapped me on the shoulder and said, "Ms. Brooks?"

I guess I shook my head yes.

"Are you hurt?"

I guess I shook my head no.

"Can you talk?"

I guess I shook my head yes.

"Can you tell me what happened?"

Then I heard Greg's voice. "Baby? Wendy, baby, are you

hurt? Baby, talk to me. Are you hurt?"

I looked up at him, and I guess I shook my head yes, because he said, "Where are you hurt?"

I replied, "Jessi's pregnant for Rashad."

I heard the officer yell back, "Whoever Jessica is, she's pregnant. Tell the medic Jessica is pregnant."

I saw Walter walk up. He took my purse, while Greg picked me up and put me in the car. There were people in the neighborhood that I had never seen. The ambulance drove off as another one pulled up.

I saw Rashad being put in the police car, and he had blood on his shirt. One of the girls that Chrissy hung with was being put in another police car, but I didn't see Jessi or Chrissy anywhere. When I woke up, I was at Greg's house and my mother was in bed with me.

"Hey, Momma."

"Hey, baby, how you feeling?"

"Like I've been hit by an eighteen-wheeler truck."

"You'll be alright. You're the strongest big-little girl I know."

"Where's Greg?"

"He went to your house to get you some clothes for the week. He tried to plan a shopping trip for you, but I told him you probably would not be in the mood. So, he said he would pick out you some good stuff to wear to work." She chuckled as if she was pleased with his attempt to dress me for the week.

"Momma, how is Jessica?"

"I don't know. She has called your cell phone several times, though. I didn't answer because I didn't know what to say to her. Given your relationship, I think the first person she needs to talk to is you."

"What should I say to her?"

"Depends. Are you going to forgive her for what she has done? I mean, Greg said you told him she was pregnant for Rashad. Is that true?"

"She said she didn't know if it was Travis' or Rashad's, but the fact that she has been sleeping with him while I was gone hurts me to the core, Momma."

"I know, baby, but people make mistakes."

"Momma, a one-night stand is a mistake. She has been living in my house for the last three weeks, sleeping with my ex-boyfriend. The man that beat me and treated me like shit, excuse my language. But, he was horrible to me, and I stayed for the wrong reasons, and the minute I turn my back, she's with him. Why? You tell me why?"

In shock after what I had just said, she replied, "I can't, but maybe she can, if you let her. You deserve that much at least, and then decide. But, pray first because she is your best friend."

My cell phone rang again, and it was from Jessica's cell.

"Hello."

"Hi, Wendy."

"Momma Reins?"

"Yes, how you doing, baby?"

"I'm okay. How is Jessi doing?"

"She's still not in the clear yet, so we don't know. That damn girl stabbed her in the stomach, and she was in surgery for hours. Do you know what happened? Did you know she was pregnant?"

"Momma Reins, Jessica moved in with me because Travis hit her. I promoted her on the job so she could afford to move out. When I went on a business trip for about three weeks, the entire time she was living in my house and sleeping with

Rashad."

"Your Rashad?"

"Yes, ma'am, my Rashad. Well, my old Rashad. We're not together anymore, but still."

"I can't believe her ass. That's why she got stabbed? Over your man?"

"Well, Rashad had a sexual relationship with my neighbor, too. That's how I found out about Jessi and Rashad; my neighbor called me in New York and told me. I told Jessica that I had to stay another week, but I came home, praying what my neighbor said wasn't true. I walked in on a conversation between Jessica and Rashad discussing her pregnancy. She was telling him that she wasn't going to keep the baby whether it was his or Travis'. Then my doorbell rang, and it was Chrissy, my neighbor, letting me know that she wasn't lying. That's when Jessi and Rashad found out I was back in town and had heard their entire conversation. Chrissy and Jessica started yelling at each other, and I called the police and left. I have no idea what happened after that. I saw the police and heard the ambulance, but I don't know what happened after I walked out of the house."

"I'm so sorry, Wendy. I don't know what's going on with her, but now she's fighting for her life. I don't know if you will ever forgive her, but I know she needs anyone who cares about her to pray for her right now. So, I'm apologizing on her behalf."

"I'll be up there shortly, Momma Reins."

I hung up the phone and closed my eyes to say the prayer that would get me to the hospital and keep me from pulling the plug on my friend. *What do I say to her if I'm there when she wakes up? What if Rashad is there? What if Travis is there?*

Who do I tell about the baby? God, please help me.

"Wendy, you know you don't have to go."

"I know, Momma, but before this, she was my friend and a damn good one."

Just then, Greg's voice lit up the room. "Then I'll drive you to see your friend, and we can stay as long as you want to."

I jumped up off the bed and ran to his arms just like you would see in a Hollywood romance film. He kissed me like I had been gone for months, and I loved every minute of it. He let me know right then that I was his and he was mine, and he was going to be there for me no matter what.

*****

At the hospital, Momma Reins hugged me like I was her long lost child.

"Wendy, I'm so glad you came."

"How is she, Momma Reins?"

"She made it out of surgery. She lost the baby, but she is doing fine. She asked me had I talked to you or had you been by, but when I asked her why you would come by after what I heard, she turned her head and began to cry."

"Momma Reins, this is my boyfriend, Greg Hamilton. Greg, this is Jessi's mom, Ms. Reins."

"Pleased to meet you, Ms. Reins. Sorry the circumstances, but a pleasure anyway."

"And he's a handsome little ole thing, too, Wendy."

"Thank you."

"Keep him away from my daughter. Looks like she has a problem with understanding what belongs to someone else is off limits to her."

"Momma Reins…"

"I'm so disappointed in her, and once she's better, I'm

going to let her know exactly how I feel because I didn't raise her like that. And as big of a whore as her father was, we talked about that."

"It's in the past, Ma. Just let it go, and I'm going to try and do the same."

"Past my ass, Wendy. That was just a few hours ago. That's dirty, and I don't like it. She has never heard me talk about how I slept with nor did anything with one of my closest friend's exes."

"Momma Reins, it's okay. Don't upset yourself, please."

"I'd a whooped her ass if I was you."

Greg had to interject because she was really getting upset. "Ms. Reins, let me take you to get some coffee."

"Thank you, sweetie. I could use some vodka, but if coffee is all they have downstairs, then coffee it is."

"Momma, what room is Jessica in?"

"She's in room 562."

"Thank you."

"No, Wendy baby, thank you. Thank you for letting the Lord put a forgiving heart in your spirit."

I smiled and walked off to find the elevator. I asked the Lord to give me the right words to say past, "Bitch, you got some nerve making it through surgery." I really didn't want Jessica dead, but after all I had done for her, a slight coma would have worked for the time being.

Okay, fine. Sure, I'm glad she made it out; glad she would get a chance to tell me why she would do me like this. What did I ever do to her? Then after she explains, I can pray another prayer for her punishment. Wait, Wendy. Check yourself. You are not God. You have done your share of dirt, too. Get it together.

"Hey, Jessi."

She turned her head to look at me and began to cry. I walked over and wiped her eyes.

"How you doing?"

"I'm okay. Wendy, I–"

"Shhh. It's over and done with. You just need to get better and get out of here."

"No, please, let me talk."

"I don't want to know, Jess. I just want you to get out of here, okay? I love Greg, and I'm going to marry him. Rashad was a part of my past; Greg is my future. You will be my friend forever. And I'm sorry you lost your baby. You would have been a great mother."

"You of all people should know I was NOT keeping a baby that belonged to Travis or Rashad. I was wrong, Wendy, and I didn't sleep with Rashad the entire time. Most of the time, he slept in your bed alone. I guess waiting for you to come back and change your mind. The first night, he came by to get his clothes. We had a few drinks and slept together that night and maybe three other nights. I was wrong, and I'm so sorry."

"One time was too many, and we both know that. But, you're my friend and I love you. I can't say it was all Rashad's fault, but I know he and liquor are a bad combination. It's a bad combination for you, too, sometimes, but we have been through hell and high water together. So, we are together to stay."

There was a knock on the door and Travis walked in.

"Hey, Wendy."

"Travis."

"Baby, how you doing?"

"I'm fine."

"See what happens when you go off and try to leave a

brother? You get into all kinds of mess."

"Whatever."

"Now would be a good time to tell me how you got stabbed at Wendy's house, why Rashad is in jail, and why you didn't tell me I was going to be a father?"

I looked at Jessica and she looked at me.

"Travis, they gave her some medicine for pain, so come on. I'll tell you what happened in the waiting room, and when she wakes up, you can come back in."

She started crying again. I got up and kissed her forehead. Jessica knew then that I would take care of the talk with Travis.

Chapter Eighteen
What If?

"Baby? Baby?" I heard Greg shouting for me from the shower.

"I'm in the shower, baby." Before I could say another word, he was in the shower with me fully dressed. "Greg, what are you doing? That's a thousand-dollar suit."

"Kiss me."

So, I did.

"No, kiss me like you mean it."

I gave him a few more little pecks while I undid his pants, pulled his dick out, and stroked it with my hand. Then he stuck his tongue damn near down my throat.

"Greg, what is wrong with you?"

He picked me up, slid me down on his dick, and we started fucking right there in the shower. His suit was surely ruined, but it seemed like he didn't care. I guess whatever he was so excited about gave him the notion he could buy twenty more suits if he wanted to.

"Shit, baby." He squeezed my body tightly, while sliding me up and down on his rock-hard dick. "Yeah, baby, fuck me. Fuck me just like that, Wendy."

He looked me in the eyes, and it felt like his dick grew in size and width. It filled my pussy up like water in a balloon. I knew something was up. He bounced me faster and faster, then stopped. He opened the door to the shower and carried me to the bed while still inside of me. He laid me down, quickly finished undressing, and buried his head in my pussy. I could feel his tongue pressing its way inside me. As I wrapped my legs around his head, he shoved them back to the point where they were damn near touching my ears. I came instantly. He plunged right back inside of me and pulled my body close to his.

"I love you, Wendy. I love you so much!"

"I love you, too, baby. Right there! Shit, Greg, right there."

"Wendy, baby, I'm about to cum. I'm about to cum for you, girl!"

"Me, too, baby! Yeah, don't stop, Greg. Yeah, yeah. Fuck!"

We both let out the biggest sigh of pleasure that two people in love can release. He kissed me on my lips and smiled.

"I do love you, Wendy."

"I know that, baby, but what's wrong? What were you trying to tell me before your dick so rudely interrupted?"

He laughed and kissed me again. "Baby, you're not going to believe the call I got today."

"If you would have just asked me that instead of busting into the shower and putting your dick in me, I could have guessed a while ago."

"Listen, baby."

"Okay, who called you today?"

"Ted Lawson."

"Ted Lawson? Your real estate agent?"

"Yes, and guess what else?"

"Gregory Hamilton, just tell me!"

"Okay. The property I bid on for the hotel, I won. It's mine. It's ours. I can start building in sixty days if I want to."

In excitement, I climbed on top of him, kissed him, and said, "I'm so proud of you, baby."

"W. Brooks Hotel & Spa. That's the name of it."

With a confused look on my face, I asked, "What do you mean W. Brooks?"

"I told you I love you. I want this to be the first of *our* projects."

"Greg, I can't let you do that. I mean, you're telling me that you want to name your hotel after me?"

"Well, I thought about doing another club in Raleigh, North Carolina, but then I said let me see if I can do bigger. I have been bidding on the property for almost a year, and finally, it's ours."

"You keep saying ours. What is that, Greg?"

"That is me saying I want to spend the rest of my life loving you, if you'll have me."

"What?"

I got off him; he sat up and got right back in my face.

"Wendy, this isn't for play for me. I'm not dating you to just date you. I'm dating you to keep you. Remember that?"

"What if I'm not ready for marriage?"

"So. I'm not going anywhere until you are. Love doesn't mean right away. It grows over time. It gets stronger, deeper, and it means more and more with time. I'm not going anywhere because I love you."

This time when he said it, the words sent chills through my body.

"But what if we don't make it? What if you find someone else before I'm ready to be married? What if–"

He cut my words off with a kiss. "Wendy, I'm not going ANYWHERE. Hell, what if we *do* make it? I mean, what if

Schelle Holloway

there is no one else and all I want is you? Why is that so hard for you to believe? Why do I have to keep saying that to you? I love YOU. I want to spend the rest of my days loving YOU. You know everything about me, the good, the bad, the in between. You know Greg Hamilton, and he loves you. Whenever you're ready, I'll be here."

I felt a tug at my stomach, and right then, all I could do was cry. I tried to hold all my emotions in, but I couldn't.

"I'm scared, Greg. I'm so scared."

"You're supposed to be, and my job is to ease all that. I got you, baby. I want to marry you. I want you to have my children. I want us to vacation with your mother, and Ms. Ethel can come, too."

I looked at him and laughed. "You know she's going to want to bring her or her little boyfriend."

"Whatever it takes to make you happy, Wendy, that's what I'm going to do. Do you understand that?"

"I do."

"Wow. That sounds so good rolling off your lips, girl."

I blushed and kissed him again. "I have to get ready for work. I have a meeting with Mr. Wallace this morning. I'm guessing he wants to do a follow up from the New York trip."

"Get going then."

When I got up to walk away, he pulled me back into his lap. "You know I want to make love to you again, right?"

"That's too bad. I'm already running behind schedule because of your great news."

He grabbed both of my breasts as if I had not said one word.

"Baby, I have to go."

He stuck his finger in my pussy and then put it in my mouth. Once he slid his finger out of my mouth, he turned me around to face him and kissed me as if he wanted to taste my saliva mixed with my pussy juice.

"Baaabbby," I whined, while feeling his dick getting hard underneath my ass. "Greg, please."

Since he ignored my request to let me go, I said fuck it. My pussy was already throbbing with the desire to have him again. So, I reached around, grabbed his dick, and put it inside of me. He laid back on the bed and closed his eyes in pleasure. I leaned back and rode his dick in gratitude, thanking him for giving me five more minutes of what we both really wanted. It was hard playing hard to get when the dick was this good.

He grabbed my waist and helped my hips dance on his dick. He bit his bottom lip so hard that I thought I could see his teeth prints on his skin. His sighs made me explode on the inside, and he must have felt it, because he opened his eyes and gave me the biggest smile of approval.

Next, he lifted me up, bent me over the bed, and went in again. This time he grabbed a hand full of my hair and pulled my ass back and forth as if his new name were Cowboy Hamilton, and I loved it. He banged me so hard that I had to bury my face in the linen not to scream from the pain and pleasure I was being served. He reached around to my neck and lifted my head.

"Don't cheat me. Let me hear what you feel."

I immediately obliged. Shouts of mind-blowing sex rang out from my mouth.

"Fuck me then. Wait, you're hurting me, Greg."

"No, I'm not. You like this shit."

"Baby, shit! Oh, baby, right fucking there. Don't stop."

"Why? You like that shit?"

"Yeah, baby, I like it."

"No, you don't." With his grip still on my hair, he pulled my head back and said, "Tell the truth."

If I say the wrong shit, he may fuck me TOO hard, if there is such a thing.

He got in my ear and said, "I love it, baby. This is my shit, and I love it."

He reached for my titties with his other hand, which made his body slump over mine, and that gave me some comfort. So much so that I reached down and began to stroke my clit because I wanted to cum again. He could feel it and began to call out to me.

"Wendy, baby, shit. You're squeezing my dick. Stop that, please. You gonna make me cum."

I knew I had his ass. "Shhh."

"No, baby, for real, stop. I don't want to cum yet. Fuck."

With my head down, I smiled while listening to him beg,

"What is it? Talk to me, baby." I backed it up on him and squeezed that shit some more. "What is it?"

"Fuck you, baby. You gonna make me cum. Shit. Shit, Wendy." He stood right up and started banging my pussy as hard as he could. "Fuck you, Wendy. You ain't right. You gonna make me…shit. I'm cumming, baby!"

He grabbed my body from the back, stood me up, and wrapped his arms around me tightly, like I was scared of something and he was protecting me. He bounced me on his dick a few more times, and then I got that last good pump. He froze in place.

"Baby? Greg? You okay?"

He kissed the back of my neck. "I love you."

I didn't move. "I love you, too, baby."

After slowly letting me go, he grabbed my hand, walking

me into the bathroom. He opened the door to the shower that was still running and escorted me in. He grabbed my ponytail holder off the counter, pulled my hair up, and put my shower cap back on. I thought he was going to get in with me, but he closed the door and walked away. I had never seen him act this way, so I didn't start showering.

Instead, I opened the door to go out and get him to shower with me, but when I went back into the room, he was on his knees in a praying position. My emotions ran wild. I didn't say a word. I just turned and went back to my shower.

I closed my eyes and said, "Lord, I don't know what I have in Greg Hamilton, but you know." Then I smiled, took my shower, and got on to work, late!

*****

"Mr. Wallace, that's great news."

"Yep, even while you were out of town, your team worked the magic that you taught them and put us in the number two spot for the region and number five in the nation."

"Well, I only do what I can do when I can do it."

We both shared a laugh of confidence.

"Well, Wendy, that's only one reason I wanted to meet with you. Because you do what you do so well, we want to offer you a traveling expertise trainer position."

"Excuse me? Traveling?"

"Yes. You will travel from company to company and train their revenue departments for three weeks max, pending on where they fall in the region. Then come back here to base, report in, and head back out again."

"That means training others to take our position in the region. How am I supposed to keep our place if I spend all my time out of the office training others?"

"You will only train those at the bottom. I think they just want the bottom ten companies. You don't have to decide today, but it has been proposed. They will pay for all of your travel, lodging, and food of course; whatever you need."

"For three weeks at a time, Mr. Wallace? That's crazy."

"No, that's business. You are the best in the company, Wendy. People are paying big money for the best. What if I told you there was a seven-thousand-dollar pay increase for this position that will be added to your annual salary? It's yours; it can't be taken back. It's so many other perks to this position, too. You have got to trust me when I say you won't be disappointed in your decision. All you have to do is go and show them what you do every day. Hell, show them half of what you do every day and just kick start them, and the money and other goodies are still yours. They don't have to soar to the top; they just have to show some level of improvement. Every time they move up on the quarterly report, you get a bonus. I'm talking like five thousand dollars per company. You do the math. I've never been selfish with giving; I always put the best people in high places. You work too damn hard not to be rewarded for your work. Three weeks out, one week in, and then you go back out and start over until you have hit all ten companies. Then you're done. Just think about it."

"Mr. Wallace, my mother has cancer. I can't be away like that. If something were to happen, I couldn't get to her. She really needs me right now, and I just don't think I can deal with all the travel and–"

He cut me off. "Take her with you. Find the chemo locations in the areas, if that's the issue, and I will make arrangements for a two-bedroom condo for each location."

"Mr. Wallace, you can't do that. I don't want her to have to be in the house all day while I'm out working and–"

He cut me off again. "You'll have a rental car equipped with a GPS, and let your mother have shopping sprees in every city."

"Mr. Wallace–"

"Wendy, you're the one for this job. I'm not going to let you 'excuse' your way out of this. What if this is your opportunity to take your title to another level? Don't sell yourself short. Take the rest of the day off and go talk to your mother. Talk to Mr. Limo Man, as well, because if you're serious about him, he will need to know what you have been offered. He will have to be able to deal with his woman being gone."

"He wants to get married, Mr. Wallace."

"Lucky-ass man. See, even he knows you're the best."

I blushed and replied, "I'll talk to my family, but ultimately, the decision will be mine. I want to talk to my team, as well."

"Done deal, but, Wendy, can you give me a timetable on a decision? A day? A week? A month? Lord knows I hope not that long, but I mean, take your time."

"I'll be in touch soon."

"Take tomorrow off, too. Come back on Wednesday, and I will have more details laid out on paper. Then you can take off Thursday and Friday and think about it over the weekend. Maybe Monday when you come back to work, we can work on a decision."

"Thank you, Mr. Wallace."

"I know it will be hard, Wendy, with your mother being ill, but you know mothers. They want what will make their children happy."

"I know."

"Alright, Ms. Brooks, I'll see you on Wednesday."

"Yep."

"Hey, do you know when Jessica is due back into the office?"

"Yes, sir. She will be back next Wednesday."

"Good deal."

I got in my car, but I had no idea where I wanted to go first. *Maybe I should cook dinner tonight at Greg's and invite Momma over so I can tell them both at the same time. Nah, that won't work. Number one, I ain't cooking, and number two, I ain't cooking. Let me just go tell Momma first.*

"Ma, where are you? Well, why didn't you answer the house phone? Okay, well, I'm going to stop by. Why not? Ma, you okay? Don't lie to me. Fine, I'll call you later."

Okay, so it's the middle of the day. She didn't answer the house phone but answered her cell phone. Says she's at home, but doesn't want me to come over? That smells real stank. Good thing I can read right through that.

I pulled up and Momma's car was not in the driveway, but her nosey neighbor Ms. Inez was in her yard working.

"Hey, Ms. Inez. How you doing?"

"Good, baby. How are you?"

"Good. You seen my momma today?"

"No, not today. Is her paper still in the box?"

"Yeah, it is."

"Then she must be still in the house. We normally come out at the same time, but this morning, I thought I missed her."

"Okay, thank you."

Now I was really worried. I peeked in the garage, and her car was in there. My heart changed beats to something scary. I clutched my cell phone in the event I had to call for help. I turned the locks, and since the deadbolt was on, she was clearly in the house. I called for her so I wouldn't scare her by just walking in.

"Ma! Momma!"

Why does she have this music so loud? That's why she didn't answer the house phone, because she couldn't hear it.

"Ma?" I looked in the kitchen. *Well, she cooked breakfast.*

"Ma?" I got even more nervous as I got closer to her room, but then I heard her talking. I stopped walking when I heard a man's voice.

"Damn, Beverly."

I know damn well...

"Come on, Timmy. Give it to me. Yeah, daddy, right there."

"Oh shit, Bev, that thang is good to me, girl."

"You like that, baby?"

"Hell yeah, girl."

"Come on, Timmy baby. Right there. Right there, daddy."

"Oh hell, Beverly, you gonna make me do it again."

"That's what you want, ain't it?"

"Yeah, girl. Give it to me then."

I almost threw up in my damn mouth. My momma was fucking Mr. Newsome from the wine tasting with Ms. Ethel. *Oh my fucking goodness. I'm scared to move. My momma's ass has cancer, and she is in here fucking.*

"Shit, Tim. Oh shit, daddy. I'm about to give it to you."

"That's it, girl. Give it to daddy."

Please, Lord, let me just get out of here without the visual kicking in. Deep breath. Turn around and walk.

"Oh, Beverly, there it is."

"Come on, daddy. Let it out."

I grabbed my ears and walked as fast as I could to the door. Just as I opened the door, Ms. Inez was about to ring the bell.

"Ms. Inez?"

"I just wanted to make sure Beverly was okay."

Loud as hell, we heard Momma. "Oh shit, Tim! That's it, baby!"

"She's fine, Ms. Inez. You go on back home, and I'm leaving, too. You may want to come back later, or tomorrow might be even better."

Ms. Inez looked at me damn near cross-eyed. I just gave her an uncertain smile, jumped in my car, and left. Hell, I don't know if she went back across the street or not, but I had to get something to drink to ease my stomach. So, I pulled up at my favorite lunch spot.

"Vodka and cranberry, please."

"Wendy, girl, you never drink this early in the day unless you have something on your mind. Are you okay?"

"Vanessa, I love you to death, but what's on my mind right now, I dare not share. Excuse me one sec. Baby, come to Victor's right now if you can. Yeah, I'm fine, but you're not going to believe this shit."

Vanessa looked at me and poured me a double shot of vodka. I nodded my head with gratitude, drank that shit like a shot, and kindly said, "Give me another one."

In no time, Walter showed up with Greg. I waved him over to the bar.

"Baby, why are you at the bar drinking and it's not even noon yet? Is everything okay?"

"I walked in on Momma fucking Mr. Timothy Newsome."

"What?"

After I explained everything to Greg, Vanessa, who was also listening, said, "Girl, shit, I see why you needed a drink," and then she poured me another one.

"Hell, pour me one, too," Greg said. "Baby, your momma is

getting her groove on right now? Damn!"

"Greg, that shit isn't funny. She's damn near sixty years old and sick with cancer. She has no damn business fucking."

"Baby, she's sick, but she ain't dead. You better still give up the booty at sixty years old, too."

I smacked him on the arm. "It's not funny. She is supposed to be resting."

Vanessa chimed in, "Hell, most women do sleep after a good orgasm. So, maybe now she IS resting."

"Fuck you, too, Vanessa. I see you and Greg think this is a joke."

"Baby, I can't believe you're this upset about your mother having sex. She's grown, and she has needs, too. Go 'head, Mrs. Beverly Brooks, do that shit."

"Greg, I better not hear any side jokes when we see her again either. I just can't believe this. How are you battling cancer and fucking?"

"Wendy, let it go, girl. At least she's still living her life. She isn't letting the fact that she's sick weigh her down and kill her spirit. You should be happy for her."

"Whatever. Can you get us a table, please?"

"Yeah, come on."

Greg continued to chuckle as we walked to the table. *I see right now he wants me to act up. I guess it could have been worse. I could have come in, found she had fallen or was really hurt, and she didn't want to tell me and get me upset. I don't know.*

"Baby, you okay?"

"Stop picking at me, Greg. I just never expected that. I was really scared that she was trying to keep something from me."

"She was. Mr. Newsome." He was still laughing.

"Laugh on. My boss wants me to travel again to ten cities three weeks out of each month, and the last week I come back and do my report before heading head back out. So, it will be roughly ten months of travel," I blurted out.

"What?"

"Oh, your ass ain't laughing anymore, are you?"

"No, wait. Say it again?"

I proceeded to share with Greg everything that Mr. Wallace and I had discussed, my compensation, and my concerns about leaving my sick mother.

When I finished, Greg replied, "Wendy, there is no way in hell I want you away from me for three weeks at a time. You know what? It won't matter. I can fly anywhere I want to. Momma will be fine. I can take her to treatment here. She's not going to want to follow out behind you, especially now that she is dating."

"Fuck you, Greg."

He grabbed my hand and kissed it. "Okay, that was my last joke about Mom. Baby, do it. We will be fine. Momma and I are not afraid to fly. We want you to soar in your job. You have to be the best in the company for them to invest in you like this."

"Now you sound like Mr. Wallace."

"It's true. You're a bad chick. You're beautiful, black, intelligent, fine, motivating, grounded...I could use more adjectives, but they would all come back to you being a bad chick. Do it. You know I'm going to be here. I might have a girlfriend for every month you're gone, but those last two months I'm all yours again."

Rolling my eyes, I said, "Whatever. You really think I should?"

"Yes. Show them why they pay you the big bucks, and show them why they will have to continue to pay you the big bucks. Then when you get back, you can keep working or come and run the hotel. It's yours to do what you want with it."

"Greg–"

"Wendy."

"Fine, I'm going to run it by Momma whenever she gets her legs out of the air, and I'll see how she feels. Then I'll tell Mr. Wallace. He told me to take today and tomorrow off to think about it. Come back Wednesday, look at it on paper, take off Thursday and Friday, think more over the weekend, and make a decision on Monday."

"Good. Let's go to Miami tonight then."

"What?"

"Yeah, then on Wednesday when you get off, I need to introduce you to the staff at the club in Dallas. So, we'll go there and stay until Friday. Then come back here Saturday and take Momma shopping for new clothes since she has a new man, get you some new clothes for travel, and Sunday go to church. Afterwards, we'll make love for the remainder of the day, and then let you rest up so you can walk into Mr. Wallace's office and let him know he has the right woman for the job. Deal?"

"I love you."

"Long as we still fucking at sixty, I'll love you, too, girl."

I dipped my fingers in my glass of water and sprinkled it at his face as he leaned in to kiss me.

*****

"Hey, Ma. Yeah, we made it to Dallas. You doing okay today? Good. Ma, are you sure you will be okay with me doing all this traveling? Yeah, but you know you can come with me anytime. I know that Greg will be there with you, but you are my mother, and I want to be there if you need me. Yes, ma'am."

"Tell Momma I said hello."

"Ma, Greg says hi. Okay. Love you, too. Oh and, Ma, tell Mr. Newsome I said hello."

Greg popped me on my ass after I hung up and said, "You know that's what he's about to do to our momma."

I put my cell phone down and jumped on top of him. "You said you would stop with the 'my momma is having sex' stuff. So, stop it."

"You still haven't told your mother you caught her bumping and grinding? Shame on you. Y'all might be able to go lingerie shopping together."

I get off him and take my dress off to show him I'm completely naked.

"For what? I don't even wear it when I'm around you."

He looked at me like he had just hit a goldmine. As he stood up to start undressing himself, there was a knock at the door.

"Damnit." He slid me behind the door, with his hand properly placed so he could finger my pussy while talking through the cracked door.

"Yes?"

A woman's voice answered. "What do you mean 'yes', silly boy? Can I come in?"

"No. Can I help you with something?"

"Greg, don't play. They told me at the club you would be in town this week. So, I took it upon myself to find you. Dominique told me you normally stay here at the Embassy, so here I am."

"Who are you?"

"You can't be serious, Greg. It hasn't been that long since

you've seen me. It's Natalie. Hellooo."

I didn't know who the chick was, but she was wrecking my moment. To make sure he was focused, I pulled his hand up and started to suck my juices off his fingers. He loved that shit.

"Look, um, Natalie, whoever. I don't remember you, and I normally remember people. So why–"

He couldn't finish his sentence, because by this time, I had put his hand back in my pussy and was guiding his fingers in and out.

"Greg, I just want to come in and talk to you for a second. If this is a bad time, I can come back tonight after the club."

Fuck this shit. I came from behind the door butt-ass naked.

"No, bitch, you can't come back tonight or any other night. He's unavailable."

Her eyes got big as a deer caught in some headlights.

"Do you get it now? Goodbye."

I closed the door and turned around to find that Greg was now naked, too. Needless to say, we were late getting to the club.

*****

He introduced me to so many people that it was hard to keep up. He held my hand all night. On stage, off the stage, at the door, behind the bar, in his office, he showed me off like a first place trophy, and I loved every minute of it.

He had a nice opening songstress, and the atmosphere was so grown. The women were all fine, and the men were even finer. *Damn, Dallas is the place to be.*

"Greg, I'll be right back, baby."

"Where you going?"

"I have to pee, baby. I'll be right back."

"You want to use the one in my office?"

"No, I want to use the one the rest of the ladies use. I mean, if that's okay with you?"

"I guess, with your fine ass."

I shook my head and smiled at him.

He moved his lips and said, "I love you."

I returned the lip service. "I love you, too."

He winked, and I walked off, commanding the attention of all the men that were surrounding the bar and tables nearby.

This club is unbelievable. I knew I was going to get better than Rashad. I just had no idea this was what I was suppose to have. This bathroom is some L.A. set up, just to pee. Nice, Greg.

"Get the fuck out of here now."

I was in the stall and had no idea what was going on.

"Bitch, did you hear me? Get the fuck out and take your fake-ass friend with you. If there are any other fake-ass bitches in here that don't want to die, you better get out of here, too."

I thought it was a bad joke or that I was being Punk'd for sure. Before coming out the stall, I got my composure together and sent Greg a text message.

But I know that voice. I came out, and sure enough, it was the girl from the hotel.

"Yeah, bitch, come on out."

I looked at her, as she stood there in a nice dress, nice shoes, cute bag, and a fucking gun in her hand. I looked at her in confusion.

"What the fuck is your problem?"

"You. You're my problem."

"I don't even know you. So why in the fuck are you in here waving a gun at me?"

"You don't know me, and Greg don't remember me. I bet if I shoot yo' ass, he'll remember me then."

"Look, I don't know what kind of relationship you and Greg had, but it's over. He's moved on, and maybe you should try that."

"Don't you dare try and give me advice on Greg."

While not really listening to her, I started to wonder what the hell was taking Greg so long since I had texted him before I walked out of the stall.

"Tell me what you think you've done that was so good that he forget about me?"

"Look, I don't know where you and Greg's relationship went wrong, but it had to be before he and I got together."

A few women came into the bathroom, and she immediately turned the gun on them.

"Get the fuck out of here!"

Screams erupted as they pushed their way back out of the bathroom.

"Do you think it's because you're tall? Because you have a nice ass and tits? Or maybe because he thinks your pussy is so good he just don't want anybody else's?"

"Maybe it's because I'm not a psycho holding people at gunpoint because a man doesn't want to be with me. Did you and Greg even date, or was it your imagination?"

She walked right up to my face with that gun pointed directly at me. "Don't get smart, bitch. I'll blow your fucking brains all over this fucking bathroom."

I just looked at her and took a deep breath, refusing to shed one tear.

Greg's voice finally rang out in the bathroom. "Natalie, what the fuck are you doing?"

"Oh, nigga, now you know who I am?"

I started yelling at Greg as soon as I could get words to

255

speak. "Greg, I don't know what you did to her, but she's holding me at gunpoint in this fucking bathroom."

"Calm down, baby. I'm sorry."

She turned the gun on him. "You need to apologize to me."

"For what? I didn't do a damn thing to you."

"You lied, and I hate liars."

"What the fuck did I lie about? I didn't even remember your damn name, so how in the fuck am I supposed to remember anything about you? You're in here with my fucking lady at gunpoint. For what?"

"You said I was pretty. You said you'd like to get to know me better, and you said you would call me."

I looked at the crazy bitch and shouted, "You got me in here on some dream of being with Greg? Because he gave you the 'I'ma call you' line? Are you fucking kidding me?"

"Shut up, bitch!"

Just then, a police officer entered the bathroom. "Ma'am, I need you to lower that gun and put your hands in the air."

"Oh really?" She grabbed me and put the gun to my throat. "How about you lower your fucking gun or I'll shoot her ass, then him, then you."

"Ma'am, please don't make me shoot you."

Greg started to walk towards us as tears began rolling down my face.

"Don't cry, baby. I'm not going to let anything happen to you. We didn't come here for that. Natalie, what do you want?"

"Everything you promised."

"I didn't promise you shit."

The officer moved closer. "Ma'am, you get one more chance to drop the gun."

She pointed the gun and shot him in the leg. "Shut up! Now

throw me your gun and handcuffs. Then slide your ass out the door and tell anyone that if they come back in here, I will kill everyone in this fucking room. Now, get the fuck out!"

The officer looked at me and slid out the door, leaving a trail of blood. I just shook my head and looked at Greg, thinking this was the end for both of us.

"Now, Ms. Pretty Bitch...Ms. I Got Greg Hamilton, get your ass over there and sit in that chair in the corner."

I looked at her, and while wiping my eyes, I told her, "You know they're going to kill you, right? You just shot a police officer."

"Oh well. When you fuck with a person's head, that's what you get. Now, back to you, Greg. Go on. Tell me I'm pretty again like you did the first night we met."

"Fuck you. Crazy bitch got me in here on some bullshit. No matter what I fucking said to you, I didn't want your ass then, and I don't want you now. Why you think I didn't call?"

"Greg!" I called out to him. "Just tell her. I don't care. Tell her."

He looked at me, but didn't have a bit of fear in his eyes. I could hear the people clearing out of the club. I could hear the walkie-talkies of the cops who were gathering outside the door.

"Hello." She snapped her fingers for Greg to talk. "I have plenty of bullets in this gun. I'm waiting."

"Natalie...you're pretty."

"You can do better than that. Come on."

"Natalie, you're very pretty."

"And?"

"And I'ma call you so we can hang out or something."

"Maybe we should fuck right now since that's probably all you wanted anyway. Mr. Club Owner who thinks he can just

257

talk that talk, and women fall to their knees for you."

"I'm not fucking you. I didn't want to fuck you then. Bitch, I pass up plenty of pussy. That ain't what my life is about no fucking way. I don't know where you got that shit from, but I don't just fuck anybody."

She turned the gun back to me. "But you'll fuck this bitch, huh?"

"She's about to be my fucking wife."

I closed my eyes because I knew that didn't do anything but infuriate her.

"Oh, you gonna marry this bitch?" she yelled.

She pulled the trigger, and the shot rang out. I couldn't feel any change in my body, but I was afraid to open my eyes to see Greg.

"Answer me, motherfucker!"

"Yes, I'm going to marry her."

When I opened my eyes, he was still standing there. No blood; he was still there. I looked at Natalie,

"Natalie, please don't do this. Okay, Greg may have led you on a little bit, but now you're going to go to prison and for a long time if you hurt either one of us. I mean, you already shot a cop. Don't make this situation worse. Please."

"You know what? Since he's going to marry you, he might as well have one more night of fun, right? Pull your dick out."

"Fuck you."

"I was thinking the same thing. Now, pull it out."

All I could think was, *This bitch is crazy.*

"If you think I'm going to fuck you in front of Wendy, you might as well fucking shoot me. I will not disrespect her to give your sick ass any satisfaction."

Just then, a voice called out from the other side of the door.

"Natalie Hayes, this is Charles Barrel. May I come in?"

She shot the gun in the air. "Does that answer your fucking question? Stay the fuck out of here or they both die tonight."

"Just tell me that Mr. Hamilton and Ms. Brooks are okay."

Greg shouted to the officer, "We're fine. All of us are fine. Just please don't come in here. Natalie, listen to me. I apologize, okay? I apologize for leading you to believe that I wanted to be in any kind of relationship with you or however you took it. That's my bad. Wendy doesn't have anything to do with this. I mean, you want me? That's fine. Just let her leave. Then you and I can sit and talk about how to get you out of this mess."

"You think I'm stupid, don't you?"

"Hell no. In fact, you have to be smart as hell to get a gun past my security. I'm pretty pissed about that. So, I know you have to be very intelligent."

She gazed into his eyes as if he gave her a great compliment. "I do love you, Greg."

"Natalie, no you don't, because if you did, we wouldn't be in here like this. You wouldn't have that gun, and my girl wouldn't be over there thinking about how she's going to dump me when we get out of here."

"Well, she can leave. I just want you anyway."

"I'm not leaving. So, if you want him, you might as well be ready to have me, too."

"Get out!" She turned the gun on me. "Get out if you want to live to see another day!" she screamed. "Get your ass out right now. And you tell that officer if he comes in here before I'm done with Greg, he'll take him out in a body bag."

"Greg, I'm not leaving you."

She shot the gun in the air again, causing shit to start falling from the ceiling.

"Get the fuck out of here!" she screamed at me again.

Greg pulled me to him and kissed me. "I'll be out there in a minute," he said, then pushed me towards the door. "Go, Wendy, please, and tell the officer what she said. Tell him please don't come in."

With tears running down my face, I told him I loved him and walked out.

As soon as I exited the restroom, I walked over to the officer that tried to come in the second time.

"Are you going to get him out alive? I need him out alive."

"Ms. Brooks, we plan on getting him out alive, but this woman is very unstable and unpredictable."

After what seemed like hours, I heard commotion behind me. Greg was walking out with no pants on and his hands cuffed behind his back. I pushed my way through the crowd as they took off the handcuffs that Natalie had put on him.

"Baby, are you okay?"

"Wendy, I'm sorry. I'm so sorry."

"Shhh. Are you okay, Greg?"

Seconds later, they escorted Natalie out in handcuffs.

"I'm pregnant now with your baby, Greg, and when I get out, we can be a family," the disillusion bitch shouted.

Before I knew it, I grabbed a beer bottle off the table and hit her across the face. I started kicking and stomping on her with my stiletto pumps, causing blood to splatter everywhere. Quickly, the officers grabbed me and wrestled me to the ground.

"Get the fuck off her," I heard Greg yell. "Move!""

He grabbed me and took me to the other side of the club. That's when I saw Walter running towards us. Walter grabbed me and took me upstairs, while Greg tried to put on the pants Walter handed off to him. A police officer walked up to Greg, they exchanged words and a handshake, and then he ran up behind me and Walter.

"Baby, are you okay?"

All I could do was hug him and cry.

"Shhh, it's okay, baby. I'm right here."

"Greg, did you fuck her?"

"Baby, we don't have to talk about this right now."

"Just answer me. Did you fuck her? You came out with no pants on, so I don't know. Just tell me. Did you fuck her?"

"Baby, you've been through enough tonight. Let's just go back to the hotel, shower, get something to eat, and try to forget this night."

My tone changed and I began to yell. "Greg, I'm only going to ask you one more time."

The same officer that Greg shook hands with came into his office.

"Greg, can you come here for a second, please? We need to get a statement from you, and you, too, Walter. Ms. Wendy, as soon as they return, you all can go."

I looked at Greg. "Tell me."

"I'll be right back," he told me, then they all headed out.

I guess he forgot he showed me everything about this club, security and all. I immediately pulled up the bathroom cameras.

"I know it's here," I said to myself, as I proceeded to press the rewind, play, and fast forward buttons until I found what I was looking for.

There it was on the screen. *She was holding the gun to his head while handcuffing him to the chair. Oh my God, this bitch is sucking his dick. And he was hard. Fuck, Greg. Oh my God.*

Then I heard Greg's voice behind me. "Wendy, I didn't have a choice. She had a gun to my head."

I hadn't even heard him come back in the door.

"All you had to do was tell me."

"I couldn't."

"Why?"

"Because!" he yelled. "Because I came, Wendy. She handcuffed me to a chair, fucked me at gunpoint in my club, and I had a fucking orgasm. I didn't know how not to cum. I tried to hold it; I tried to focus on something else so I wouldn't, but I did." He dropped to his knees and began to cry. "If I could have killed her right there in that bathroom, I would have. But, all I could do was pray that you wouldn't leave me if you found out."

"If I found out? You weren't going to tell me?"

"Wendy, how do you tell the woman you want to spend the rest of your life with that a woman fucked you at gunpoint and you had a fucking orgasm? That's sick. I was too scared to try and fight back because I didn't want to die, so what did I do? I came for the crazy bitch."

"Greg, I love you. I didn't give a fuck what you had to do to get out of that bathroom alive. I just wanted you out. But, the thought that you weren't going to tell me hurts me."

He approached me. "I wanted to die in there because I knew you would leave me if you knew the truth."

"That bitch was crazy, Greg, okay? I could have died tonight, too, and I wasn't worthy enough to know the truth? I know you didn't want to fuck her, but to flat out be ready to lie to me about it should have never been an option."

"I was ashamed, Wendy. What the fuck! I couldn't protect me or you. How am I supposed to feel about that? I'm a man. A grown fucking man that was raped in his own club by some psycho bitch with a gun. There's your fucking truth. Fuck that. Fuck all this shit."

He started throwing stuff and tearing up his office. When I tried to grab him, he pushed me on the ground and kept tearing up the office. That's when Walter came in.

"Greg!" He stopped in his tracks. "Stop! Let's go. Let's just go."

Greg walked right past me on the floor. I dropped my head. When I looked up, an outstretched hand waited to help me up off the floor.

"It's gonna be alright, Ms. Wendy. Trust me. It's gonna be alright."

*****

When we pulled up to the hotel, they were waiting at the door with our bags.

"What's going on, Greg? Why is our stuff outside?"

"Walter moved us from this hotel since this is where Natalie came first. He didn't want anybody bothering us. He got us a room downtown. Is that okay?"

"As long as I'm with you, I don't care where we stay."

He slid over just a little bit and laid his head in my lap.

"I'm sorry, Wendy. I'm so sorry."

I rubbed his head with my tears streaming again.

"Me, too. I'm sorry, too."

After we checked into the magnificent hotel, I went straight to the bathroom. I came out and reached for his hand.

"Come on, baby. I started the shower for you."

"I just want to be alone for a few minutes, if that's okay."

"So you want to shower alone?"

"If you don't mind."

"Go ahead, baby. Take all the time you need, Greg. I'll be right here. I'm not going anywhere."

I went to the window and looked out at the beautiful view, when my cell phone beeped with a text message from Deacon Fredricks for me to call him.

"Hey, Deacon Fredricks, is everything okay?"

"Yes. I just wanted to check on you. I had a horrible feeling in my stomach, and you're the only one I know who trouble seems to chase down. Are you okay?"

I smiled in pleasure. The Lord had one of his angels checking on me. *Here I am trying to be strong for Greg, and the Lord sends one of his soldiers to be strong for me.*

"I'm fine now. Greg and I—"

"Greg? Who is Greg? Is he the reason I have only seen you at church one time in the last couple of weeks?"

"I have a new position at work. I'm out of town three weeks at a time, and then the fourth week, I'm in town. So, that's when I come to church."

"Too busy for God? Wow!"

"It's not like that, Deacon Fredricks. And I have been praying on a regular, thank you. So I get my time in with God, especially when I have been a bad girl."

"Good. So how have you been dealing with the other thing?"

"What other thing?"

"Wendy, you know exactly what I'm talking about. Have you had any episodes since we talked about it last?"

"Deacon Fredricks, I can handle my life. I have so much going on that I don't have time to fantasize about anyone or anything. And my man gives it to me on a regular, fulfilling all my dreams. So, like I said, I'm fine."

"Will you see me when you get back then?"

"For what? What part did you misunderstand? I am fine."

"Then coming to see me in my office should be a piece of cake. I just want to do a follow-up visit with you."

"I'm sorry. I don't recall the first visit for you to encourage this follow-up, but if it will get you off my back before I leave town again, I'll stop by."

"Leave town? Where are you headed now?"

"Deacon Fredricks, look, I have to go. I'll try to stop by before heading to Washington, but I won't make any promises."

"That's all I ask. You think you are okay, but busying yourself doesn't take away what is buried inside of you. So, please make every effort to get to my office before you leave."

"Goodnight, Deacon Fredricks, and...thanks for checking on me."

"You stay on my mind, Wendy."

There was a silence on the phone, as if both of us were waiting to see what the other would say next. So, before putting my foot in my mouth, I just hang up. Greg was still in the shower, and I had begun to worry about him.

"Greg? You okay, baby?" I asked after knocking on the door.

"Yeah, I'll be out in a few. You okay?"

"I'm fine. Just missing you out here."

"I'll be out in a sec."

I leaned on the door to listen and see if he was on the phone, but I didn't hear him saying anything. So, I went and sat on the bed. I picked up my phone and sent Deacon Fredricks a text message back.

Thanks again. Didn't know how much you really cared. Sorry for being a butthead; it's just been a long day. After composing the message, I pressed the Send button.

The longer I waited on Greg, the sleepier I got. I closed my eyes with Deacon Fredricks' kind, caring voice in my head. I opened them, quick. For some reason, I didn't want to fall asleep with thoughts of him on my mind, as this would lead to something terrible with Greg in the other room.

My mind took me to thoughts of his lips, his arms holding me, his scent, and the way he walked. The entire night was on one side of my head, and he was growing stronger on the other. As I thought about all the other times I've had him in my head, my body grew weak. My eyes closed again, and my body began to tingle on the inside.

I jumped up out of the bed and tried to walk it off. While sitting in the chair by the window, I tried to let the view calm my body down, but it only made me think of romance, lovemaking, and passionate screams of pleasure. Unconsciously leaning back in the chair, I saw Deacon Fredricks' face walking towards me in the window. I turned around and asked him what he was doing there. He put his finger over my lips to silence me, then ran that same finger into my mouth for me to taste. I looked him in the eyes and stroked it back and forth like I would do his dick had it been in my mouth.

He let out the biggest sigh of pleasure, which turned me on even more. I reached for his pants, and his dick had already taken the position for the night. I wanted to put it in my mouth, and as I went down to do so, he grabbed my face and kissed me with so much passion that my body got weaker. He picked me up and put me on the desk. Then he sat in the chair in front of me. He reached around and slid his hand down my spine, and I arched by back in pleasure. This gave a direct path for his face to taste my pussy. I put my head against the wall and let him have his way with my body.

"Yeah, baby! I missed you so much."

He came up and silenced me with a kiss, and I could taste my pussy juices all over his mouth as expected. Just as I was catching my breath from his mouth consuming mine, he pushed his dick inside me, taking my breath away again. I don't know if he filled Mrs. Pam's pussy up, but his dick inside of me fit like a hand in a glove, and I loved every inch of it.

"Right there, baby. I've been waiting for you to fuck me like this again. Right there."

I heard him call my name right in my ear.

"Wendy?"

"Yes, baby?"

"You like it?"

"I love it, baby. Give it to me. Right there."

He had my body pulled so close to his that I could almost count the beats of his heart. He was grinding and moving like any young boy fresh in some new pussy, but he was every bit of forty-nine years old. His pace picked up, and his strokes became longer and more direct. If he were aiming for my g-spot, he was hitting it, and I was going to cum all over his dick within minutes if he kept that up. In one instant, he turned my body around and bent me over the desk. The same dick that slowly stroked my pussy seconds ago began to aggressively thrust inside of me.

He grabbed my hair unexpectedly and began pulling it with force. I could feel him breathing on the back of my neck.

"Is this the dick you've been wanting?"

"It is. I wanted it so bad."

"I missed you, Wendy. This pussy is so good to me. I want it all the time. Tell me I can have it all the time. Tell me."

"You can have it. You can have it whenever you want it. Just fuck me. Fuck me, please."

I must have been really giving it to him, because his voice changed. It was deeper and much more passionate than when he first spoke to me.

"I'm sorry, Wendy."

I turned around and silenced him with kisses.

"Open your eyes, baby, so you can see me. I love you, and I'm so sorry."

I wanted to open my eyes, but instead, I just reached down, grabbed his dick, and shoved it right back inside of me as he let out a sigh.

"What are you sorry for?" I asked. "Fucking me this good is nothing to apologize for."

"But do you forgive me?"

"Yes, Mark, I forgive you."

"Mark? Who the fuck is Mark?"

I immediately opened my eyes to see Greg standing in front of me with a very confused look on his face.

"Who the fuck is Mark?"

I backed away from him and sat down on the bed.

"Answer me, Wendy. Are you cheating on me with a man named Mark?"

"No, not really."

"What the fuck does not really mean? Here we are making love, and you call me another man's name, and you're 'not really' cheating on me. Tell me what the fuck is going on before somebody gets hurt, Wendy."

"I'm sorry, Greg."

His voice got louder. "Who the fuck is Mark?" He got closer to me, and the look in his eyes demanded for me to answer him and answer him now.

"Mark is a deacon at my church."

"You're fucking a deacon at your church?"

"No. I'm not really fucking him."

"You tell me right now what the fuck is going on, or I'm walking out of this door and never looking back. What the fuck, Wendy? I love you, and the best you can do is fuck another man? A fucking deacon?" He started pacing the floor like he was about to explode in an uncontrollable rage.

"If you'll just let me explain, Greg. Please, just let me explain it to you." I reached out my hand to get him to sit down beside me. "If you love me like you say, you'll let me tell you what is going on with me. Just give me that, and then you can decide what you want to do next."

He grabbed two towels out of the bathroom, handed me one, and then sat down beside me. I took his hand, and he wiped his eyes.

"Greg, I do love you. And no, I have not slept with any other man or woman physically since we became official, but mentally, I cheat on you all the time. It's not that you don't satisfy me either. But, if I close my eyes with a particular person or thought in my head, I will fantasize about them or it, which results in one or numerous orgasms. I do it in public sometimes, in the shower, at work, in my car, wherever. It just happens. Tonight, you caught me in the middle of sleeping with a deacon from the church who is a psychiatrist and has been trying to help me with this. He seems to think if I saw him on a regular, he can teach me how to control this thing in my head."

"Is that what happened to you that night I met you, when you came back to my office?"

"Yes. And the day I was at your house after we left the

video store, and the day on your floor in your office at the house. It used to happen all the time, but then when we started dating, it slowed up, but it didn't completely stop. Tonight, Deacon Fredricks called to check on me, and it just stayed in my head. I closed my eyes while waiting on you to come out of the bathroom, and he showed up in my head. I could feel him, and I really don't know when you slipped in, but in my head, I thought I was sleeping with him."

"Did this happen when you were with Rashad?"

"It started right at the end of our relationship. I hadn't slept with him for like three months before we broke up. So, I don't know if I used it to take the place of the sex I wanted, but it has been happening since then. I have slept with men, women, men and women at the same time; all in my mind. But, I will have very strong orgasms that excite me. I feel bad sometimes because I can't control it once it starts, but the sex is so good during that time that I forget about not being able to control it. Does that make sense?"

"So let me get this straight. I satisfy you, but you also have thoughts in your head that you can't control, where you sleep with men and women for sexual pleasures, too? You have wet dreams all day, every day?"

"Some days I don't because you and I have been together, and I'm fine."

"So, I'll never be able to fully satisfy you? You'll always have the desire for someone else?"

"No, you always satisfy me. I'm not out there having physical sex with these people; it's just mental. People fantasize all the time. I've never acted on any of my thoughts since we've been together."

"So, if we stay together, I will always have to compete with the person in your head that you're fucking on any given day?"

"No, no, you won't, because I want to get some help. I want to be better. I hate that it came out like it did tonight. But, I have been dealing with this since before we got together, and I have never made this mistake of calling out someone else's name."

"Would you have ever told me? Or would you just have continued to be an unfaithful bitch?"

"Bitch? So we are name calling now? I open up to tell you about something that has been tearing me apart, and the best you can do to show me you care is call me a bitch? Fuck you! I could be some of the crazy whores you've dealt with in the past, fucking your friends and taking your money and shit, but I've never. I may be a lot of things, but a bitch I'm not. I have a problem, okay? I don't know why or how I got it, but I slipped and let you into my fucked up head. I wanted to tell you. However, I just couldn't bring myself to say I sleep with you and tons of other people in my head. So don't you dare go judging me. I could be doing worst things."

"I'm sorry. I'm sorry for calling you a bitch, but, baby, can you imagine how I feel right now? I'm making love to my woman, and I get called another man's name. How is that supposed to go? Any other man would have killed you and left you here in this room for room service to find you."

"Greg, I have fantasized about you like this, too, and I have never cheated on you physically since we became a monogamous couple. I will see a doctor when we get back home. You can come with me so you can try and understand what's going on."

"So, for right now, when we're intimate with one another, I'll always have to wonder if you're with me or if you're thinking I am someone else."

"No, baby, every time I have been with you, I've been with just you. This normally happens if something triggers me mentally. I don't want this to ruin anything we have. So, whatever it takes for me to get better, that's what I'm going to do, but only if you promise to do it with me. Will you? Will you go with me?"

"Only if you promise to tell me EVERY TIME you have an episode and who it was with, where, why you think it happened, and what you were feeling right before it was brought on. I want all the details."

I laughed. "Okay, but it might turn you on to know half the shit that goes through my mind when this thing takes over, but I promise."

"Answer this question for me."

"Anything."

"Is the deacon better than me in your dreams?"

"Hell no, but he is good. He's older, and for an older man, he's nice. However, you throw down in this pussy, baby."

"Go get in the shower and wash his lust off your body. As a matter of fact, I'm going to wash him off for you. Purify your thoughts so I can finish what I *thought* I started."

I jumped up like a kid getting ready for a bubble bath. "Thank you, Greg. Thank you for understanding. I knew you were a Godsend, but I just didn't know to what extent."

"Baby, we were held at gunpoint tonight, I fucked a psycho with a gun to my head, and I interrupted you fucking a deacon in your head. Hell, I might need to see someone, too."

We shared a hug, laugh and a kiss to seal our reality of what had us in the moment, and yeah, that shower I was supposed to get…I never made it past the desk. This time, we both knew EXACTLY who I was fucking, because he was taking my body places it hadn't been before. He made me say his name over and over again with every strong stroke, and I loved every minute of it.

Sorry about that, Deacon Fredricks, but my man takes precedent tonight.

Chapter Nineteen
Where Do We Go From Here?

Things had been going great for Greg and me since we made it back in town. We decided to let what happened in Dallas stay in Dallas. The hotel was coming along great, and my first trip out of town for three weeks was not so bad. Mind you, the staff I was working with looked like little creatures from Mars, but nonetheless, I gave them the training needed to get their revenue department back in the race for next quarter's numbers.

Jessica moved out of my place, and we were working on mending our relationship, which wasn't easy. Still, I loved that girl. Rashad's ass was still a mess, though. I had seen him leaving Chrissy's house when I went to my house to put the "For Sale" sign up. I just laughed to myself and said, "What the hell ever." If that's the best he could do, so be it.

Momma was doing well with her chemo. She only had three more treatments left, which made my being out of town less stressful.

By now, you know Greg got me to sell my house. I was torn between leaving that sign up and taking it down. I loved my little house. There were some good memories and some bad, but it was MY house.

My hot little señorita had been still begging for more pussy from me, but I hadn't been in the mood. So, I smiled, flirted, and kept it moving.

It was the day of my appointment with Deacon Fredricks; I had missed the appointment we had originally scheduled before I went to Washington. I planned on asking him for a referral to see another doctor before Greg came with me to my future appointments. I just felt it would be more comfortable for everyone.

I thought about having a drink to relax before I went to my appointment, but then thought, *Hell, it's Deacon Fredricks. You've seen his dick for crying out loud. Why are you nervous?*

"Hi, I'm Wendy Brooks. I have a four o'clock with Dr. Fredricks."

"Hi, Ms. Brooks. Give me one second to get your paperwork together for you."

"Thank you."

Deacon Dr. comes from the back escorting a very beautiful young lady out. She hugged him and expressed her gratitude with a very big smile. She nodded and looked me up and down as if I were in competition with her.

I wanted to tell her, *Chile, please. If I wanted him, I could have him.* Instead, I picked up my purse and walked off like I had fucked him minutes before and the pussy she tasted on his lips belonged to me.

His admin stood to her feet. "Dr. Fredricks, my son's daycare called. He's not feeling well. They tried to let him finish the day, but now, he's thrown up. I have to go and pick him up now."

"No problem. Can you lock the door for me? I think Wendy is my last patient today anyway."

"She is, and I have pulled all the patient charts for

tomorrow."

"You are a jewel. See you in the morning, and I hope little man gets to feeling better."

I followed him to the back, but to a different room this time. When I turned around, he was right in my face.

"Can I have a hug, please?"

I hugged him, but for some reason, I didn't want to let him go.

"Wendy, just tell me you are okay?"

I pulled back and looked at him. "I'm okay with the exception of the fact I was having sex with Greg and called him your name. Look, I can't see you as my doctor. I need a referral because he wants to come to these appointments with me, and I can't bring him here."

"What? Wait. You called him my name while you were having sex? How?"

I turned to walk away, but he grabbed my hand. "What happened?"

"Remember when you called that night to check on me, when you said you had that feeling in your stomach that something was wrong? Well, Greg and I had a very bad night, and when you called, he was in the shower. When we got off the phone, I checked on him, and then I sat on the bed to wait on him. But, thoughts of you took over my mind. I tried not to close my eyes, but I did. And…"

"And what?"

I could feel my heartbeat change; it began beating faster with the thoughts of that night coming back to me. I went to sit down on the couch, and he sat beside me.

"Go on, Wendy."

"You appeared in the window. You kissed me so gently. I

tried to ask you what you were doing there, but you wouldn't let me talk. You put me on the desk in the room, and you tasted my pussy like you had done so many times before in my mind. You kissed me and then put your dick inside of me slowly, and all I could do was let out a passionate moan to let you know it was good."

"What else happened?"

"You fucked me. You fucked me so good. I don't know when Greg came in the room and took over my body. I mean, your voice changed, but the questions you and Greg were asking in pleasure began to run together, and the sex took me to another level. He asked me something, and when I answered, I called him Mark. I thought he was going to kill me. But, I made him think back to the other times it happened in the past and he was there. We talked about it. I reassured him that I had not cheated on him and had no intention to do so. I told him it was all mental for me. He asked me how he was supposed to compete with that."

"Did you tell him he doesn't have to? You only want those people for that moment. You love him before, during, and even after the orgasm. So, he really has nothing to worry about."

"Try telling that to a man who has just heard his woman call them another man's name. I just don't remember ever calling names before. I don't know what happened that night to let me get comfortable enough to call your name."

"Maybe you really wanted me to be there. You know, fucking you. So much so that you said what you really felt."

"But, Deacon Fredricks, I don't want you past the lust when I see you or hear from you. You're a great man. You love your wife and represent what a Christian man should be. This is not worth losing my man, your wife, your position in the church, nothing."

"Was I good that night?"

"Are you staying focused as a doctor, or are you turning into a man?"

I was scared to hear his answer, but I wanted to know. I wanted to know if he could separate the two. I wanted him to stay my doctor, because anything other than that would have led to us fulfilling my fantasies right then and there.

"Was I good that night?"

"You're good every time I'm with you. And that's why I need not come back here again. I'm probably going to be looking for a new church to attend, as well. You're my biggest temptation. I cannot and will not jeopardize your life or destroy mine, because right now, it is going so well. I love Greg. He wants to marry me, and I'm trying to let go of my fears so I can tell him yes and be his wife. That's why I am going to fix this thing in my head so I don't lose what I know has been sent to me by God. I have to–"

"Kiss me."

He leaned in and kissed me.

"What are you doing? No. Please don't do this to me."

He leaned in and kissed me again. This time, I received his kiss with an open mouth. His tongue slid in my mouth enough to touch mine. I could feel my body changing, and by changing, I mean my pussy had begun to throb with anticipation.

"Deacon Fredricks, please stay my doctor. I need you to be my doctor right now."

"I want to be whatever you need me to be. Let me be that person. Let me be the man you've dreamed about. Let me be myself with you right now."

"Deacon Fredricks, I love Greg. You love Mrs. Pam. You

are a deacon at our church. You are a professional, and right now, I feel like you're taking advantage of me."

With every word I said, he kissed me in a different place on my body. *This is real. This is not a dream. He is here in living color, and he's doing things I have dreamed about on several occasions.*

"Mark–"

"That's better. Let me make love to you, Wendy. We both want this; we have for months. We both don't want to hurt the people we love, but we will never have this chance again, especially if I give you that referral to another doctor. Let me make it real for you."

Before I could answer, he had pushed my dress up to my thighs and his face was buried in my pussy. His mouth was just like I remembered. This time, he made it his business to let me know he was really there. He put my legs over his shoulders, pulled my body closer to the end of the couch, and pressed his tongue directly on my clit.

My phone began to ring. When I reached for it, he shoved my entire purse down the couch until it hit the floor. I grabbed his head because he was making my pussy jerk with pleasure. *I don't remember this part of my dream.*

"Mark, please stop. I don't want to hurt anyone. Please, just let me go."

He came up and kissed me. I knew that taste. He stood up, and his dick was out of his pants. It was just as I remembered. He took my head and pulled it to receive his dick in my mouth.

I don't think I resisted, not even for a second. The thought never crossed my mind not to suck his dick like I imagined I had. He leaned back and gave moans like he hadn't been orally satisfied in years. His dick was chocolate, hard, and big, and I

280

gave him some of my best head. Yes, that shit that used to make Rashad leave money for me the next day.

"Wendy, stop, please. I don't want to cum now. I want to feel your pussy. Please stop."

I gave it one more good stroke, and he dropped to his knees and pulled me back to the end of the couch. While looking me in the face, he put that same chocolate, hard, big dick inside of me, and oh my goodness! That was EXACTLY what I remembered. I gasped for air because it was real this time.

His office phone rang, but he was so deep inside me that he never even looked over at his desk in concern, until he heard Mrs. Pam's voice.

"Hey, baby, I'm pulling around back because the front door was locked. I brought your shirts from the cleaners for your office. Your car is here, but I guess you've run off to be with your young mistress. I love you. See you when she drops you off." She laughed as she hung up.

He never took his mind off me. He kept fucking me as if nothing was going to keep him from cumming or making me cum. As he began rubbing his finger across my clit, I felt it coming on. I couldn't let out any signs that I was going to cum all over his dick because I had no idea where Mrs. Fredricks was in the building. He kept pushing his dick inside of me.

I heard the back door close. He fucked me harder and harder. He put his finger over his lips as if to tell me to be very quiet, but his dick was doing things on the inside of my pussy that I just couldn't keep to myself. I opened my mouth, but nothing would come out. He pointed down for me to look at the cum from my pussy that covered his dick. Then he kept fucking me, while putting his finger back over his mouth.

Mrs. Pam's voice rang out in the hallway. "Mark? Baby,

you here?"

He reached in his pants to turn his cell phone to vibrate, and as he took his finger off the button, he showed the phone to me where she was calling him. He put his finger back to his mouth. A tear ran down the side of my face. He wiped it away with his finger, stuck it in his mouth, and then in mine. My pussy came instantly, and I squeezed his dick with intent to make him scream.

His entire facial expression changed, and his body buckled. I could hear Mrs. Pam walking the halls and turning all the doorknobs. He looked up at me, put my right titty in his mouth, and pushed deeper inside of me. I gasped for air, and he shook his head, as if to tell me I don't get to even breathe. I just had to take his dick.

She turned the knob to the room we were in. "Hmm, he must be gone. I wonder who he is with. Dangit. I forgot I'm supposed to take Ms. Shirley to the store."

We heard her heels hurrying out the door. She locked the door, and when I heard her car alarm disarm, I began throwing my pussy on his ass like I needed my mortgage paid. He finally released all the words he had been holding.

"Fuck, Wendy. What the fuck are you doing?"

I didn't say a word. I just squeezed his dick again.

"Shit. Damnit. Stop that, please."

I kept throwing my pussy, and this time, I did a fucking hip twist and squeeze. I slid his dick out to the tip and then shoved my pussy all the way down on it.

"Fuck." He pulled out fast as cum shot everywhere. He stroked his dick maybe three times and looked up at me with the remaining cum in his hand.

"You fucked me against my will. My mouth said no. I don't

give a fuck what my body said. I should press charges and have you arrested, but the punishment of you not getting this pussy ever again is punishment enough."

I got up, grabbed my purse, and walked to the door. I wanted to turn around and look back at him, but I wouldn't have been a bad bitch if I did. I just shook my head and walked out. I got in the car, dug my phone out, and made one phone call.

"Greg Hamilton?"

"Hey, baby. How was your day?"

"Will you marry me?"

"What?"

"I said, will you marry me?"

"What's wrong, baby?"

"Is that a yes or a no?"

"Wendy, you know I want to marry you, but what's wrong?"

"I'll see you at the house then. I'm going to see Momma, and then I'm coming home to see you."

"Okay, but are you okay?"

"Yes, I'm in love. I'm in love with you, and I want to be your wife."

"Okay. I'll see you at the house. I-I love you, Wendy."

"I love you, too, baby."

I pulled off with a feeling of completion, but what I almost didn't see was Mrs. Fredricks pulling up to the front of the building, until I checked my hair in my rearview mirror.

When I arrived at Momma's, I wanted to call Deacon Fredricks to see if everything was okay, but I was done with him. I had my mind made up; new church, new start, and a new life. Greg Hamilton it is. *Is that your final answer? Yes!*

"Ma? Momma?"

"I'm upstairs, baby."

I run upstairs full of energy and with a smirk on my face when I hit the door.

"Well, why are you so happy?"

"How you feeling, Momma?"

"Why you smiling like that, Wendy?"

"I asked you a question first."

"I'm fine. Now what's up?"

"I'm getting married. I'm going to marry Greg and be Mrs. Wendy Hamilton."

She jumped up and hugged me. Then, she started screaming loudly.

"Ma, calm down."

"Baby, you're in love, and that's something to scream about. Oh my goodness! Wait until I tell Ethel. I *am* going to have some grandbabies. Thank you, Lord."

"Ma, wait. It will be a while before you get grandchildren. Plus, you just finished treatment. You need to take it easy."

"I can look at dresses with you sitting down. I can call florist and churches and look at invitations all sitting down. I'll be taking it easy while helping you plan the perfect day."

She hugged me again, and this time, I didn't let her go.

"I'm scared, Momma. I have this thing that I'm dealing with, and sometimes it controls me."

She tried to pull away to look at me, but I didn't let her.

"What thing, baby? Are you on drugs?"

"No, ma'am. It feels like it sometimes, though."

"Well, what is it? What is it, baby? Why are you shaking? Talk to me, Wendy."

"In my head sometimes…I-I see people. Then I think about them sexually, and if I close my eyes in the thought, I have sex with them. The bad part is I touch myself, make noises of pleasure, have an orgasm right where I am, and don't snap out of it until someone makes me open my eyes. I want to get help for it before I marry Greg so he won't leave me because he thinks I desire other people."

"You told him?"

"Yes, ma'am, but only after I called him another man's name during sex with him."

"Oh no, baby. Are you okay?"

She slowly pulled away to look me in the eyes and wiped my tears away.

"It's okay, baby. None of us are perfect, and you're going to be an awesome wife. You'll get through this because you want to be better. Some people are content with staying in their mess. Greg loves you. He loves you, flaws and all."

"He told me that."

"All you need to do is find one of them sex therapist. I hear they have them all over now. And I'll be praying for you and Greg. Don't let this keep you from being happy, and don't keep any secrets from Greg. He's not going anywhere."

"He told me that, too."

"Do you believe him?"

"Yes, I do."

"Then you pray, too. You pray that God will deliver you from this, and you pray for patience for Greg."

"I will. I love you, Momma."

"Did Rashad know?"

"No. It actually didn't start until right after we broke up this last time."

"Okay. Well, it doesn't matter. You'll be fine. And you're going to be a beautiful bride."

"Thank you, Momma."

We hugged like life had started over for me again.

*****

"Greg?" I knew he was there. I saw Walter pulling away. I run upstairs and all but tore the door down to his office. And there he was on one knee holding a box.

"Now that I know you're for real, Wendy Brooks, will you marry me?"

I dropped down in front of him. "For better or for worse? For richer or poorer? In sickness and in health? I will. I do. Forever and ever. I will not let my fears keep me from being all I can be in your life. I love you."

"I love you, too, and I know you want help for the issues you're having. I also know Mark Fredricks is a deacon at your church and a psychiatrist on 4th Street, across from the Cancer Center where we took your mother on her first visit. Maybe that's what led to you being so hot and bothered that day you fucked me in the car. I also know you visited him today. What I don't know is what happened there that would push you to accept my invitation to be my wife. So, love me enough to tell me. Did you sleep with him? Did you live your fantasy and now you have the closure needed to move on? Please, just tell me the truth."

My entire facial expression changed. My heartbeat sped up, and I didn't know what to say next.

"Just tell me, baby. I love you. I just need to know. I don't want to go into this marriage with any secrets."

"Are you going to marry me regardless of what I say?"

"I love you. If you tell me that's what you needed to get over this, then I have to live with that."

"So you would just give me a freebie?"

"Some people wouldn't understand my reason for it, but I don't care about people. I care about you. As long as we understand it, that's all that matters. So, tell me."

"I love you, Greg. No, I didn't sleep with Deacon Dr. Fredricks. He gave me a referral for a new doctor. He told me he understood and how happy he was for us, and that he better get an invitation to our wedding. He also said he hopes to see you at church soon. He told me to always honor your request with not hiding these fantasies if and when I have them."

He stood up and hugged me tight. I knew if we started kissing, it would lead to sex, and I had Deacon Fredricks' scent all over my pussy.

"Let's go out and celebrate," I quickly suggested.

"Where?"

"Anywhere. I'm going to shower and put on the sexiest dress that you pick out, because I'm about to introduce myself to this town as the soon-to-be Mrs. Gregory Hamilton."

He kissed me, and in excitement, he ran to my closet. "You said a dress? So, a thong and bra alone are out of the question?"

He looked back at me as I was taking off my shoes, and I smiled.

"Clothes, baby. Pick clothes for the public. You get the thong and bra only when we come back home. And they have a thirty-second maximum to stay on my body upon entry into the house."

"Shit, if you make it out of the car, you'll be lucky."

I ran into the bathroom and turned on the shower. I took off my clothes and looked in the mirror as I was pulling my hair up. Then I said a silent prayer.

"Lord, forgive me for what I have done. If you just keep this buried under a thick rug, I promise never to lie to him again."

"Shit, baby, you scared me."

"Who are you talking to?"

"The Lord."

"What you tell Him? Thank you for this fabulous husband you're about to have?"

"That's exactly what I told Him. And if you get out, I can finish my conversation with Him."

"But what about this dress?"

"Not in the mood for all those straps. Try again."

"Damn. Okay. Hurry up."

He ran out like a kid in a toy store going to check the price on his top pick toy, hoping it was on sale so he could get it.

"Okay, Lord, forgive me for that one, too."

I jumped in the shower, and he jumped in right after I got out. We were dressed and ready for the world.

*****

Oh my goodness, why was the sex so good last night, is the question I asked myself on the way to the airport. I almost touched myself in the back seat with the thought. Walter would surely enjoy that.

He's too sweet. Guess I shouldn't torture him like that. Okay, so I have three weeks away from my fiancé; Momma is dating heavily; and I haven't heard from Deacon Dr., thank God. I'm about to blow Cincinnati away, and when I get back, I have my first appointment with my new doctor. Then I'm off to meet with the wedding planner. Life is good; love is good. And now there's an unknown number on my cell. Who in the world is it?

"Hello?"

"Wendy?"

"Yes, this is Wendy. Who's speaking, please?"

"This is Pam Fredricks."

I swallowed silently, but I knew she could hear the hesitation across the phone lines.

"Hey, Mrs. Pam. How are you?"

"I'll be just fine if you can tell me the pussy scent I found in my husband's underwear two days ago doesn't belong to you."

"Excuse me?"

"I saw you leave his office Friday after I was there. I checked every door, and they were all locked. He's never done that before. I've always been able to walk freely in all of his offices. But, Friday...Friday I was locked out. I left and parked across the street because it didn't make sense. Then, not even ten minutes later, you stroll out. So, I'm going to ask you again before I go up to this church and tear it down. Did you fuck my husband?"

"No. No, ma'am. I mean, I was there, but I had no idea you were there. I did a meditation exercise with headphones, and he took some notes, wrote my referral, and I left. That's it. Mrs. Pam, Deacon Fredricks wouldn't do that to you. Come on now. You know he's a good man."

"Good doesn't mean he's not human. But, if I find out you fucked him or anybody else fucked him, it's on, and I don't play fair. I don't give a fuck about that clinic, that church, or anything else. As much shit as I have put up with being married to him, let me find out. And you know I will. I'm a woman."

"Well, good luck with that, Mrs. Pam. Who would have thought you were a deaconess with a mouth like that? Be blessed."

I hung up before she could say another word. My mind said to call him, but then I thought about what she said about being a woman. So, my second mind said she was sitting right there with him trying to see if I would call him with what she just dished to me.

Walter got my luggage, and I went to board the plane. *As far as I'm concerned, good luck on finding the bitch who fucked him, because I don't know her. If she didn't see me on the dick, then I wasn't there. She will NOT fuck up this lie for me, but I will shoot him a text on what I told her just to be on the safe side.*

*Wow, nice airport, Cincinnati. Damn, look at his ass. What is the correct spelling of Cincinnati again? It's not **Sin**cinnati with an "S", is it? That's too bad. Okay, okay. All work and no play is bullshit! When is that doctor's appointment again? Get it together, Mrs. Soon-to-be Hamilton.*

"Open your eyes. Now, Wendy Brooks!"

The End…Or is it?

Writer/Director/Producer/Actress & Author
Schelle Holloway

Schelle Holloway, a native of Gulfport, Mississippi, relocated to Cary, North Carolina after the devastation of Hurricane Katrina swept the Mississippi Gulf Coast in 2005. Holloway's writing talents were brought to fruition when she finally realized moving back home was not an option. After a seven-city tour with her first stage play, including a trip back to the Gulf Coast with the production, she was surely on her way with this hidden talent.

Holloway has written and produced dinner theatres, directed other stage plays, as well as written more of her own. She has written and executively produced an independent film and a talk show that is seen locally in Raleigh, NC. She is a motivational speaker and a strong advocate for young people in her community.

During her career shift, Holloway has worked with and interviewed several international artists along with a host of other local talented artists and well-known people of her community. Holloway looks forward to opening a community theatre in the near future to give an opportunity to those who started off just like her and only need an open door to start living their dream.